RAVE REVIEWS F
FRANCIS RAY

THE WAY YOU LOVE ME

"As always, Ray leads her readers on a mesmerizing journey of drama and love. . . . *The Way You Love Me* confirms the fact that Francis Ray is, without a doubt, one of the Queens of Romance." —*A Romance Review*

"Fans of Ray's Grayson and Falcon families will be thrilled with the first installment in the new Grayson Friends series. . . . Told with such grace and affection that this novel is a treat to read." —*RT Book Reviews* (4 stars)

"A romance that will have readers speed-reading to the next tension-filled scene, if not the climax."
—*Fresh Fiction*

ONE NIGHT WITH YOU

"The steam the lovers create is a pleasure to behold. Ray never disappoints!" —*RT Book Reviews* (4½ stars)

WITH JUST ONE KISS

"Heartwarming and fu

NOB

"A story that tugs at the heartstrings. —*RT Book Reviews*

"Fast and fun and full of emotional thrills and sexy chills. Everything a racing romance should be!"
—Roxanne St. Claire

"Not only does Francis Ray rock in this book but also you see a whole different side of racing that will keep you on the edge of your seat." —*Night Owl Romance*

"A wonderful read." —*Fresh Fiction*

UNTIL THERE WAS YOU

"Ms. Ray has given us a great novel again. Did we expect anything less than the best?" —*RT Book Reviews* (4 stars)

"Crisp style, realistic dialogue, likable characters, and [a] fast pace." —*Library Journal*

ONLY YOU

"Francis Ray's graceful writing style and realistically complex characters give her latest contemporary romance its extraordinary emotional richness and depth." —*Chicago Tribune*

"It's a joy to read this always fresh and exciting saga." —*RT Book Reviews* (4 stars)

"The powerful descriptive powers of Francis Ray allow the reader to step into the story and become an active part of the surrender . . . If you love a great love story, *Only You* should be on your list." —*Fallen Angel Reviews*

"Riveting emotion and charismatic scenes that made this book captivating . . . a beautiful story of love and romance." —*Night Owl Romance*

"A beautiful love story as only Francis Ray can tell it."
—Singletitles.com

"Readers will find a warm and wonderful contemporary romance with plenty of humor and drama. Adding a fun warmth and reality to these characters and a plot that moves quickly add all the needed incentive to read this fun book." —*Multicultural Romance Writers*

IRRESISTIBLE YOU

"A pleasurable story . . . a well-developed story and continuous plot." —*RT Book Reviews*

"Like the previous titles in this series, *Irresistible You* is another winner . . . Witty and charming . . . Author Francis Ray has a true gift for drawing the readers in and never letting them go." —*Multicultural Romance Writers*

DREAMING OF YOU

"A great read from beginning to end, it's even excellent for an immediate re-read." —*RT Book Reviews*

"An immensely likable heroine, a sexy man with a heart of gold, and touches of glitz and color, [this] is as unapologetically escapist as Cinderella. Lots of fun."
—*BookPage*

YOU AND NO OTHER

"The warmth and sincerity of the Graysons bring another book to life . . . delightfully realistic." —*RT Book Reviews*

ST. MARTIN'S PAPERBACKS TITLES
BY FRANCIS RAY

All That I Desire

FRANCIS RAY

St. Martin's Paperbacks

This is a work of fiction. All of the characters, organizations, and events portrayed in this novel are either products of the author's imagination or are used fictitiously.

ALL THAT I DESIRE

Copyright © 2013 by Francis Ray.

For information address St. Martin's Press, 175 Fifth Avenue, New York, NY 10010.

ISBN: 978-1-250-02382-7

Printed in the United States of America

St. Martin's Paperbacks edition / November 2013

St. Martin's Paperbacks are published by St. Martin's Press, 175 Fifth Avenue, New York, NY 10010.

10 9 8 7 6 5 4 3 2 1

Lovingly dedicated to all of my loyal readers who patiently waited and never lost hope that Rio's story would be written.

Acknowledgments

Again, to my incredible readers for their support and well-wishes during the process of writing this book. You rock!!

Prologue

Skylar Dupree, event director for Navarone Resorts and Spas, had never been impulsive. But now as she watched the approach of two couples and one lone man from the second-floor turret window of Navarone Castle, Skylar contemplated taking the biggest gamble of her life.

As the pampered only child of divorced, overprotective parents, Skylar had wanted for little in her life. What she now desired—what she'd longed for, dreamed of, the past two years—might be impossible to attain. And cost her a job she loved.

Unlike her highly successful parents in Boston, she wasn't cut out to be a lawyer. When a family friend showed her an ad for an assistant to the event director for Navarone Resorts and Spas—headquartered in Tucson, Arizona—she had jumped at the opportunity.

Six weeks after she'd been hired, she met Blade Navarone at the grand opening of his latest resort. With him were his two personal bodyguards. One in particular, Rio Sanchez, caught her attention the instant she saw him.

He was tall, fallen-angel handsome, with razor-sharp cheekbones, long curly black hair that he wore tied at the nape of his neck, and flat black eyes. Much to her surprise, since she had loads of male friends but nothing serious, Rio piqued her curiosity and heated her body.

The other guard, Shane Elliott, might socialize, but Rio never did. He always kept himself apart, always watching. He seemed unapproachable. Hard. She'd observed more than one woman start toward him only to stop a few feet away, then beat a hasty retreat. She well understood why.

Rio was handsome enough to draw attention, but the unblinking flat eyes made any sensible woman feel as if she might be getting in over her head. Skylar felt that way herself.

In the two years she'd known Rio, she'd caught him a couple of times watching her. The problem was, she couldn't be sure if it went deeper than just doing his job.

Skylar wanted to know the man behind the unreadable facade that never smiled, make him stop looking through her, calling her Ms. Dupree. It was more than her wanting him to notice her or treat her differently than he did all the other people, besides Blade and Shane. She didn't think Rio had anyone.

Blade and Shane had wives, but who comforted Rio? With his broad shoulders, quick reflexes, and reported skills as a fighter, he acted as if he didn't need or want anyone.

She might have believed that if she wasn't looking at Rio with Blade and Shane and their wives. As always Rio walked apart, unsmiling, as the two couples laughed and held hands. She didn't know there were tears on her cheeks until Ruth Grayson, Blade's mother-in-law, handed her a tissue. "No man should walk this earth alone," she said and excused herself.

Skylar might have been embarrassed, but she liked Mrs. Grayson and knew she could keep a confidence. Skylar looked out the window again and came to a decision: Rio wouldn't walk alone any longer if it she could help it. It would be risky, emotionally and professionally.

If Rio felt she'd crossed the line professionally, she'd be out on her ear. She would be risking everything for a man who had never smiled at her, had never given her any indication that he felt anything more for her than the stones surrounding the castle—except for those two occasions.

Suddenly Rio looked up at her. She felt the familiar leap of her heart, the warmth curling through her, the need to touch, to soothe. She smiled. He didn't smile back, just continued inside behind the others. He was a tough man. That was all right. She turned from the window.

One day he would smile back.

Chapter 1

Skylar Dupree wasn't the risk-taking type, but neither was she the type of woman to falter once she'd made up her mind. The only other time in her twenty-six years she dared do anything remotely defying tradition was leaving law school. Yet that had been more for self-preservation. Her parents were pragmatic; she tended to be more easygoing and laid-back.

Skylar paused on the curved stone staircase of the thirty-five-room castle. Easygoing wasn't going to cut it this time, not if she wanted to grab Rio's attention.

Just the thought sent her heart rate skittering out of control. Rio could look straight through you with hard, unblinking black eyes. He exuded danger. Nothing seemed to bother him. She could count on one hand the number of times she'd seen him smile, and those times had been when he was with his closest friends, Blade and Shane. As far as Skylar knew, he'd never bestowed upon anyone else a smile, let alone his laughter.

The task she'd chosen for herself was scary. Since Shane's marriage, Rio was head of security for Blade's business as well as Blade's personal bodyguard. Even Rio's security team had a healthy fear of the man reported to be deadlier than a viper, and just as stealthy. She'd heard one of his men refer to him as "smoke" because of his elusiveness.

Skylar had flown in that Sunday afternoon from Navarone Resorts and Spas's headquarters to go over the final preparations for a charity auction and ball to benefit the Music Department of St. John's College, where Mrs. Grayson was chair. The auction was two weeks away. The big draw to get the right people to come was that the auction would be held in Navarone Castle, near Santa Fe, a place heretofore off limits to anyone but close family and friends.

Much had been speculated about the home of the billionaire, which had a real moat, a working drawbridge, a helipad, and a lake. Sierra, Blade's wife, might have owned the castle before her marriage, but Blade ensured their privacy by buying up all the surrounding property within fifty miles. You might get on the property, but with its constant patrols, you were quickly escorted off, which gave Navarone Castle even more of an air of mystique.

Continuing down the stairs with her iPad clutched to her chest, Skylar stepped into the comfortable great room. Sitting in sky-blue leather chairs and love seats were Blade, Sierra, and her mother on one side. On the other were Shane and his wife, Paige. Rio, arms folded, standing by the immense stone fireplace, glanced up. Her heart did a fast jitterbug.

Rio looked incredibly handsome in a long-sleeved white shirt with the cuffs rolled back to show strong wrists. He had a silver watch on one arm and a wide silver band on the other. His jeans delineated the long, sleek muscles of his thighs and made Skylar's mouth dry.

In Tucson he'd always worn tailored clothes, the same

as Blade. Here, Rio was more casual. The curly black hair she'd dreamed of running her fingers through was held at the base of his neck with a silver clip. His bronzed, hard body was honed to perfection.

There was nothing in his midnight-black eyes that indicated he desired or felt anything at all for her. Skylar stared back at the flat eyes that seemed to see right through her and stiffened her spine.

One day he'd look at her with desire.

"Hi, Skylar." Sierra rose from her seat and went to greet Skylar. "I'm sorry we weren't here to meet you."

"That's all right." Skylar smiled. She and Sierra had hit it off immediately. "I enjoyed looking around the castle again. You have a beautiful home."

"Thanks." Sierra glanced back at Blade. "We like it."

Skylar's smile increased. One place she'd bet was off limits was the grotto downstairs that was Sierra and Blade's secret place.

"Please have a seat." Sierra took the other woman's arm. "Can I get you anything?"

"No, thank you." Skylar greeted everyone as she took a leather chair. Everyone spoke. Rio nodded.

"Is everything going as planned?" Ruth asked.

Skylar knew Ruth could have asked that question earlier, but hadn't. Mrs. Grayson also didn't let on she'd seen or talked with Skylar before. She smiled her thanks.

"Yes, Mrs. Grayson. In fact, we're ahead of schedule. As planned, the auction will be by invitation only. Thanks to Lance's help, a printed color catalog with the starting bid for each item has already been sent out."

"Good thing," Sierra interjected. "Because he and Fallon are off on their honeymoon."

"Still discussing if she'll be able to go scuba diving

due to her pregnancy." Blade glanced at Sierra. "She's almost as strong-willed as another woman I know."

"Aren't you and Lance the lucky ones?" Sierra grinned and kissed Blade on the cheek.

Skylar cut a sideways glance at Rio. His arms remained crossed, his gaze somewhere over her head. He wasn't going to make this easy. Back to the business at hand.

"I personally called everyone to ensure they received the catalog and still plan to attend." Skylar pulled out the guest list and stood to give it to Rio. "This week, four of the invitees asked if they could bring a guest. It was to be expected that some would ignore the one-month time limit to invite a guest. I know you'd want to check the people out before I committed."

He crossed to her in his effortless stride that reminded her of a stalking cat. Long, lean fingers took the list without looking at it. "Thank you." His voice held no inflection.

Trying not to sigh, Skylar retook her seat. She needn't have bothered wearing a tangerine-colored dress that complemented her complexion and hazel eyes. However, she wasn't giving up.

"The items will be arriving by special courier or delivery service starting Tuesday. I'll be here to check and sign them in. I'll return each day until we have all the items in place," Skylar told them. "We've already selected the room where they'll be displayed."

"That's too much trouble," Sierra said. "It would be easier and make more sense if you stay here."

"I couldn't agree more," Blade said.

"I couldn't," Skylar said, surprised by the invitation. While they were planning the auction, she'd always flown in and out of Santa Fe.

"We have plenty of guest rooms." Sierra leaned against Blade. His arm immediately circled her slim shoulders. "We're leaving for a new Navarone property in the morning; you're welcome to stay here."

Skylar didn't know what to say. She was very aware that a lot of trust had gone into the invitation. If Rio stayed, she might run into him more. The thought had no more than materialized when she discarded it. She was not going to impose on Blade and Sierra's kindness to go after Rio.

"It won't be any trouble," Skylar finally said. "I don't mind the trip."

"We won't take no for an answer," Blade told her.

"You're staying and that's final," Sierra said firmly as if the matter was settled.

"Please." Ruth leaned forward in her seat. "What you're doing is to help my Music Department. We'll benefit from your hard work. I'll always be thankful. You could have passed when I asked if you had any ideas on how to raise funds. You didn't. You even offered to take vacation time to help."

"I appreciated the professionalism, but as I said then when you mentioned what you would be doing, using your vacation time won't be necessary," Blade said, his gaze direct.

Sierra patted his knee. "He's even gotten over being a little miffed that you thought you had to ask. He forgot all men are not as wonderful as he is."

Blade smiled at his wife, then Skylar, and she breathed a bit easier. She well remembered the harsh look on his face that day in his office. She hoped never again to see it directed at her and remained silent.

"Stay," Blade said. "It would make up for my poor behavior."

Blade wasn't above apologizing. He just seldom had to. Shane had a grin on his face as he held Paige's hand. No one had to tell Skylar that Blade's love for Sierra and hers for her mother were the reasons behind the apology.

Skylar recalled Ruth's words, *No man should walk alone.* Her gaze went to Ruth again as she wondered if she was trying to give Skylar a gentle push in Rio's direction.

But as Blade's bodyguard, he went with him everywhere or was at least nearby. Was he staying this time? She had her answer seconds later.

"To ensure the auction pieces remain safe, Rio is staying," Blade told her.

"I should be going with you." Rio unfolded his arms, his attention on Blade and Sierra.

Sierra lifted both hands in a fighter's stance. "Don't worry, Rio. I promise to take down anyone who looks suspicious."

Shane was the only one who laughed. He ignored his wife's nudge.

"You checked out the island; the men there were trained by you or Shane. You and Shane made sure my name is buried so no one outside the company knows we own the property," Blade reminded him. "From the vantage point on the island you can see a boat miles away. We'll be safe."

"That's why I should be there—to make sure."

"I want you here." Blade rose to his feet and went to Rio. "This is important to Mrs. Grayson. There's some valuable merchandise coming. I trust you to ensure it's kept safe."

Rio remained silent. Skylar's eyes and everyone else's were on Rio and Blade. No one, absolutely no one—outside of Sierra—went against Blade's orders. She sensed

Rio might be the second. Protecting Blade and Sierra was more than a job to him.

Shane went to the two men. "I'll fly down with them and check it out."

Rio's gaze slowly tracked to Shane's and stayed there for a long moment before returning to Blade. "If you'll excuse me, I'll begin checking on the list."

Skylar blew out a breath as Rio's long strides took him from the room and up the stairs to the command center on the second floor of the castle's front wing.

"You shouldn't tease him," Ruth said to Sierra.

"Who said I was teasing?" Sierra lifted innocent eyes to her mother.

Ruth shook her head once, then stood and pulled a set of keys from the pocket of her denim skirt. "Come on, Skylar. I'll drive you to your hotel to get your things."

Sierra stood, her arm going around her mother's waist. "Since I've seen how Skylar packs, I'll send a driver with the SUV."

Ruth smiled at Sierra, then Skylar. "She likes clothes as much as you do."

"You never know what you might need." Sierra spoke to Skylar. "We'll wait dinner for you."

Skylar smiled. Sierra and her mother weren't taking no for an answer. "I graciously accept. I'll be back as soon as I can."

In less than fifteen minutes Skylar had checked out of the Casa de Serenidad Hotel. Thank goodness she had been so anxious to get to the castle that she hadn't begun to un-pack. Outside, she climbed into the SUV, and they headed back to Navarone Castle.

Skylar wasn't the impatient type, but she was anxious

to get back. She wondered if Rio ate with his men or Blade and Sierra. Everyone had someone, except him. But he didn't seem to need anyone. He certainly wasn't afraid to speak his mind—to anyone.

"Back again," the driver said, startling Skylar out of her deep thoughts.

"Thank you." She got out of the vehicle and walked to the back. She almost winced at the amount of luggage being unloaded. Besides the large trunk, she'd brought five large suitcases. It had taken her weeks to decide what to wear in the hope that Rio would stop looking through her and be just a little bit interested. With him staying and checking in the merchandise with her daily, it might just happen.

"Mrs. Navarone instructed me where to place your luggage. Please, go on in."

"Thank you again, Jefferson." Skylar picked up her overnight kit.

"I can take that as well." The driver closed the back. "Don't worry, Eli is sending someone to help. Besides, we're both used to helping Mrs. Navarone load and unload for trips."

Skylar placed the case on the stone driveway and laughed. "That's very kind of you. Thank you."

The driver tipped his hat. "No problem."

Skylar went up the steps and rang the doorbell. There was a key pad for a code, but she didn't know it.

The door opened. Eli Patterson, the house manager, stood there in his black suit, freshly starched white shirt, and shiny leather shoes. Of medium height, he had a lined, fatherly face and a balding head.

"Hello, Mr. Patterson," Skylar greeted.

"Hello, Ms. Dupree. I'll assist with your luggage," he

told her. "Mr. Navarone asked that you see him in his office as soon as you returned. This way."

Unsure of what was going on, she followed the house manager past the wide foyer, then left to an arched door at least fifteen feet tall. Opening the door, he stepped aside.

Thanking him, she entered the office, an immense room lined with bookshelves, a fireplace, and tall windows with silk burgundy draperies. On the slate floor were handwoven area rugs. Blade sat behind an antique mahogany desk with ball-and-claw feet. Her eyes narrowed on seeing Shane and Rio standing on either side of him.

"Thank you for coming, Skylar. Please have a seat." Blade indicated the chair in front of his desk.

Skylar sat down in the straight-back chair, upholstered in a deeper shade of burgundy than the curtains, demurely crossed her legs, and placed her clutch in her lap. She'd learned not to jump to conclusions just because she was summoned by Blade, and not to ask questions.

"One of the men on the list you gave Rio is Sherman Tennyson, a venture capitalist. Several months ago, Tennyson used my name to entice backers into buying property. The deal folded." Blade's black eyes hardened. "A lot of good men lost money. Tennyson put the word out that it was my fault."

"No." Skylar's voice was barely above a whisper as she placed her hand on her galloping heart. People who made huge mistakes at Navarone were out the door.

Shane picked up the story. "Blade has been able to overcome the lies, but Tennyson lost a lot of his credibility, along with money he could ill afford to let go."

Blade's fist clenched on top of his desk. "Tennyson hates my guts, and the feeling is mutual."

Skylar came to her feet. "Mr. Navarone, I just checked

to ensure he had the funds to purchase if he chose. I apologize."

Blade waved her apology aside. "There's no need. You foiled Tennyson's plan." He leaned back in his chair, the sides of his mouth kicking up. "You didn't just okay the names as he probably expected because the auction is in two weeks and he has money. Instead you had the foresight to give Rio the list of names before committing. You did well."

"I agree," Shane said. "Good thinking."

From Rio there was nothing. Trying to keep from looking at him, she retook her seat. "Should I call Mr. Hampton, the man who had asked if Tennyson could attend?"

Blade's smile was like the sharp edge of a knife. "I'll take care of it. That's all."

Eternally thankful she wasn't the unfortunate man, Skylar came to her feet. "I'll go change for dinner. Good-bye."

"Good-bye," Blade and Shane said.

She told herself not to turn, but a force stronger than her will had her glancing over her shoulder at Rio to see if there might be a spark of admiration. She saw nothing but eyes devoid of warmth. Unconsciously she narrowed hers before turning to leave the room.

Stubborn man! He might not know it, but he'd only made her more determined!

Chapter 2

A little after six Sunday evening, Rio debated going downstairs to dinner. If he did, he'd be subjected to Skylar's haunting hazel eyes following him everywhere. He'd never run from anything. The idea that he was considering it now, and because of a woman he could pick up with one hand, set his teeth on edge. The problem was, she also made his body hard.

Cursing under his breath, he stepped from a cold shower. What was it about her that he couldn't dismiss, couldn't ignore?

Absently, he ran the large bath towel over his body. He'd better find his answer. Being around each other for the next two weeks would be unavoidable. He planned to be there for the deliveries as well. They were expecting more than one and a half million dollars in paintings, jewelry, and other donated items. He wanted no doubts, no questions if something expected didn't arrive or arrived damaged. Each item would be documented and verified in multiple ways. Cameras would be on, but film could be altered.

He knew this was important to Mrs. Grayson and her students and, as Blade said, there was no way to sneak onto the island. Even at night the sound of an engine carried. They'd be safe. He wasn't sure about himself. He reached for his black boxers. The threat of physical injury had never bothered him, and it didn't now. There was something much more dangerous here.

Snatching his shirt from the hanger, he pulled it on then stepped into his slacks. There was nothing to do now but see it through. The day had never arrived that he couldn't outthink a woman. He slipped on his Italian loafers.

Opening the bedroom door, Rio quickly bounded down the stairs and into the small dining room. Blade and Sierra sat at the head and foot of the table. Next to Sierra was Skylar. On the other side was Shane, between Paige and Mrs. Grayson.

Rio almost faltered when Skylar's hungry gaze collided with his. He wished she'd stop that.

"Good evening," he said, his steps slowing on seeing that the only seat left was the one next to Skylar. The place for the third chair had been moved, and a serving cart was there in its place.

"About time," Shane said. "Paige is starving."

His pretty wife simply looked at him. He kissed her on the cheek and grinned. She shook her head and smiled back. Skylar had watched the exchange. Paige loved and respected him too much to correct him about teasing Rio.

"Martin outdid himself as usual for Sierra," Blade said. "He would have left long ago if it wasn't for her."

"He's irreplaceable and we all benefit," Sierra said. "Especially since I can't cook."

Laughter came from around the table as Rio took his seat and stared across at Ruth Grayson, another woman who made him uneasy, but for an entirely different reason. He pulled his napkin into his lap as she said grace.

He lifted his head and stared into her eyes when she finished. She stared back. You never knew what the woman was thinking. She was ruled by love, and that made her unpredictable. When he'd helped save Sierra's life when she was kidnapped, he'd gotten on Mrs. Grayson's marriage hit list. She had married off all five children, just as she'd predicted. To this day Sierra believed she'd picked Blade by herself. Rio wasn't sure if Blade knew the truth, but Rio and Shane did.

If that wasn't enough, she'd turned her attention to Shane. He'd caved like the rest before him. There were others as well, but she could take Rio's name off the list.

Murmurs of appreciation and compliments went around the table as the chef and his two helpers served them prime rib roast, red potatoes, and broccoli with hollandaise sauce on fine china. Homemade yeast rolls were passed around the table as Martin looked on with pride. He'd been the executive chef at the Mansion in Dallas until Blade had hired him away from the famous five-star hotel.

"You never cease to amaze and delight," Sierra murmured after tasting the beef. "We'd be lost and starving without you."

"Thank you, Sierra." Martin bowed his head and withdrew.

Rio picked up his fork and hoped Mrs. Grayson wasn't planning anything. As he'd told Shane, home and hearth wasn't for them. Shane hadn't listened. But Shane knew where he came from. Rio didn't. Skylar could send out signals until all that beautiful hair on her head turned gray; it wouldn't do her any good. He wasn't looking back.

It was all Skylar could do to eat and carry on a sensible conversation with Rio sitting next to her. They'd never been this close for any length of time. She thought of the movie scenes she'd seen where women took off a shoe and rubbed a foot against the side of a man's leg. Or other parts of his body. She blushed. She wasn't that brave. Yet.

She leaned forward to pick up her water glass and swayed the tiniest bit toward Rio. He smelled delicious, like man and soap. She wanted to lean closer to his hard, lean body. Heat shot through her.

She bobbled her water glass, took a hasty gulp, and choked. That would teach her to lust after a man while drinking.

Sierra, sitting at the end of the table, patted Skylar gently on the back. "Are you all right?"

Embarrassed, she tucked her head and mumbled, "Yes."

"What time are you leaving again, Blade?" Mrs. Grayson asked.

Skylar sent the woman a look of appreciation for getting the conversation started again. She'd better pay more attention to what she was doing than to the silent man beside her.

"Around nine tomorrow morning." Blade braced his forearms on the table. "The plane is scheduled to leave at nine forty-five from the airport. We'll refuel in Atlanta and continue on to the island."

"We're taking the chef and Blade's houseman with us." Sierra sipped her sparkling water. "But don't worry, Skylar, the house manager will be here as usual. One of the downstairs maids will take over cooking duties."

"That's very thoughtful of you, Sierra." Skylar placed her glass on the table. She might get to eat with Rio again. "Thank you. And I'll keep you informed as to how the bidding goes. The Web site will start accepting bids at midnight tonight. I expect a flurry of interest for the offerings from your relatives and friends. They were extremely generous and accommodating."

Ruth nodded and looked at Paige. "One of the board of regents told me, if her granddaughter doesn't win the bid to meet your brother and sit in on a recording session with him, her life was over."

Paige beamed with pride. "Who would have ever thought when Zachary was learning to play all those instruments and driving me and Mother crazy, he'd be so famous and popular?"

Skylar smiled. "Rolling Deep, aka Zachary Albright Wilder, is the top music producer in the country. He's even more sought after since his and his wife's album, *A Father's Love,* went triple platinum. Laurel's solo performance on the violin will also be a hot item."

"Zachary's desire to produce Laurel's next album is what brought them together," Paige told them.

"But it wasn't easy for them," Shane said.

Paige turned to him and cupped his cheek with her palm. "Nor for us, but love found a way for them and for us."

"Add our names to that list." Sierra tipped her head and lifted her glass toward Blade.

He lifted his glass to her. "Sometimes there's only one chance, one choice."

Skylar couldn't help glancing at Rio. He was calmly eating his prime rib as if all the talk of love and devotion meant nothing to him.

"I'm blessed to be surrounded by talented and loving people." Ruth looked at Rio. "Everyone deserves that special someone their heart can't refuse or deny."

Rio lifted his head to meet her gaze, then placed his knife and fork on his plate. "If you'll excuse me."

Skylar masked her disappointment that he was leaving

by cautiously drinking her water. The man couldn't even take time to finish his meal. Was he that against love?

"Rio needs to take time to have a little fun." Sierra made a face. "He knows he has competent men, but he personally checks the perimeter of the house nightly before he allows himself to go to bed."

"He's a man who takes his responsibilities seriously," Blade said. "I'm glad to have him."

"I'll always be thankful to him, and to you, Shane, as well," Mrs. Grayson said softly.

Shane tipped his head.

Skylar got the feeling that she was missing something, but then Blade's chef entered the room rolling a glass-topped silver cart. She felt worse on seeing huge slices of lemon pie, probably as delicious as they looked. The meringue was at least six inches high. Rio had missed his dessert. She didn't like the idea of him going without. She'd just have to do something about it.

Two hours after he'd left the dining room, Rio entered the house again. He'd checked with each sentry posted on the grounds, those in the guardhouse, and the ones by the draw-bridge that was always down.

Rio's foot hit the bottom step of the stairs. He stopped, sensing more than seeing a small figure going up the stairs. Even in the dim light from the wall sconce at the top of the flight, he recognized the tantalizing shape of the woman he'd been trying to forget.

"What are you doing?"

Skylar shrieked, whirled around, and lost her balance. He quickly covered the distance and caught her by the arm to keep her from falling. She stared up at him with wide, frightened eyes. He tried not to notice the heat of her tempting body burning though her thin pink robe and gown, and failed miserably.

"I asked you a question."

She moved the cloth-covered plate closer to his face. "It's lemon pie. You—you didn't eat dessert. I—I thought you might be hungry. I was going to leave it outside your door."

Lemon pie wasn't what he wanted. Looking into her beautiful eyes that had gone from frightened to needy, he realized he wouldn't even have to ask. She was his for the taking.

He took the pie from her unsteady hands. "Go to bed. Now."

Skylar turned and ran up the stairs. He didn't move until he heard her door open and slam shut. *That's right, keep running for both our sakes.*

In her room, her back pressed against the door, Skylar's breathing was as off kilter as her heart rate. She hadn't expected to see Rio. As she'd told him, her plan had been to leave the pie by his door.

Initially he'd scared her. She'd quickly become embarrassed because she'd been in her thin nightgown and robe. However, as he held her against his strong, coiled body, fear and embarrassment had turned to a growing need to press closer to his arousing warmth.

She gulped.

Just before he'd taken the pie from her and told her to go to bed, she'd finally seen emotions swirling in Rio's dark eyes, a fiercely burning desire that made her shiver, her skin heat. Yearn.

She shivered again. She might have taken on more than she could handle.

* * *

The next morning, Skylar wasn't surprised not to see Rio at breakfast. She was almost glad. She wasn't sure she was ready to see him again. She was still a bit unsteady from the night before. If the man could shake her that much with a look, what would happen if he kissed her?

"Skylar, are you all right?"

Skylar jumped and stared at Sierra, who stood by the open back passenger door of the SUV that would take them to the airport to board their private jet. From the odd way Sierra was staring at Skylar, she must have zoned out. "Sorry, I have a lot on my mind."

Sierra glanced behind her. "I'll say."

"Call me when you finish the recon," Rio said.

Skylar's gaze snapped back to Sierra, but she was already getting in the SUV with Paige. Blade and Shane were talking with Rio a short distance away. Had Sierra meant Rio? Skylar felt her face heat. Had she been that obvious?

"The house will run as smoothly as if you were here," Eli, the house manager, said. "Don't worry about the auction merchandise. The staff won't reveal anything."

Skylar breathed easier. Sierra had meant the auction. Her secret was safe.

"I know, Eli," Blade assured the older man. "Let's go, Shane. Rio, I'm depending on you. You've never let me down."

"And I never will," Rio replied.

Skylar stepped back as Blade and Shane got into the SUV with the tinted windows. She waved good-bye. Behind their vehicle was another identical black SUV. She watched until the first one started across the drawbridge, then she turned for the house. She wanted to look at the Web site again. As she'd expected, bids were already coming in when she'd checked it after getting out of bed. The regent's granddaughter might be disappointed. Rolling Deep's bid was already at twenty-five hundred dollars.

"Ms. Dupree, I need to see you."

Skylar was so annoyed at Rio for still being so formal with her after scorching her with his eyes last night that she didn't let her mind think he meant anything but business when he said *need*. She faced him with cool eyes and a cooler voice. "Yes."

He held out a key and inclined his head toward a black BMW SUV in front of the nine-bay garage. "You'll need transportation."

"Thank you." She took the key and continued into the house, wishing she could look back and see his face. Two could play his game.

Shortly after twelve, Skylar was on her way to meet with the president and board of regents of St. John's College along with Mrs. Grayson, the chair of her Music Department, and other professors in that department. Thankfully, the BMW had an excellent GPS system. Twenty-five minutes later she waved at Ruth standing on the sidewalk in front of the music building and continued to the parking lot across the street.

As she drove in, a young man waved and beckoned. Skylar parked in the spot he indicated, directly across from the music building. She climbed out and extended her hand to the smiling man. "Hi, that's what I call service. Skylar Dupree."

He blinked, stared. Skylar kept her hand extended. She got that look sometimes from men because of her hazel eyes. If she was all that, as her sorority would say, she wouldn't have so much trouble getting Rio's attention.

"I believe they're waiting for us," Skylar said, trying to get things moving.

"Oh." He flushed and grasped her hand, pumping it a couple of times before releasing it. "Ah, I'm Greg Harris, I'm to escort you to Professor Grayson."

"Hi, Greg. Thanks for meeting me."

"My pleasure." Greg grinned. "All I can say is I'm glad I'm a music major."

"I'm sure she's glad to have you as a student as well," Skylar replied and took the paved path across to the street, then crossed to meet Ruth. She was dressed in a beautiful dove-gray suit with silver earrings and high heels instead of her casual clothes. She'd been dressed similarly when she'd visited Skylar and asked for her help. She could be as fashionable as her daughter when she wanted.

Skylar extended both hands and hugged the other woman. "You look fabulous."

"Sierra, Morgan, and Pierce's doing. They think I have to have as many outfits as they do." Mrs. Grayson leaned closer. "Days like this are the only time I need them."

Skylar lifted a brow. "A tough crowd?"

Mrs. Grayson hooked her arm through Skylar's. "Not in the least. It's just good to remind them that I could always run with the big dogs, even before my children married well."

Skylar chuckled. "No wonder Sierra is so outspoken and independent. My mother and grandmothers are the same way. You'll meet my maternal grandparents at the auction. My paternal grandparents are in Europe on an extended holiday, but both are very interested in bidding on your daughter-in-law Phoenix's sculpture."

"That's good to hear. You've worked very hard on

this," Ruth said. "You'll be rewarded in more ways than you can imagine."

Skylar glanced at Mrs. Grayson, thinking once again that she'd missed something.

The women walked through the door Greg held open, nodding their thanks. He passed them and continued down a long hallway. Students clutching books, cell phones, and backpacks passed them.

"This brings backs memories." Skylar gazed at the pictures on the wall, stopping at one with Sabra Raineau Grayson surrounded by smiling young people. "Your daughter-in-law is a beautiful and talented woman. The bid to sit in the front row on the opening night of her new Broadway play and have dinner with her later has already reached over a thousand dollars."

"Probably Pierce. My son trusts Sabra, but not the man who might take her out." Mrs. Grayson tsked. "It took some hard talking on her part to get him to leave his name off the dinner engagement."

"I understand Sierra met Blade when she took Sabra's place at another auction because she had recently married Pierce." Skylar continued down the hall. "Isn't it wonderful how a chance meeting can lead to love?"

"Isn't it." Ruth stopped a couple of feet from where Greg stood in front of double doors. "But there's something also to be said for allowing love to grow over time."

Skylar jerked her head around to stare at Ruth, but she'd already released her arm and continued to Greg. When she looked back at Skylar, she wore the same warm, friendly expression she always did. Skylar chastised herself for being overly sensitive about Rio. She had to stop this. Sierra, and now Ruth.

Just because Ruth had said *No man should walk alone*

didn't mean she knew Skylar had the hots for Rio. Yet as she entered the room full of people waiting for her, she couldn't quite be sure.

Skylar pulled away from St. John's College two hours later, a full hour longer than had been scheduled for her to explain the auction. Everyone there had been excited and grateful. She thought the reasons for the lengthy meeting were mostly to do with the delicious food that Brandon Grayson, owner of the renowned Red Cactus restaurant, had unexpectedly showed up with, and the regents and other teachers angling for invitations to the auction.

Ruth became the woman of the decade when she passed out the coveted invitations to the regents and to her staff. Rio had cleared all of them weeks ago. For a moment Skylar and Brandon thought they would hoist his mother into the air.

Ruth had been right about one thing: Those were some very big dogs there. The regent whose granddaughter wanted to win the bid for Rolling Deep was the president of one of the largest banks in the area. The silver-haired woman had topped the bid to three thousand dollars. Her eyes had been narrowed at the time. Skylar and Ruth had shared a smile. The woman didn't plan to lose.

Skylar's contentment with the event faded in the slow traffic out of Santa Fe. The new cook said she'd serve at six. It wasn't likely Rio would show up for the dinner. And if he did, he'd ignore her as usual.

But he hadn't last night, a small voice said. So what? He could have reacted that way to any woman in her night-gown; it didn't mean his reaction had been for her. This morning when she saw him on the castle grounds, he'd been his stoic self.

She eased on her brakes as the green light turned to yellow. The car on the other side of her went through the light. She heard the screeching of brakes and glanced into her rearview mirror. That's all she needed. Rio would have a fit if the BMW was in an accident.

She blew out a breath and glanced out the window. Eli Patterson, the house manager, stood in front of a bar with another man. The stranger had his back to her, but he was around six foot two in a gray suit that fit his broad shoulders perfectly.

She couldn't hear what they were saying, but from the man's wild gestures they were arguing. Her suspicions were confirmed when lifted his hand and pointed his finger at Eli. The house manager's face blanched. The bigger man took Eli's arm and hustled him into the black Lincoln pulled up beside them.

Poor man, she thought. No one should be bullied. She wasn't the only one having a bad day. The light changed and she pulled off.

Skylar ate dinner alone as expected, but refused to give in to the melancholy that had gripped her earlier. Perhaps it was seeing the house manager an hour ago with his head down. The bully was probably kicked back someplace having a great time, just like she was probably the farthest thing from Rio's mind.

She stabbed her citrus salad and nibbled on a piece of lettuce and orange. Keeping her head down wouldn't get her in Rio's arms. She wasn't sure what would, but there'd be no more feeling sorry for herself.

Her shoulders straightened. She wasn't half bad looking, had a good sense of humor, and was intelligent enough to have worked her way up to director of events in fourteen months. Most men would be thrilled to have her. She dug into her salad with renewed gusto. Before the night of the auction, Rio would be, too.

Tuesday morning, Skylar dressed in a calf-length black skirt with a five-inch slit above her knees on one side and paired it with a white crepe blouse with long flowing sleeves. On her feet were toeless four-inch heels. Each time she moved, the skirt shifted against her skin and a glimpse of her leg, covered by sheer black stocking, was visible.

She put her hair in a chic chignon. Around her neck was the double strand of pearls her parents had given her when she graduated from high school. She put on her pearl ear studs, grabbed her iPad, and left the room.

Her first confirmation that she had achieved her goal of looking sophisticated and sexy was when one of the guards on the stairs stopped in his tracks as he saw her. She smiled. "Good morning, Eric."

"Ah, Skylar." His eyes roamed appreciatively over her face. "You look very nice."

"Thank you." She folded her arms around the iPad. "A woman always likes to hear that."

He opened his mouth, his smile growing, then his shoulders straightened and the smile faded. "Please excuse me."

"Of course." Skylar stepped aside to let him pass, but in such a way that she could look back up the stairs. She wasn't surprised to catch a glimpse of Rio. She continued to the small dining room for breakfast and took a seat. She wasn't trying to make Rio jealous or get his men into trouble; she just wanted him to notice her as a woman.

"Good morning, Ms. Dupree." The cook, Mary, placed

a glass of cranberry juice and a glass of water by the place setting.

"Good morning, Mary," Skylar greeted. "What are you going to serve me that will tantalize my taste buds and make me have to work out?"

The pretty young woman beamed. "Eggs ranchero. My family loves it when I cook it for them."

"I'm sure I will as well." Skylar placed the cloth napkin in her lap as the cook rushed out of the room. She was reaching for her juice when the hairs on the back of her neck stood up. Slowly her gaze lifted to Rio's. It was all she could do not to lean back, away from the force of his hard gaze.

"The first delivery is scheduled to arrive in twenty-eight minutes."

Before she could comment, Rio left as quietly as he'd come. Skylar sagged in her chair, then sat up and glanced at her watch. Eight fifty-seven. She wasn't going to be late. It was her responsibility to check each delivery to ensure it matched her master list and see that it was placed in the designated spot.

"Here you are, Ms. Dupree." Mary set the plate on the table.

"It looks fantastic. Thank you." Skylar blessed her food, then picked up her fork and began to eat. If Rio thought he could rattle her, he had better think again.

She forked in another bite. Rio was incredibly gorgeous with the body of a Greek god, a noble bearing, the instincts of a seasoned warrior. Women were drawn to the mystique that surrounded him. It was exhilarating to be near a man that exuded that much power. When he turned those cold black eyes on you, you were snared and immediately knew you might find endless pleasure

in his arms—but there was also danger. Continue at your
own risk.

Rio might have thrown her at first, but she was made
of sterner stuff. Her ancestors were Moors, Creoles, and
free people of color. Some were warriors as well. Others
had toiled in the hot sun, done backbreaking work, all
with the goal of achieving wealth and independence.
They hadn't had it easy, but each generation had accomplished more than the next. No Dupree or Carrington—
her mother's maiden name—ran from hard work or a
challenge.

Game on!

Chapter 3

Skylar was sitting at the table beneath the open tent when the first delivery truck rolled across the drawbridge. There were one hundred items up for bid. Neither she nor the Navorones wanted delivery people traipsing in and out of their home. Nor did they want to risk photos being taken inside. The exterior was already well documented.

The simple solution was to accept the delivery in the courtyard. Once a donation arrived, the tracking number would be checked, then the package opened to validate the item with the driver present. Merchandise didn't always make its way to the final destination.

The driver jumped out of the truck with a package in his hands. "This is the first of four. I don't see why this delivery has to be different," he muttered.

Silently Rio took the twelve-by-twelve box, scanned the label, placed it on a long folding table a few feet from Skylar, and opened the box with a box cutter. Removing the packing, he carefully pulled out a Baccarat crystal vase valued at twenty-five thousand dollars.

Skylar found the vase and marked it off her list. "One down and ninety-nine to go."

"Yes." Rio placed the rose-colored vase aside.

Skylar stared down at the screen of her iPad. At least he was talking to her.

"Here are the other three." The driver stopped with a cart. "Who is going to sign?"

"I will." Skylar placed the iPad on the table.

"I'll take care of it." Rio stepped past her and signed, giving the scanner back to the driver. He picked up the top box. "Please step over here while I open the other packages."

"Hurry up. I got a schedule to keep," the man snapped.

Rio had turned away but swung back so fast the driver stumbled, swallowed.

Skylar bet the man wouldn't pop off again like that. She picked up the next box. "Shall I open it?"

Rio finally moved to place his box beside hers. One of his men placed the other one on the table. No one spoke as he opened each.

"They all check." Skylar spoke to the nervous man. "Being courteous never goes out of style. Good-bye."

The man went to his truck. Once there he sneered. Skylar smiled at him. "Have a wonderful day."

The men standing with her laughed. She didn't even have to look at Rio to know he hadn't joined in with them. He was too serious. He needed to have some fun, and Skylar was going to be the person to show him how.

Rio personally took the four deliveries into the designated room. All the furniture had been stored so people could easily browse the collection. Skylar had even acquired locked jewelry cases. There were also stands for the expected art pieces. After placing the crystal pieces in their designated spots, he went back out. He'd gotten no more than a foot out the door before he heard the unmistakable sound of Skylar's laughter.

No emotion showed on his face, but inside was a different matter. He shouldn't care that she had such an easy way with his men. She was just another employee.

If only he could make himself believe that. He was actually ready to warn Henderson off when Rio caught the known womanizer and Skylar on the staircase that morning. Her tone had been light, almost flirtatious. Henderson wasn't the type of man to let an opportunity with a beautiful woman pass.

A man with less control might have cursed at that admission. Rio continued to the tent. No woman was ever going to get the best of him. He'd mastered his body years ago, just as the Man With No Name had taught him.

"Another delivery is due in thirty minutes." Skylar looked at her watch again. "It's finally happening. I called Ruth while you were inside and told her about the first delivery."

He didn't know what to say to her. He'd never been one for small talk—with a woman or a man. She looked at him as if he were her whole world one moment or as if she wanted to crawl into his lap, then other times as if she wanted to comfort him. He didn't need anything from her—except to stop looking at him with such innocent desire and sinful expectations.

"Everything all right on the island?" she asked.

"Yes," he answered, hoping that would end the conversation. She was sitting in a chair with her long, shapely legs crossed. The slight breeze loosened strains of her thick, lustrous black hair from the chignon and molded the white blouse to her high, firm breasts.

"I know you wanted to be there." She twisted toward him, revealing more of her elegant legs. "But I'm glad you're here."

Rio mentally shook himself. Her striking hazel eyes wistfully stared up at him, not hiding any of her desire. Didn't she have any sense? He might ask himself the same thing. "I'll be back before the next delivery."

Rio made a strategic withdrawal to the command center. Every good soldier knew there was no shame in retreating to regroup. No matter what, Skylar Dupree would not breach his defenses.

Rio was there to watch the items being unloaded as the day progressed. The deliverymen and -women cast nervous glances at him. He unpacked each box or package, carefully handling delicate crystal pieces as easily as he did sturdier items with his large hands.

Skylar remembered those hands on her and, from the sudden narrowing of his eyes when their gaze happen to meet, Rio did also. She might have rejoiced that she'd gotten another reaction out of him if her knees hadn't been shaking.

"I'll take that into the display room while you have the driver sign." Glad her voice was steady, she picked up the box with the signed Waterford limited-edition vase and went inside the castle.

Five minutes later, more in control of her emotions, she came out of the room with the auction pieces and saw the house manager, Mr. Patterson. He didn't look any happier than he had the day she'd seen him in town.

"Mr. Patterson, life can change for the better at a moment's notice."

If anything, his frown deepened. He stared at her in puzzlement. "What are you talking about, Ms. Dupree?"

Skylar wasn't sure what her response should be. She didn't want to embarrass him. "It's just my observation. I better get back outside."

The next morning as she left breakfast, she met Eli standing just beyond the doors of the small dining room. "Good morning, Mr. Patterson."

"Good morning, Ms. Dupree. Would it be possible to have a word with you?"

"Of course," she said and followed him to the library. He closed the door behind them.

The poor man looked worried. She hoped it didn't have anything to do with what she'd said to him yesterday.

He glanced away as if unable to find the words, before finally facing her. "What you said about life changing at a moment's notice has been bothering me all night. I had the feeling that it wasn't just random conversation. Am I right?"

She hesitated. She should have kept her mouth shut. Especially since Rio had gone cold on her again.

"Please, I need my sleep," he said, a slight smile on his lined face.

She knew exactly what he meant. She had tossed most of the night. "I saw you in town."

His expression didn't change.

"With the man outside of the bar Monday," she rushed on when his eyes widened. "I didn't mean to spy or anything. I was at a stoplight and I happened to glance over."

"I see," he said slowly.

She truly felt bad. She placed a consoling hand on his

arm. "He was mean to bully you. If there is anything I can do to help, you only have to ask."

His complexion paled. His shaky hand fluttered to his chest.

Afraid he was having a heart attack, she took his other arm. "Mr. Patterson, are you all right? Do you want to sit down?"

"No. No. I . . ." His hand lowered, and he glanced away for a moment. "What you saw was a private exchange. The man is an unwanted friend of a friend. I realize I have no right, but please don't tell anyone what you saw. It . . ." He swallowed. "It might cause problems."

She certainly knew about keeping secrets. She'd be mortified if it became public knowledge that she was lusting after Rio. "I didn't see anything."

Her cell phone rang. "I have to take this. Hello. I'll be right out." She ended the call. "This conversation never happened."

"Thank you, Ms. Dupree."

She touched his arm one last time, then rushed outside and to the tent. Rio was at the receiving table cutting open a large rectangular box. "Good morning."

"Good morning." He never looked her way or paused in what he was doing. Moments later he drew out a beautiful painting by Kara Simmons-Landers, a newly discovered artist.

Used to his short answers, she walked over. "Breathtaking, isn't it?"

His dark head slowly turned. His dark eyes revealed nothing. "You mark it off the master list?"

She hadn't. She'd been caught by the beauty of the man and the picture. "I'll do it now." Picking up the iPad, she entered the date and time of the painting's arrival.

Her head lifted and she saw Rio opening the other packages as the driver patiently waited. It was the same delivery service that first driver had belonged to, but she'd never seen the impatient first deliveryman again. She started to ask Rio about it, but decided to let it go. She had more important things to take up with him.

For the rest of that day and all the next, Rio was even more distant. By the end of the working day on Thursday, Skylar had had enough. She patiently waited until the last delivery truck left at six thirteen. Two of Rio's men took in the framed pictures with a personal letter from famous individuals donating dinner or time with them.

Skylar didn't speak until the two men were out of hearing range. She went to Rio, who was putting the paper and boxes in a recycling bin. She gazed at his prime rear for a couple of seconds, then shook herself. "Rio?"

Slowly he straightened and turned. "Yes?"

"Why don't we drive into town for dinner? My treat."

"I'm busy," came his flat answer.

She barely kept the smile on her face. "I didn't tell you the time."

"Doesn't matter," he returned, not missing a beat.

All right, perhaps she had to spell it out for him. "I'd like for us to get to know each other better," she said, thinking what a horrible line that was, but it was the truth.

He crossed his arms as if bored. His flat expression never changed. "You were vetted and cleared by me before you were hired. I doubt if there is anything more to learn about you. As for my life, it's boring." His arms dropped to his sides. "If you'll excuse me."

"Fat chance," she snapped.

He simply stared at her, which angered Skylar even

more. "I've tried. I really have tried to understand you, but you're impossible."

"Ms. Du—"

"All of your men call me Skylar, why can't you? It isn't that difficult to pronounce." She didn't give him a chance to answer. She jabbed her finger into his broad chest and had the brief satisfaction of seeing his eyes widen in surprise. "I won't wait around forever for you to figure out what you're missing." She turned, then quickly wheeled back. "And for your information there might be some things about me that you don't know that would blow your mind!"

Her nose in the air, Skylar stalked to her room, giving her hips a little something extra. Today was the final straw. She was not about to twiddle her thumbs and let Rio keep ignoring her.

She took a long bath, lotioned and sprayed her body with V, the most expensive perfume in the world, and applied her makeup. She slipped on a red backless mini dress, stepped into five-inch stilettos, put on silver chandelier earrings encrusted with diamonds and a matching necklace and bracelet. Snagging her red clutch, she was out the door. She was not waiting on Rio a second longer.

Downstairs, she went in search of the house manager. She'd already told Mary at lunch that she had plans for dinner. She found Eli in the kitchen drinking coffee.

When he saw her, he sat the cup down, stood, and shoved the chair back under the table.

Sad to say, he didn't look any more at ease to Skylar. She knew how he felt. Some problems just wouldn't go away.

"Good evening, Mr. Patterson. I have dinner reservations at El Matador. I'm not sure what time I'll be home."

"Very well. Are you going alone?"

Her chin came up a fraction. "Yes."

He stared at her a bit strangely. "Drive carefully."

"Thank you. I will." She started for the garage, hoping that she'd see Rio. She'd show him.

Luck was on her side. He was still outside talking to one of his men. Her head high, she passed him without a glance. She got into her SUV, then backed out of the garage and drove past him, wishing she could see his face. She wasn't sure if she looked in the mirror he'd see her looking back.

Waving to the guards at the guardhouse, she headed to town. She'd show him!

Hands on his hips, Rio stared at the back of the SUV. He could shake Skylar until her perfect white teeth rattled. They both knew she wasn't the type of woman to pick up men, but that didn't mean men wouldn't try once they saw her, or that she wouldn't consider trusting one.

A mad woman was a dangerous woman.

He turned to go inside to the command center and saw one of his men still staring at the SUV with a rapt expression. Rio wanted to dunk him in the lake. "Finish here. I'm going inside."

Rio went straight to his personal computer in the command center and brought up the location of the SUV. All of the cars had tracking devices on them. He could find her. He started to rise, but sat back down.

He wasn't running after any woman.

Halfway through what should have been a marvelous dining experience, tired of telling men she didn't need their company, Skylar accepted that her ultimatum to Rio hadn't worked. She'd gambled and lost.

"Check, please."

"Certainly." The attentive waiter handed her the bill. "Would you like anything boxed?"

"No, thank you." She gave him the black folder and waited for him to return with the receipt so she could sign and go back to the castle. She'd accomplished nothing except making herself look foolish or, worse, desperate.

"Hello, gorgeous." The man braced his manicured hands on the chair across from hers. "You sure I can't buy you a drink? Last chance."

Skylar simply looked at the man, who had been the most persistent of them all tonight. He'd tried to pick her up shortly after her arrival. When that hadn't worked, he'd sent over a glass of champagne, which she refused. Now he was back again.

"And this is your last chance. If you bother me again, I'll alert management and call my boyfriend, who can bench-press two hundred pounds and not break a sweat."

The man jerked upright, the easy smile gone. "I was just—"

"Not another word or I'm making a phone call you aren't going to like."

The man beat a hasty retreat to his table.

"Here you are." The waiter handed her the bill holder. "I took the liberty of telling the valet to have your car ready."

She placed the receipt in her purse. "How? I have my claim ticket."

"Some guests are memorable. Have a good night."

To some men, perhaps. Rio wasn't among them. The waiter held the chair as Skylar rose to her feet. "Thank you and good night."

Outside, her SUV waited for her. Tipping the attendant, she saw two couples still waiting for their cars. At least someone had noticed her. Unfortunately, it wasn't the right person.

Fastening her seat belt, she pulled out of the restaurant and headed back to the castle. She glanced at the clock. Eight thirty-eight. It was too early to return. He'd know she had a crappy night. However, she wasn't about to hang out someplace to make him think otherwise.

She flicked on her signal and passed a car going ten miles below the speed limit. At the best of times, she'd never been able to drive slowly. Her father said she had a lead foot, just like her mother.

Skylar smiled. She loved her parents and missed them, but she loved her job and was happy. Well, relatively happy. She stopped at the signal light and glanced into her rearview mirror. An SUV was behind her with its high beams on.

She detested drivers who drove with their high beams on in good weather. She pulled off and changed lanes. So did the driver behind her, cutting off a car to do so.

She frowned. Some people shouldn't have driver's licenses. Her thoughts returned to her parents. It was difficult to believe they'd been divorced for three years. Sure, they'd argued at times, but they made a habit of never leaving the house or going to bed unless it was settled.

Until that last time they'd argued bitterly. Her father hadn't been able to say anything to keep her mother from filing for divorce.

Skylar thought they'd always be together, just like her maternal grandparents who lived in Boston, and her paternal grandparents in New Orleans. She was learning that love was hard to find and harder to keep.

Skylar eased her foot off the gas. All the slow cars

must be out tonight. Signaling, she passed a creeping Impala and got into the far lane, the lane she'd use to turn onto the road leading to the castle. She didn't like changing lanes because the potential for an accident was higher.

She glanced into her rearview mirror and frowned. The SUV with the high beams had changed lanes as well and was behind her. Strange.

She wasn't the paranoid type, but her uncle had hammered it into her head that paranoia was a good thing and could save your butt. Skylar changed lanes. The SUV changed with her.

Her heart rate kicked up. She remembered stories of men following women home and assaulting them. Wouldn't they be in for a surprise once she reached the castle? If she made it there. Before she reached the castle, she had to drive through a lonely five- or seven-mile stretch of road.

She glanced in the mirror again. The beams were so high, all she could detect was that it was some kind of dark SUV. Perhaps she was overreacting. They could have changed lanes for the same reason she had. One way to find out.

She slowed down until she was ten, then fifteen miles under the speed limit. The car behind her matched her speed. She couldn't deny it any longer.

She was being followed.

Chapter 4

"Don't panic. Don't panic. You're in your car. Other people in cars are in front of and on the side of you." She eased back into the inside lane. No way was she leaving the city limits.

Yet Skylar's hand trembled as she reached for her purse and pulled out her cell phone. She wished she'd synced it to the radio. It was answered before the second ring.

"Rio."

Skylar sagged with relief. "I think someone is following me. Their high beams are on."

"Are you sure?" There was a fierce sharpness in his voice.

"When I slow down or change lanes, so does the SUV. The police will act faster if the call comes from you."

"Already done. We have your location. I'm on my way."

Just hearing he was coming bolstered her resolve to keep it together. "Thank you."

"Which lane are you in?"

"The inside."

"Good. Skylar, there's only one more light before you reach the edge of town."

He'd called her name, settling her fraying nerves. The

sound of his car's engine through the phone calmed her even more. He was coming. "I'm almost there."

"Don't catch the light," Rio advised. "When it turns green—"

"Make a U-turn and floor it back to town," she finished for him.

"Put the phone in the seat. The Beemer has enough juice to make the turn, but I want both of your hands on the steering wheel. The police are on the way. You're safe in the car."

"Please hurry."

"Nothing is going to happen to you," he said, his voice a mixture of anger and resolve.

"The light is red. The SUV is a car length behind. I'm putting the phone down." She placed the cell phone back in her purse so it wouldn't slide onto the floor. "It's green." Her sweaty hands flexed on the steering wheel. She didn't know if Rio still had his cell phone on or not, but it was comforting to think he did.

Both hands gripped the steering wheel as she eased off, then gunned the BMW. Her car was approaching sixty when she made a sharp U-turn and floored it back to town, thanking God that there had been no oncoming traffic. She threw a glance in the rearview mirror as the speedometer reached eighty.

Her heart thumped. The SUV was right behind her. Increasing her speed, she whipped around a car, hoping the police showed up before she had to make a decision to run a red light.

The SUV was gaining on her. Up ahead she saw the light turn red. "You're safe in your car." She heard Rio's voice and drew in a deep breath. She passed another car, hoping to shake them. The SUV stayed on her like a burr.

"Green. Turn green."

The light flashed green three car lengths away. Skylar glanced to the right and left to ensure that some driver wasn't running the light in the opposite direction, then zoomed through it. She didn't know where the police station was located so she was going back to the restaurant, a straight shot from—

Police sirens. Up ahead she could see their running lights flashing. She glanced in the rearview mirror to see the SUV dropping back, then turning down a side street. For one insane moment, she considered following it to try to get the license plate number.

Common sense prevailed as she pulled to the side of the road and put on her emergency lights to signal the police. She didn't know how many were in the SUV or if they had weapons.

Two police cars converged on her. One parked beside her and the other catty-corner, hemming her in and protecting her at the same time.

She had the foresight to unlock the door just as a brawny policeman opened it. He tipped his black Stetson. "Dakota Rodriquez, police chief, Ms. Dupree. You're safe."

She swallowed, nodded. "The SUV following me turned to the right one street back."

"Is there any thing else you can tell me about the SUV?"

She clamped her hands in her lap and shook her head. "The high beams were on."

Dakota spoke to the policeman standing nearby. "SUV turned a block back. Check it out."

"Right, Chief."

"Ms. Dupree—"

"Are you all right?"

Her head jerked up on hearing Rio's strong voice.

His muscled body filled the doorway of the vehicle. She wanted so much for him to hold her, but she was afraid if he did, she'd become a blithering idiot.

His callused hand tenderly skimmed down her bare arm, sending heat and comfort. She shivered. She'd waited so long for him to touch her with more than disinterest. His sharp eyes narrowed on her face when she didn't answer. "Yes," she finally managed.

"Rio, I need to ask some questions if we're going to find this joker," Dakota said.

For a long moment, Rio simply stared at Skylar. "You did good."

"Rio," the police chief repeated.

Rio turned his body so she could see the police chief, but he didn't move away. The chief glanced from one to the other. "Do you have any idea who might have been following you?"

"No. I—I—" She swallowed and clutched her hands in her lap.

"This is only the third time she's been to Santa Fe," Rio said. "She's Navarone's event director. She flew in Sunday afternoon on the small jet to run an auction at the castle for Mrs. Grayson's Music Department. She has no other connections here besides that."

The police chief looked from Rio to Skylar again. She twisted uneasily. "When the SUV turned off the highway, I thought about turning around and following to get a—"

"Are you crazy?" Rio grabbed both of her arms. His black eyes blazed. "You trying to get yourself—?" His teeth clamped together, his fingers slowly uncurled.

Killed. "No. That's why I didn't follow them."

"*Them.* You think it was more than one person?" Dakota's attention sharpened.

"It's just a figure of speech," Skylar told him. "I couldn't tell how many, the sex or race. The lights were too bright."

"Chief, I didn't see anything," the other police officer said. "With more to go on . . ." His voice trailed off.

"Ms. Dupree, where were you coming from?" Dakota asked.

She cut a glance at Rio. "Dinner at the El Matador."

"Alone?" Dakota continued.

Skylar looked at Rio again. Had his eyes sharpened? "Yes."

"Forgive me, but you're an attractive woman dining alone and wearing some serious jewelry. Unfortunately, some men look at that as an opportunity." Dakota tipped his hat back. "Any problems at the restaurant?"

She touched her diamond necklace and sat up straighter. "You don't think it was one of them, do you?"

"Them." Dakota took out a pad. "Perhaps you better give me their descriptions."

Without looking at Rio, she told the police chief about the five men who'd tried to pick her up, ending with the one who had been the most persistent. She wanted to slink away. This could have been her fault.

"That's enough, Dakota." Rio faced the other man. "I'm taking her back to the castle."

Dakota scratched his ear. "Will you be available tomorrow to come down to the station, Ms. Dupree?"

"We're expecting shipments for the auction and we both need to be there to sign them in." Rio placed his arm on the top of the BMW, effectively blocking Skylar from the policeman. "There's a gap between one and three. We'll come in then."

"Thought you might be coming." Dakota slipped his notepad back into his shirt pocket. "Sorry, Ms. Dupree, that you had a bad experience in my town. We have good people." He tipped his hat. "Good night. See you both tomorrow." Both police cars pulled away.

Rio reached inside the SUV and grabbed the key. "We'll go back in my car. I'll send someone back for yours."

Skylar picked up her purse and twisted around to get out. Her dress inched up to mid-thigh. She didn't seem to notice. Rio did. He took her arm and helped her, touching more bare skin, skin that could be easily bruised and abused. Just the thought sent rage pulsing though him.

He opened the passenger door of the Jeep, felt her tremble. His gut twisted violently. No power on earth could have kept him from pulling her securely into his arms. "You're safe, Skylar. You're safe."

"I'm sorry," she murmured, her arms wrapped tightly around his waist, her breasts pushing against his chest. "The men at the restaurant—"

He stiffened. She dropped her arms. He didn't want to think of what might have happened if she hadn't been more alert. "Let's go."

Wordlessly, Skylar got inside the Jeep, her hands clamped in her lap. If Rio ever caught whoever did this to her, they would pay and pay dearly. Closing the door, he got inside the Jeep and drove off.

Rio thinks it's my fault. Skylar was miserable. During the drive she kept her face averted. She had bought it all on herself by trying to entice Rio. What must he think of her?

As soon as the Jeep stopped in front of the castle doors, she got out. One of Rio's men was there to open the front door. "I'm glad you're all right, Skylar."

"Thank you," she murmured, her head down as she

continued toward the stairs, very aware that, although she couldn't hear him on the carpet-covered risers, Rio was behind her.

She didn't stop until she reached her bedroom door. She drew upon her fledging courage and slowly lifted her gaze to his. It had to be said.

At least he wasn't looking through her any longer. "I'm sorry. I didn't mean to cause any problems. I just wanted you to stop looking at me as if I didn't exist."

The tears glistening in her beautiful eyes make his insides clench. He pulled her to him, his cheek resting against the top of her head. "Don't. It's not your fault some bastard can't accept a no! You're safe. I'm not going to let anything happen to you."

"I—I thought you were angry with me." She gripped handfuls of his shirt.

"I was angry at the man who scared you." Feeling his resistance weakening, he slowly stepped away from temptation and dropped his hands to his sides.

Staring up at him, her fingers uncurled. She sent him a watery smile.

His hands clenched and flexed to keep from pulling her into his arms again. "Go to sleep. If you get scared, just call."

She looked up at him through a sweep of her thick eyelashes. "Can I call you if I'm not afraid?"

Frustrated by her unwavering persistence, he shoved his hand over his head. "Why can't you let it go?"

"Because I've watched you for two years." She grinned. "I'm tired of watching and ready to do some touching."

Despite the situation, Rio threw back his head and laughed. The next instant, her arms were around his neck, her hazel eyes staring up at him and sparkling with happiness.

"I've always wanted to hear you laugh, among other things."

He sobered. His hands anchored her small waist. "I'm not a forever kind of man."

"I know that," she said. "I'm not asking for forever. I just want to be there for you now."

No woman and few men had ever affected him so deeply, been so unselfish. *I just want to be there for you now.*

"You ever heard of kissing it to make it feel better?" she asked.

"Go to bed, Skylar."

Her smile trembled. "Hearing you say my name helped make me not so scared. I'm glad you were there in the control booth."

His hands flexed on her waist. "I was monitoring the car's movement."

She grinned. "You were?"

His finger grazed her nose. "It doesn't take that long to eat dinner unless . . ."

She placed her hand on his wide, muscular chest. "Not ever going to happen. I was waiting for you."

"And rebuffing men."

She shrugged. "They weren't you."

He shook his dark head. "This is not going to happen."

"We'll see. Good night, Rio, and thanks for coming for me." The door closed. For a long time, Rio stood there with a wistful look on his face. On the other side of the door, Skylar was smiling.

The next morning Rio found a small envelope stuck to his door. Even before opening the thick vellum paper and pulling out the note card with Skylar's name, he'd known it was from her.

Good morning. I hope your schedule is free to have breakfast with me at eight thirty, lunch at one. We'll go from there.

Skylar

He should just write BUSY on the envelope and leave it outside her door. He couldn't. With Skylar's soft heart, he'd hurt her. He stopped in front of her door. She was wealthy and cultured with a lineage that could be traced back several generations. He had no idea who his parents were. She was outgoing; he kept to himself unless he was with Blade or Shane. They didn't have anything in common.

It didn't seem to matter. There was this awareness between them. He might have been able to resist her, if not for last night. Thinking of her being frightened and alone sent fresh rage shooting through him.

The door opened. Skylar stood there. Her eyes widened in surprise, then her gaze ran over him like silent fingers. Her head lifted. She wore a scarlet-colored dress and looked much too tempting. "Good morning, Rio. I see you got my note."

She wasn't for him. "I might—"

She held up both hands, effectively stopping him. "Don't tell me that after my harrowing night you're going to refuse my invitation?"

His brow lifted. She looked beautiful, happy, and ready to take on the world. He crossed his arms. "That's beneath you."

She shrugged her elegant shoulders. "A woman's gotta do what a woman's gotta do."

Before he thought better of it, he reached out and swept his hand over her hair. This morning it was unbound and flowing down her back, and it felt like strands of silk. "You're not going to let it get you down, huh?"

"It would give whoever it was too much power." Shutting her door, she stepped closer. "Besides, it did something I couldn't do."

His hand dropped. "Skylar, this is not going anyplace."

"We'll see." She hooked her arm through his. "We're about an hour early, but I'm a pretty good cook."

He found himself going down the stairs with her. "Why are you up so early?"

She tossed him a grin. "Waiting for you to pass. I wasn't sure you'd accept."

He stopped in the middle of the foyer. "I always meet my men for a report first thing each morning."

"I just thought of something. You live here, but where do the other men stay?" she inquired.

"In the barn."

"Barn!" she yelped, staring up at him with disbelief.

His lips twitched at the indignation in her face. She really did have a soft heart. "Converted barn, I should have said. You should know Blade treats his employees well."

She looked abashed before recovering. "Maybe I could follow you and have breakfast with you there."

"Off limits to women," he informed her. "Although Sierra has tried. Not even she has been inside."

Skylar glanced up at him with a grin. "Man cave, huh?"

"It suits its purpose."

"I'll bet."

He wasn't sure if that was a compliment or not. "How did you know not to keep going?"

"Training."

He paused on the landing. "It wasn't in your record."

She stuck her tongue in her cheek. "Told you you might have missed something."

Rio lifted a brow at the impossibility of that.

Skylar rolled her eyes. "All right. My maternal grandmother's purse was snatched when I was twelve. She was angrier than a wet hen and determined she'd never be vulnerable again. Uncle Joshua, my mother's bother, was home on leave from the navy. He taught her and my mother self-defense. I went with them and kept on learning. That's why it wasn't on any of my records. We trained quietly at home."

"Joshua is in the Secret Service now, and for a while so was his daughter," Rio said. "I'm sorry for her loss."

Skylar pulled her arms free and tucked her head. "We were all devastated."

He wanted to take the grief from her eyes. "Your family is very close."

Her head lifted. "Is there anything about me and my immediate family that you don't know?"

"It seems I know plenty about you."

"A woman likes to have some secrets." On tiptoes, she kissed him on the cheek. "Is twenty minutes enough time for you to be back for breakfast?"

They both knew he hadn't accepted. She was looking at him again as if he were the only man on the planet. "Make it thirty."

She grinned. "I'd kiss you again, but I don't want to push my luck. See you in thirty."

He could have stopped the kiss if he'd wanted. That was the problem. He wanted her and, each time he saw her, the wanting increased. He'd have breakfast with her because she'd been through so much. She might appear soft, but Skylar had a hint of steel in her spine.

He watched her until she disappeared, then headed for his men's quarters. He had a job to do.

Skylar didn't sigh or throw up her hands or pout when Rio returned with his stoic face firmly in place. She hadn't thought it would be easy.

"Please have a seat." She motioned to the chair beside hers. There were two place settings side by side.

He pulled out her chair. "Thank you." She took her seat and waited until he sat beside her. Tucking her head, she said grace and then placed a huge omelet on his plate. There was already a steaming cup of coffee and a glass of orange juice for him. "How did the report go?"

"Fine."

Skylar picked up her fork. "Is there anything else you'd like me to get for you?"

"No, thank you."

Skylar quietly ate her breakfast, determined to act as normally as possible. "Over half of the items are already here. By next Tuesday, everything will be in place and we'll have the other three days to make sure everything is ready."

"Yes."

She wasn't giving up. "What day will Sierra and Blade return?"

"Next Friday."

She tried to think of a question that couldn't be answered with one word. She smiled and leaned over to whisper in his ear, making sure he'd feel her warm breath on his skin. "What would you do if I got up from my chair, slid into your lap, put my mouth on yours, my arms around your neck, and kissed you until my head swam? Shall I find out?"

He went still. His hand on his fork clenched.

Skylar couldn't be sure, but she thought his breathing accelerated. Hers certainly had. She was seriously considering biting his earlobe when he abruptly rose to his feet.

His nostrils flared as if he was having trouble drawing in air. "Thanks for breakfast. I'll be outside."

"I'll be there shortly." Rather pleased with herself, Skylar sipped her juice. Rio didn't run from anything or anyone, but he'd certainly made a quick exit. He wasn't as disinterested as he pretended.

"You can run, Rio, but you can't hide. I'm coming after you and, what's more, you're going to like it. Eventually."

Chapter 5

Rio wasn't having a good day. Thus far, Dakota hadn't come up with anything on the car. He was headed out the door on another call and would talk to Rio when he and Skylar came in that afternoon.

The clear, husky sound of Skylar's laughter was like a prod to Rio's back. Arms crossed, he kept staring toward the driveway for the next delivery. For a woman as delicate and cultured as Skylar, her laugh was bedroom-husky. It made a man's mind wander where it shouldn't.

"Skylar, you're a mess," Conner exclaimed, his laughter joining hers.

Rio refused to look over at the happy trio. Henderson was there with them. Skylar had enough sense and was woman enough not to try to make him jealous. She was just being her usual friendly self. In Tucson, she'd donated time and money to a women's shelter. She'd flown home last year on Christmas morning because she'd helped with shopping and wrapping presents for the women and children staying there. The twenty-foot fully decorated tree in the front room had been from her. She cared about people.

She'd just picked the wrong one this time. *I've watched*

you for two years. I'm ready to do a little touching. He'd laughed last night. He wasn't laughing now. Skylar was proving to be more tempting than he had anticipated.

"Rio, I see the last delivery truck. We can make our one o'clock appointment," she said cheerfully.

He straightened and looked at her. "I can't make it. We'll leave at one thirty to go see Dakota."

Her hazel eyes narrowed. Her chin lifted. "Of course." She came to her feet and turned to Conner and Henderson. "Time to get back to work, gentlemen."

Both men saluted her. Rio walked from beneath the tent to meet the driver. Skylar was not going to get to him.

Five minutes later he wasn't so sure about the delivery driver. He couldn't seem to keep his eyes off Skylar. Usually she stayed beneath the tent and waited for Rio or one his men to bring the packages to the unpacking table. This time she was there when the man brought out the first box. He actually stopped in his tracks.

"Thank you."

Seemingly oblivious to the man's stare, she took the small box from his hands and went to the unpacking table.

"We'd like to get this done this year," Conner said.

The man jerked as if coming out of a trance. "Yeah. Sorry."

Conner and Henderson loaded their dollies and wheeled them back to the table. Skylar, ignoring Rio, unpacked the diamond-and-ruby brooch. "This is exquisite."

Not as exquisite as you, Rio thought, and turned to help unload the dolly. They were almost finished when the driver approached with another box.

"This is the last one."

"Thank you." Skylar smiled at the man. "Would you like something to drink while we open these?"

"I'd appreciate it." The man looked as if he'd just won the lottery. He stepped forward and Rio reached for the box. The man's gaze met his. The driver's eyes widened. He stumbled back. The box slipped from his hands.

Rio caught the package and mentally cursed. He knew his expression was ice-cold and dangerous. He also knew the reason he looked that way.

"Ah, sorry." The man wiped his now sweaty face. "I think I'll pass on the drink."

There was absolute quiet as the packages were opened. Rio called out the items to Skylar, and she checked them off the master list. After the driver signed, Rio gave the man a large tip and handed him a cold bottle of water. He swallowed, took the money and water, nodded, and rushed back to his truck.

When Rio looked around, Skylar was gone.

"Where is Ms. Dupree?"

Mary, the cook, jumped and swung around from the kitchen sink, her hand going to her heart. Seeing it was Rio, she still looked ready to bolt.

"Sorry, I didn't mean to startle you." He really didn't like frightening people unless he meant to.

Mary slowly lowered her hand. "That's all right. I didn't hear you come in."

"Have you seen Ms. Dupree?" he asked again. He'd expected her to come out after she finished her lunch. He'd gone to the men's quarters and checked in with Blade.

"She's gone."

"Gone where?" he asked, barely managing to keep his voice even and non-threatening.

Mary shook her dark head. "She just said she had busi-

ness in town and that I didn't have to cook lunch or dinner
for her."

She wouldn't, he thought, but he was already moving
to his Jeep because he knew she would go to meet Dakota
without him. He spoke into the wrist radio. "Where's Skylar's car?"

"Five miles from here, headed north into town," came
the answer from the control room.

Two of his men had gone to retrieve her car last night.
He hadn't thought to tell them not to let her leave unless
he was with her. Opening the front door, he rushed toward his Jeep. He wouldn't underestimate her again, but
neither should she underestimate him.

Skylar followed the policeman to Dakota's office. She
would show Rio that she didn't need to depend on him or
any other man. She'd been taught to be the perfect hostess
for her husband, but never subservient to him. The nerve
of him trying to scare the poor deliveryman half to death
after ignoring her all morning. She'd show him!

"Here it is, Ms. Dupree," the young officer said. "The
chief is expecting you."

"Thank you." She knocked on the half-glass door.

"Come in," said a male voice.

Skylar opened the door and saw the police chief rise
from his chair behind a neat desk. She extended her hand.
"Chief, it's—" She whirled around to see Rio leaning
against a file cabinet. "What are you doing here?"

He straightened and came to within a foot of her. "I
told Dakota we'd be here."

"I'm perfectly capable of being interviewed without
you. Thank you, but you can leave."

Rio looked at Dakota, who leaned against the front of

his desk, his lips twitching. He was glad someone found the situation amusing. "The chief might have a question or two for me."

This was not working out the way she'd planned. "You weren't the one being followed."

Anger glinted in his dark eyes. "I was the one you called."

She knew the anger wasn't directed at her, but at whoever had been in the SUV. "Because I knew the police would respond quicker to you than to me." The words were barely out of her mouth before she realized she might have insulted the police chief. He and Rio seemed to be on good terms. She glared at Rio for making her speak without thinking and faced the police chief. To the man's credit, he still wore that patient expression he'd had on last night and when she'd just now entered his office.

"Chief Rodriquez, I didn't mean to disparage your department," Skylar told him. "However, if I had called the 911 operator, he or she would have wanted to be sure I wasn't imagining things, ask questions about the car, the reason I might be followed, before dispatching a police car. I was one signal light away from the last one out of town. I made the call that would get help the fastest."

"The right one, as it turned out." Dakota motioned to a chair in front of his desk. "Please have a seat."

She looked from Rio to the door.

"Not happening," he said flatly.

If Blade couldn't intimidate Rio, she certainly couldn't. She took a seat. She sensed him moving to stand just behind her. "Have you been able to find out anything more?" she asked.

Irritation flashed across the policeman's face. "Unfortunately, not much. As you said, the car went down a side street. One of my men questioned the valets at the restaurant, and none recalls getting an SUV after you left."

"The restaurant has cameras," Rio said.

"The tapes should be delivered to me before five today," the police chief answered, "I located the man you said was the most persistent because he'd been that way with other women that night. The manager asked him to leave. He paid with a credit card. He drives a small compact and didn't leave the restaurant until at least an hour after you did."

Skylar didn't want to ask if he'd been able to find the other men. Rio wasn't so hesitant.

"What about the others?"

"Another dead end with three of them." The police chief looked at Skylar. "From your descriptions of the men and their clothes, I was able to find them. They were still at the bar, still betting who could pick up a woman in the shortest length of time."

"Juvenile and crude. Women have more sense," Skylar said.

"The fifth man?" Rio asked.

"Nothing. A waiter thought he recalled a man wearing a black-and-white-checkered jacket, but couldn't be sure. The restaurant was very busy. We'll look for him on the tape," the chief told them. "Have you thought of anything else, Ms. Dupree?"

"No, nothing." Skylar sat back in her chair. "I told you everything last night."

Dakota glanced over her head at Rio and leaned forward. "Any old disgruntled boyfriends?"

She did not want to answer that. It would be too much to ask Rio to step out. Then she realized that those close to Blade had few secrets from his personal bodyguard and chief of security at Navarone Resorts and Spas. "I haven't dated in some time." Like not in the past two years, and very little before then. She had lots of male friends, but they were just that, friends.

"I see," Dakota said, when it was obvious he didn't.

Skylar glanced at her watch. "If there are no further questions, I need to get back to the castle."

The police chief came to his feet and around the desk. "That's all for now. Thank you for coming."

Skylar stood. "Thank you. I wish I could be of more help."

"You're safe. That's the most important thing."

"And you'll stay that way," Rio said from behind her, steel in his voice.

Despite her wish to show Rio she didn't need him, she had a desire for the man. She didn't have a shred of doubt that he'd protect her with his life if necessary. The thought of him being hurt sent a chill through her. "Let the police handle this."

From the blank look he gave her, Rio wasn't going to listen. "Stay in touch, Dakota."

"Will do."

Taking her arm, Rio headed for the door. Skylar had no intention of creating a scene in the police station. Once she reached her car was soon enough to set Rio straight.

Luckily, once they were outside, he walked in the direction she'd parked the car. However, when they reached the spot, instead of her black BMW there was a red Toyota. "Someone stole the car!" she yelled, unable to believe it.

"It's back at the castle," Ro said calmly. "I had it picked up."

She stared at him, then swung her purse at him. He caught it with his hand. She lifted her foot to kick him, then stomped it instead. She might have a black belt, but she was no match for Rio's quick reflexes. "You should have told me."

"You should have waited for me." He stepped closer. His eyes blazed. "Be annoyed at me, but be smart about it. The nut from last night could have been random or he could know you and be waiting for you to leave the castle."

Fear overrode the anger. "I've been trying to make myself believe it was random."

"Until we know for certain, we have to assume it wasn't. That means you don't go anyplace from now on without me or one of my men." He continued down the busy street until he reached his Jeep. "When we reach the castle, you're getting another car."

Rio hadn't said so, but obviously she was changing vehicles in case the person or persons in the SUV would recognize her last one on sight. He stopped on the passenger side and opened the door.

"Nothing is going to happen to you."

"Nothing better happen to you, either, or you'll hear from me." She faced him with her back to the Jeep's seat. "I mean it." She poked his chest with her finger to make her point. "We both stay safe."

He caught her hand. "Little warrior."

She was undeniably touched. "You better believe it. Now come on, let's grab some food and get back before the next delivery."

His thumb grazed her hand before reluctantly releasing it. "Already taken care of. Mary said you told her not to cook for lunch or dinner."

She stepped closer, her arms going around his neck. "Does the invitation go for dinner as well?"

His hands splayed on her small waist. He wasn't sure if

it was to keep her from getting closer or to touch her. "Brandon is waiting."

"So am I." She didn't move.

"Brandon doesn't like it when people are late for their reservations."

She cocked a brow, withdrew her arms, and reached for the door handle. He was faster, but it also placed her slim backside against his front. She stilled. Since she was unpredictable, he moved back.

Tossing him a grin, she climbed inside. "One day you won't be able to or want to move away."

He gave her a flat look. Her grin widened. She had an easier time climbing in this time because of her flared skirt. It slithered back on her thighs when she crossed her long legs. He closed the door with a snap, went around, and got inside. That's what he was afraid of.

They must have been watching for them. As soon as the hostess spotted Rio and Skylar, she picked up a cell phone. Rio couldn't imagine allowing her to have it ordinarily.

A waitress greeted them. "Good afternoon, I'll show you to your table. Your food should be out shortly."

"How many times has Brandon called?" Rio asked, his hand in the small of Skylar's back as they followed the waitress.

She glanced over her shoulder. "Twice in less than two minutes."

Rio grunted. "Someone was poking."

Skylar looked at him, then patted his arm. "Everyone can't be a good driver."

"Here you are," the young woman said, her lips twitching. "Brandon is probably on his way."

Skylar slid onto the red, tufted barouche bench at the

end of the family table and patted the seat beside her. "I won't bite."

Yes, you would, he almost said, then took his seat. No man or woman had ever gotten the best of him, and it wasn't going to start now.

"About time." Brandon set down a platter of smoking beef and chicken fajitas, piled atop grilled onions, and red and green peppers.

Another waiter brought their drinks, chips, flour tortillas, and salsa. "Rio. Skylar. Happy to see you back."

"We're a minute early," Rio said.

Brandon grinned and leaned against the edge of the booth. "My watch must be off."

"Thanks, Brandon." Skylar reached for her purse. "I appreciate the rush. Would it be possible to get an order for chips and different dips to take back for Rio's men?"

"Put that away. That goes for you as well, Rio. You're helping Mama."

"Thanks again. I really appreciate it." Skylar returned her billfold to her purse. "She's an awesome woman. I'm happy to help."

"Was there something else, Brandon?" Rio asked, already knowing the answer.

"Rio, this is the first time you've brought a guest. Top shelf." Bandon straightened. "If you need anything, just grab any passing waiter or waitress. Later."

"Try this." Skylar held a chip laden with queso.

"I can feed myself."

She rolled her eyes and inched it closer. "Come on, humor me."

He took a small bite of the chip. Immediately she crunched on the chip until it was gone, then licked her lips. "Good, but I know something that's even better."

He reached for his drink. Skylar might be more difficult to resist than he'd thought.

"Here you go."

She held a fajita to his mouth. He was not falling for that again. He took it from her hand and took a bite. "Eat. We have thirty-three minutes to get back."

"Then perhaps I should drive." He took another bite, but when he lowered his hands she took both of his wrists in hers. "I can also be stubborn. I just want to see if it tastes as good as I remember."

Me or the food? He looked up to see Mrs. Grayson turning away. Ordinarily he'd let her leave. He was on her marriage hit list.

Skylar bit into his fajita. "Almost as good until I get to taste the real thing again."

Rio placed the fajita on his plate and rose to his feet. He needed a third party here to make Skylar behave, even one who had a bull's-eye with a capital *M* on his forehead. "Mrs. Grayson, please join us."

"Hello, Rio and Skylar. I don't want to intrude," she told him.

Skylar cleaned her hands on a napkin and scooted out of the seat to hug the older woman. "Impossible, Mrs. Grayson. Especially since you're the reason this fantastic food is on the house."

"Thanks for keeping me updated. I can't wait to see the entire collection. Thank you, Rio, for staying and ensuring its safety." Mrs. Grayson smiled at Rio.

He shook his head once. Not happening. It didn't faze her.

"Please have a seat and join us." Skylar motioned to the U-shaped booth. "There's more than enough food."

"That's kind of you, but I have an appointment. Brandon said you were coming for a late lunch and I just wanted to say hi and thank you." Mrs. Grayson took Skylar's hands. "I can't cook as well as Brandon, but I'd love for you to come over tonight for dinner. If you don't have plans?"

"Do we have plans, Rio?" Skylar asked.

The women stared at him. He should just say no.

"Trying to surprise me, huh?" Skylar faced Mrs. Grayson. "Why don't you come out and I—" She stopped abruptly. "It will be dark when you leave Navarone Castle."

"I left the other night and it was dark, but don't worry."

Rio knew Skylar was thinking about the incident last night. "She always has an escort to her door, the house is checked, and she'll be safely inside with the best security system in the world before my man leaves."

"Thanks to Rio and Luke. I appreciate the security system, but the man following me is unnecessary. However, no one listens to this old woman," Ruth said, with a sigh.

Brandon snorted. "If any of us called you old, you'd brain us. Watch out when she pulls the old card." He kissed his mother on the cheek and placed three large take-out bags on the seat. "That should hold the men."

"Thanks," Skylar said.

His mother patted his cheek. "I love you, too."

"You're welcome to come over tonight and look over the collection," Skylar said. "Or do you want to wait until Tuesday afternoon when everything is finished?"

"Tuesday will be fine." Ruth hugged Skylar again, and patted Rio's arm. "We'll talk later and firm things up. Enjoy your meal." She walked away with Brandon.

Skylar sat back down and reached for Rio's fajita. "Eat up. The clock is ticking."

Rio took his seat, picked up a flour tortilla, and prepared

a fajita. Skylar didn't even seem to notice. She was up to something.

Skylar insisted on carrying one of the bags with Rio's men's food. "How many minutes?"

"Eighteen." Rio opened the back door and placed the three bags inside.

"Cutting it close. You sure you don't want me to drive?" she asked with a straight face.

"Not—"

"Happening." She opened the passenger door. "Didn't your mother or father ever teach you about compromise?"

"I was raised in a church orphanage," he said, his voice flat.

Her heart stopped, aching for him. "Then neither got to know the intelligent and wonderful man you are." She climbed inside. Her nails dug into her palms to keep from crying. "I peeked in one of the bags. I might wander over and join you."

Rio backed out. "You wouldn't get within fifty feet. Sensors."

"I sort of figured that's what posed a problem to Sierra," Skylar said, hoping she hadn't brought up bad memories earlier. "But after meeting Sierra, and knowing she's strong-willed *and* Blade's wife, how did that work out?"

"I called Blade when I saw her heading in that direction for no apparent reason and went after her." He stopped at the light. "Blade arrived while we were talking just inside the perimeter of the scanners. My men followed protocol when the scanners went off."

Protocol could mean anything from lockdown to guns drawn. Skylar would have loved to have heard that "talk" between Rio and Sierra. It was no secret to anyone who had been around Sierra that she liked having her way, and that she didn't like the bodyguards Rio assigned to her when she wasn't with Blade. She and Rio had butted heads in the past and would probably butt them again.

She glanced at Rio as he pulled off. He would give only as much information as he had to. At least they'd gotten past one-syllable answers. "All right, what happened?"

"She and Blade went back to the castle," he said simply.

There was more to it, but she'd never hear it from Rio. He was a man of principle and extremely loyal. She relaxed back in her seat. "But I'm bringing them food."

"No women."

"How about hot dogs on the grill later on tonight?" Skylar cajoled. She'd never had to work this hard for a date, but then there were no other men like Rio. "You wouldn't want me to be embarrassed when Mrs. Grayson asked me and I'd have to tell her that you stood me up." She shuddered. "I'd never be able to look her in the face again."

"You'll manage." He slowed down to turn into the Navarone estate.

"I'd manage better if you and I had dinner tonight." She wondered if she should do the finger walk up his muscular thigh.

The stubborn man ignored her. "From now until this person is caught, when you leave the estate you aren't to be alone."

"Rio—"

"Argue and you'll walk the rest of the way."

"No, I won't, because then you wouldn't be with me to protect me. Not that I don't think I can take care of myself," she said matter-of-factly.

The Jeep came to a screeching halt a yard from the black iron gate. On the other side, two men with guns drawn stepped from the guardhouse into the road. "Jaguar. Stand down," Rio radioed. His eyes were no longer cold, but burning hot with emotion. "If you suspect anything, you let me handle it. Got it?"

"Ri—"

"Got it?" he bit out.

She could argue, but she wouldn't win this time, either. Rio wouldn't back down from Blade, who was pretty scary himself. "Got it." *If he thinks I'm going to run to him and risk him getting hurt when I could hand—*

His hand on her cheek turned her face to him. "Whatever you're thinking, don't. One word from me and you're on the jet back to Tucson."

She stared openmouthed at him. Blade trusted Rio implicitly. "You wouldn't?"

"Try me."

He would, in a heartbeat. He'd do whatever it took to protect her, but she didn't have to like it. She batted his hand away and crossed her arms. "I don't think I'll be hungry tonight."

Rio started the Jeep just as the delivery van turned in behind them.

She'd show him.

Chapter 6

Skylar was giving Rio the silent treatment. That was okay. It would keep him from doing what he shouldn't—kissing her until they thought only of the need to quench the burning desire between them. He drew in a deep breath. He was *not* going there.

Nothing mattered except her safety. To add another layer of protection, he was installing another lock on her door.

He'd called Dakota at five thirty. The tapes hadn't revealed the man in the checkered jacket. The cameras were trained on the valets, the parking lot, and the back entrance, not the front or inside of the restaurant. The man could have walked from a nearby hotel or anywhere.

The only other possibility was letting Skylar watch the tapes to see if she saw the man. Otherwise they had squat—which meant they had no way of finding the person or persons who'd followed her. He hated like hell to think the bastard had gotten away—or worse, that he might come after Skylar again.

"What are you doing?"

"Putting a coded lock on your door." He screwed in the last bolt. "I reprogrammed it to have only two numbers for quicker access, and to signal when it's on. What number?" When she didn't say anything he glanced up at her. As expected, her arms were crossed. She was still ticked at him. He waited her out.

"Thirteen?"

"Too easy."

"Then why don't you pick one?" Her arms came to her sides.

"Because it has to be a number that, no matter what, you'll remember. Preferably close together," he answered patiently. Really ticked.

"Zero six." It was the month Blade had hired her.

He coded in the numbers, picked up the empty box and tools, and rose to his feet. "Come here, please."

She stopped on the other side of the door. "I know how to work the key pad. My grandparents have one, because my grandmother can never find her key."

"I spoke with Dakota. The fifth man didn't show up on the restaurant tapes," he said, hating to tell her. "The only other option is for you to watch the tapes and see if you can pick him out."

She nodded, crossed her arms again. "I'll call Dakota. If he wants, I can go in tonight since I have no plans."

Ouch! Skylar could cut a man to ribbons, but not him. "If you do, I'm going with you."

"Aren't you going to be busy?" she asked sweetly.

"I'll make the time."

"Don't bother." Her hands dropped to her sides. "Please assign Henderson or Conner."

"They'll be busy."

Skylar looked ready to blow, but he wasn't finished with her. "Keep the lock on at all times. If one of my men passes and the red light is not on, I'll be notified and we'll have a talk. Same goes if I pass and it's not on. I can guarantee that you're not going to like having that conversation."

Her gaze sharpened to pinpoints of fury. "I think we've already had that conversation."

"If Dakota decides he wants you to come in tonight, call me. If not, have a good night."

"You've made that impossible!" She went into the room and slammed the door.

Rio lifted his hand to knock on the door and remind her about arming the lock just as it flashed red. If he ever got any gray hairs, Skylar would give them to him.

"Rio, I'm fine, but can you please come to my room?"

"On my way." Replacing his cell phone, Rio left the control room fifty-seven minutes after his and Skylar's last conversation. He knew she'd gone to the kitchen and eaten.

He stopped in front of her door and knocked. He really didn't know what to expect, but at least the red light was on.

Skylar opened the door and stood aside for him to enter. As soon as he did, the door closed. "Dakota said I could view the tapes tomorrow after one."

"We'll leave after the last delivery." She could have told him that on the phone. There was something else she wanted to say.

He waited until she worked it out in her mind—he owed her that. A lot had been thrust on her. She wasn't used to being in danger. Danger was all he'd ever known.

"I don't want to go to bed with us annoyed with each other. My parents had the same philosophy—of course, look what happened to them," she finally said.

He heard the misery in his voice. It tugged at him. "My decisions were for your own safety."

She blinked, then blinked again as if fighting tears. "You were going to send me away."

"Nothing is as important as your safety," he said, trying to keep his voice flat and for the first time failing.

She walked to him, curved her arms around his waist, rested her cheek on his chest. "I was so angry with you."

He should have stopped her; he easily could have. He pulled her closer, his hands sweeping from the top of her head to the middle of her back. "You said annoyed."

He felt her body shake. She lifted her head. "Did you just make a joke?"

"I don't want you to take any chances."

"I'm not stupid." Her eyes narrowed.

He didn't want them at odds, either. Anger made one reckless. "No, you're not, but sometimes we can underestimate a situation."

"Meaning my skills against his?"

"Meaning, for whatever reason, you'd rather put yourself out there than let me do what I'm trained for," he said as patiently as he could.

She moved away from him. "So I'm supposed to wait on you? What if that's not possible?"

The thought of her facing a determined attacker made his blood chill. "Do you have any athletic clothes?"

She frowned. The question had obviously thrown her. "I think so."

Now he was the one frowning. "Didn't you pack?"

She glanced away. "Mother came to visit and helped. She's a firm believer in exercise although I can take or leave it. Mary was kind enough to help me unpack."

Rio put his hands on his hips. "You had five suitcases and a trunk."

Her chin went up. "I was more concerned with bringing clothes that a certain man would notice."

"I did," he admitted.

She launched herself at him, laughing and kissing his face. "You can certainly work my last nerve, as a friend of mine would say, but you can also make me very happy."

He just shook his head. "Meet me in front of the room across from the command center at eight thirty tomorrow in something you don't mind getting wrinkled."

"Since I know you aren't kinky, you probably want to test my technique." She kissed his chin. "Why don't we start now?"

He pulled her arms from around his neck. "Eight thirty." He left. Outside, he waiting until the light blinked red. Yep, gray hair for sure.

Saturday morning, Skylar arrived promptly at eight twenty-nine at the room in front of the command center. Thanks to her mother, she wore a gray warm-up suit and tennis shoes. Mary remembered exactly where she'd placed them. Skylar was ready to show Rio she could take care of herself, thanks to her uncle and his friend. At eight thirty, she knocked.

"Come in."

She opened the door to the room. There was nothing in it except a weight bench, Rio, and Conner. Rio wore jeans. Conner had on sweats. She felt a pang of disappointment. She had been looking forward to getting her hands on Rio's body again. "Good morning."

"Morning, Skylar," Conner greeted.

Rio, back to being stoic, nodded. "Conner will test your defensive skills."

She walked to within a foot of Rio. "Why not you?"

"I'm observing."

Her eyebrow lifted. She wouldn't dare call him chicken, but she hoped the brow said it for her.

"We're ready when you are," Rio said.

He'd gotten the message. Good. "Are there any rules?" she asked.

"Rules?" Rio repeated.

"Yes, rules. My uncle said in a fight for your life there were no rules, so I could do this"—she poked two fingers toward his eyes. When he caught her hand as expected, she went lower. He caught that one as well and simply held both hands. "Eyes and family jewels, as Grandmother Carrington delicately called them, weren't off limits."

He released her hands. "Today they are."

She shrugged, tossed her jacket aside, and sat on the padded floor to remove her tennis shoes.

"You can leave them on," Rio said.

"He has his off. Besides, a kick to the face with a shoe hurts." Finished, Skylar stood and went to Conner.

"We can do simulation," Rio said. "I just want to get a sense of your skills."

Or lack thereof, she thought. "Conner, how do you want to play this?"

"Play this?" He frowned, his gaze going to Rio.

Skylar blew out a breath. "You know, I come home one night and you've somehow managed to pick my lock and I go to the closet to hang up my jacket and you jump me, or I get into my car without checking the backseat and you try to strangle me, or you try to snatch my—"

"Skylar."

"Yes, Rio. I'd turn, but you should never take your eyes off your opponent."

Conner put his hands up to his mouth and glanced away. Skylar started to attack, but decided that wouldn't be fair.

"Now."

Conner grabbed both her arms. "Rio said family jewels were out. Right?"

His hands loosened a fraction and she slapped both of her hands on his ears. He came back with a slice of his hand. She blocked the maneuver, sent the heel of her hand into his nose, then winced.

"Stop." Rio advanced on her. "Are you all right?" He picked up her hand and examined it.

She looked at Conner. "I'm sorry if I hurt you."

"You didn't," Conner said with a smile. "You have some good moves."

"That's all, Conner. Thanks."

The man quietly left the room. Rio released her hand. "I might have known. You don't have the killer instinct."

"Tell that to Freddy Haines. He didn't take no for an answer, and his family jewels and I got acquainted in a way he didn't expect," she said with satisfaction. "You try to hurt me or someone I care about, and it's an entirely different story. No holds barred."

She had the narrow-eyed look that said *Proceed at your own risk*. He believed her. "Little warrior."

She flashed the smile that tugged at him and plastered her lips and her incredible body against his. His arms around her small waist, he lifted her off her feet. Immediately her long legs wrapped around his waist, her tongue stroking his in a hot, torrid kiss.

"My brain fuzzed." She grinned. "Let's do it again." She lowered her head for a second helping of pleasure.

Rio sat on the bench. A strategic mistake. It placed Skylar's breasts too close to his mouth, her woman's softness too close to his throbbing manhood. The woman kissed like she had waited a lifetime to taste him. It was like holding a live wire: You understood that laying it down was potentially just as dangerous as continuing to hold it.

Damned if you do, damned if you don't.

Her brain wasn't the only one not clear. He had to stop while he could. He stood with his arm wrapped around her waist and pushed one of her legs down, then her other leg. "Stop that."

"You started—oh, my! You're holding me up with one arm," she said and rubbed the tip of her finger across his lower lip. "I guess you know some of the women at Navarone headquarters have monster crushes on you. Blade and Shane are taken now, but they still get the look, too."

"Skylar—"

"I know we're not headed for the altar, I just want to enjoy this time with you." She curved her arms around his neck again. "I never thought I'd be this close to you. Kiss you." Giddy with happiness, she kissed him on the lips. "The last delivery today is scheduled for noon. What do you say, after we leave Dakota we come back here and grill those dogs? Maybe afterward take a walk?"

"Skylar."

"Nobody has ever said my name the way you do sometimes." She ran her finger over the frown lines in his forehead. "With exasperation and tenderness."

"Skylar."

"Just like that." She kissed him again.

He placed her on her feet. "What if we don't have any hot dogs?"

"I'll check. We can stop at the store on the way back. We'll even pick up some extra for your men, maybe some vegetables to grill. It will be fun. You'll see."

"I guess." Concession wasn't the same as surrendering.

Squealing, she kissed him again. "I'll cook you breakfast."

He set her firmly away from him. "I have to check on a few things."

She wrinkled her nose. "You need to have more fun, just as Sierra said."

Sierra had mentioned the same thing to Rio in so many words, but she'd added, *So you won't have time to interfere with my life.* Two seconds later she was apologizing and was actually cooperative for three whole days to prove she was sincere. He understood. She wasn't used to being restricted in her movements.

"Plan on eating before we leave. Watching the tapes could take a couple of hours," Rio finally said. "It can be boring and tiring."

"You'll be with me, right?"

"Right." He or one of his men would be with her until he was certain no one posed a threat to her.

"Then I won't be bored or get tired." She quickly kissed him on the lips, picked up her tennis shoes, and went to the door. "If you finish early, you know where to find me." The door closed after her.

Rio didn't get a chance to have breakfast with Skylar. He'd just arrived at the tent when Skylar came out of the castle's front door in one of those dresses Rio guessed she'd picked out so he would notice her. He'd have to be blind not to.

The temperature had dropped last night and had only

come up a few degrees. The chilly air wasn't enough for him or his men to change the way they dressed. They were used to being in the elements. Skylar, however, had a different idea.

Her hair was pulled back from her exquisite face in a ponytail. Onyx-and-silver earrings dangled from her ears and stopped inches from her shoulders. She lightly bounded down the steps in black leather boots with five-inch heels. The boots zipped in front, the top disappearing beneath a long-sleeved, slim-fitting red-and-black dress that was zipped in back from neck to hem. Both made a man think about how ridiculously quickly—with just three tugs—he could have her undressed and in bed.

She gave him that little grin he was learning to be suspicious of. "Good morning, everyone. This is going to be a glorious day. I just feel it."

"Good morning, Skylar," his men greeted.

Skylar took her seat and opened her iPad. The hem of the dress slid up her thighs. Rio caught himself watching to see how far the leather of the boot went and if he'd see naked flesh. Aware of what he'd been doing he turned away, then whirled back around to see if Conner or Henderson had been doing the same thing. They were staring toward the garage, the opposite direction to the road.

They looked. Rio felt his temper spike, then just as quickly cool. So had he. The Man With No Name had taught him to look inward before he judged looking outward. They were men, not robots. *His* men. They depended on one another for their lives. Skylar was a beautiful woman.

His gaze went to her. She looked up, gave him that smile that made him think about how fast he could unzip those three zippers. He'd bet she had thought the same thing when she packed the clothes. She was waging an all-out campaign against him, testing his defenses.

She'd find them impregnable. He knew his face wasn't inviting. It didn't appear to matter to Skylar. She winked, put her finger to her lips, turned it toward him, and went back to her iPad.

They weren't you.

She wasn't interested in any other man except him. Rio crossed his arms and scanned the grounds. He sighed inwardly. All right, so they weren't so impregnable. The Man With No Name had also taught him to be truthful with himself. Only then could he find the courage to face any situation.

He wanted Skylar. He could admit that and, more important, he could control the desire to have her. If, and it was a big *if,* the time came and they became lovers, it would be a mutual decision and with a clear understanding that it wasn't forever.

She was a valuable employee. She often worked closely with Blade. Rio didn't want her to feel awkward when they saw each other again after it was over—if it ever began.

No matter what she said, Skylar wasn't the easy-affair type. He doubted if there had been many men in her life. She didn't kiss like it, though. She put her whole body into making a man's blood heat, his body ache with wanting.

Skylar Dupree was a dangerous woman.

He saw the delivery truck and left the tent. He felt Skylar three steps behind him. He kept walking until he was four feet from the edge of the stone driveway. Skylar stopped beside him.

He caught a whiff of the orange blossom and amber fragrance she wore. She usually stayed beneath the tent and waited. Seems, as she said, she was ready to do some touching and was reminding him.

But what about afterward?

Skylar stood beside Rio. She might as well have been invisible. He never glanced her way, just kept his gaze on the approaching delivery truck.

She hadn't thought Rio would easily yield, but she was finding that that was what made their getting to know each other so interesting and fun. She actually admired him for his restraint. He probably knew she was his for the taking, but he hadn't acted on it. His first priority was caring for the estate, but he also was concerned about her safety.

She mattered to him. And he'd shown her. It was a big step for Rio, and she wasn't going to take it lightly.

When he'd reverted to the old uninterested Rio after she came outside this morning, she just remembered him holding her so tenderly, his passionate mouth on hers, hers on his.

She'd caught him looking at her when she sat down. Her stomach muscles had clenched at the blaze of desire in his eyes.

"I wore this for you," she said softly. "You're the reason the day is so wonderful for me. You." Louder she said as the delivery van came to a stop in front of them, "I'll get my iPad and be ready when you open the boxes."

She passed Conner and Henderson on the way back to the tent. They could have hung back for any number of reasons. She wasn't sure Rio wanted his men to know their relationship had changed. She'd try to be circumspect, but she wasn't sure about her willpower where Rio was concerned.

The man just did it for her.

* * *

Rio's conclusion that Skylar was a dangerous woman proved correct as the morning lengthened. She was in a playful mood, laughing and joking with the men, teasing and flirting with him. Every chance she got when she thought his men weren't looking, she'd touch him or rub against him. If he took an item inside, she'd offer to go "open the door" or help.

Rio would have put a stop to her tempting him, except for two things: He liked seeing her smile, and he knew looking at the tapes would bring back memories of the night she was followed.

He placed the sculpture that Phoenix Bannister-Grayson had delivered by special courier on the table as assigned. Morgan's wife was world-renowned as a sculptress. This piece was very sensual. It was of a man standing behind a woman, his arms around her waist, his lips against her neck. Her arms were folded over his, her eyes closed, her head leaning to one side.

Skylar walked up beside him. She reached out a finger and traced it over the arms of the couple. "My paternal grandparents wanted to bid on this piece. You can feel the love and happiness of the couple. *Pure Bliss* is aptly named."

"That's what you want, isn't it?"

She stepped in front of the sculpture and faced him. "I want you, however and for as long as I can have you."

He shook his head. "That isn't you."

She glanced toward the closed door, then placed her hands on his chest. "Have you ever wanted and waited for something really important for a long, long time, hoping for a chance to have it? But each day you seemed farther away than the day before, until you were almost afraid to hope any longer?"

A true friend, he almost said. "Yes."

"Did you ever get what you wanted?"

He'd met Blade and Shane in training for the Army Rangers. They'd known almost from the first that they would be lifelong friends. "Yes."

She smiled tenderly up at him. "Didn't it make up for all the time you'd waited? Wouldn't you have done anything to keep it?"

They'd been to hell and back on missions in some of the toughest, most remote places in the world, and always together. No way would one have left the others behind. They all came home or none of them did. "Yes."

"Then you should understand." She palmed his cheek. "I don't know if whatever it was you wanted still means anything to you, but I do know that, if it was truly important, it helped shape you into the man you are today. You're not a whim. I looked for two years before I leaped. I want this time with you, and I intend to have you."

A brow lifted. "Regardless of how I feel?"

"I'm hoping I can talk you into it now that I have your attention."

His finger traced the zipper in the back of her dress from the neck to the waist. "You wore this on purpose?"

"I didn't want you to change your mind about the cookout," she told him.

"This shouldn't be happening."

She wrinkled her nose. "Nothing much is happening."

"Skylar."

"Grandmother Carrington said the truth is the truth." She stepped back and took his hand. "*Pure Bliss* was the last delivery of the day. I'll fix a quick lunch and then we can go look at the tapes."

He ran his thumb across the top of her hand. "Are you all right with this?"

"As long as you're with me, I can face anything."

The weight of her words didn't bother him. The way they made him feel—protective—did.

Chapter 7

Rio and Skylar left to meet Dakota immediately after lunch. Skylar had been circumspect and kept her hands and lips to herself. She hadn't wanted to do anything that might make Rio consider backing out of their cookout.

However, on the drive there she found herself wanting to touch him again. This time she didn't see any reason for restraint.

"Things are coming along great for the auction, don't you think?" She casually placed her hand on his thigh.

Rio glanced at her hand on his leg, then at her. "Skylar."

"Remember when we talked about things we'd longed to do or have? This is one of mine," she told him. "I'd tell you the rest, but I think I should just wait."

"Skylar."

"Yes, Rio."

"We're about five miles from Dakota's office. If you don't want me to embarrass myself, remove your hand."

"Rio, I—" she started, then looked down, gulped, snatched her hand back, and faced forward for all of four seconds before cutting her gaze downward. He certainly was impressive.

"That's not helping."

She looked away. "I didn't mean to do that."

Silence reigned until they reached the police department. Rio got out of the Jeep and went around to open Skylar's door. Head down, she got out wearing slim-fitting jeans, a tailored blouse, and a jean jacket with gold buttons. She'd traded the tall boots for a midcalf pair. She hadn't wanted to waste time changing clothes when they returned. "Thank you."

He didn't move back. Her gaze stayed in the middle of his impressive chest. "What did you think would happen?"

She finally lifted her gaze to his. She couldn't read his expression, but he wasn't looking through her. "Not that," she managed. His sensual lips quirked.

"What kind of men have you been dating?" His tone was partly curious, partly derisive.

She didn't think he'd like her answer. "The regular kind."

Rio grunted, took her elbow, and started for the police station. "I spoke with Dakota while I was waiting for you to come downstairs after lunch. They'll have a room set up for us. One of his officers will run the tape."

"Then you're still staying with me?" She had been afraid he wouldn't after what happened in the Jeep.

"You're stuck with me until we find this guy."

But what about afterward, Skylar wanted to ask. For once she kept her mouth closed. She wasn't sure she'd like the answer.

Looking at the tape was as boring as Rio had told her. Even the possibility of identifying the fifth man wasn't enough to keep her mind sharp, her shoulders from sagging. The uncomfortable chair didn't help. Neither the policeman on one side of her or Rio on the other seemed to mind the tedious tape search or the chairs.

"You want me to get you something to drink?" Rio asked.

"No. I'd rather keep going." They'd been at it over two hours. Rio and Dakota decided for her to view the film from two hours before she arrived to thirty minutes after she left. Occasionally they could speed up the tape, but other times they had to go at regular speed, even slow down or zoom in.

She propped her elbow on the table and put her chin in the palm of her hand. Her sigh just slipped out.

"Please stop the film." Rio stood and reached for her chair. "Stand up and stretch."

She stood up and promptly yawned. She slapped her hand over her mouth.

"Let's go get you some sugar." Taking her arm, he led her down the hall.

"You seem to know your way around here." She followed him inside a room that had STAFF ONLY on the door.

He fed money to the machines. "It's important that I have a good working relationship with the authorities in whatever city Blade plans to be in for any length of time." He gave her a candy bar and a Pepsi.

"What about you?"

"Wouldn't want to ruin my appetite for later on."

Nothing could have revived her more. She unwrapped her Baby Ruth. "We can't have that. Let's go finish so we can get out of here."

"He's not there," Skylar said when the tape ended. She looked at the disappointment in the faces of Dakota, who had joined them thirty minutes earlier, and Rio beside her. "I'm sorry."

"Me, too." Dakota put his large hands on his hips. "It

was a long shot, but worth a try. He might have taken off the jacket."

From Rio there was nothing. "I hate that I can't identify him, but it was probably random and he's forgotten about me."

"A random pursuit wouldn't have been so persistent," Rio said, his gaze finally meeting hers.

She didn't want to hear that. "Like you said, I have no connections here except for the auction. Why would anyone be after me?"

"That's what I'm going to find out." Rio got to his feet and reached for her chair. "Let's get out of here."

Skylar stood on unsteady legs. She'd made herself believe the car following her had been random.

"I won't let anything happen to you," Rio vowed, his gaze intense.

"I know." She faced Dakota. "Thank you for everything you've done."

"We'll keep looking," he said.

Skylar knew that without more information, there was pitifully little either Dakota or Rio could do. "If anything comes up or if you need me, you know where to find me."

"Yes, I do." He glanced at Rio. "Let's stay in touch."

Rio sent him a curt nod and opened the door for Skylar. "You have the list of what you want from the store?"

"Men hate shopping," she told him.

"Maybe, but I'm hungry."

He was sticking with her until the man was found. She stepped through the door he'd opened and felt his callused hand in the small of her back as they continued down the sidewalk.

"Want to add some burgers or links?" He unlocked the passenger door and stepped back.

He was trying to take her mind off the fact that somewhere there was a man who wanted to harm her. "I'm all right."

The back of his fingers glided down her cheek. "I've seen you look better."

Despite the shiver that raced through her at his touch, she screwed up her face. "You certainly have a way with words."

His hands gently rested on her tense shoulders. "I'll never lie to you. You deserve to have it straight. I gave it to you because I know you can handle it. I know what kind of strength you have. You won't buckle or let that bastard make you afraid to live your life. You're a warrior."

Her eyes shut for an instant while she gathered her strength. "Thank you for reminding me of that." Her chin lifted. "Let's find a grocery store."

"Maybe we should order something for takeout."

"I want to grill." Skylar craned her neck, trying to spot an open parking space in the crowded parking lot of the large grocery store. People were going into the store and cars were in front of and behind them. "Let's try over there."

"We've been around twice already," Rio said but he continued down the aisle in the direction she'd pointed.

"Hail Mary, full of grace, help us find a parking space." Skylar leaned forward in her seat. "It's worked in the past when I've been desperate."

"Have you thought what it will be like on the inside if it's this busy out here?" He turned the corner in front of the store. People were coming out, but seemingly none on their aisle.

"I want to grill," she repeated, then sat up and pointed. "Brake lights up ahead."

Rio flicked on his signal and slowed. "I see it."

"Told you," she said with satisfaction as the car backed out. Then she grasped his arm as a car coming from the opposite direction—the wrong way—sped up.

Rio whipped into the spot. The man in the small sports car laid on his horn, gesturing wildly with his hand. Rio ignored him. "Mark this down because it's not happening again."

He glanced in his rearview mirror to make sure the jerk had continued on, then got out to open Skylar's door. She met him at the back bumper. "Thank you, Rio. I'll be as fast as I can."

He grunted, snagged a shopping cart between two cars, and continued toward one of the store's three double doors. Inside, people were waiting for carts and the manager on the loudspeaker was asking for available staff to retrieve them. People were in front of the deli, the flower shop, the restaurant, the gelato stand. Every cashier's line was open.

"Welcome to The Market," a young man said, handing them a circular.

Skylar took the folded paper. "Is it always this busy?"

"Saturday and Sunday are our busiest days. Big game on TV tonight and tomorrow. Plus we have great prices."

"Thank you."

"This way." Rio headed past the deli line.

"I should have asked where the meat and bread aisles were located."

"Bread to the left. Meat on the other side."

"Have you been here before?" Skylar asked, hurrying to keep up with him. He wheeled expertly around people and carts.

"I see the bread. Overhead sign for meats."

Skylar finally saw the bread, but had to squint before she could read the overhead sign for meat. "I'm glad my teachers in high school didn't have your vision." She pulled four packages of hot dog buns, four packages of sesame seed hamburger buns, and three loaves of bread from the shelf and stacked them in the back of the cart.

"Aren't you overdoing it?"

"I told you I wanted to cook for your men."

He stared at her a moment. "Grab another package of each."

Smiling, she did as he requested, then stepped beside him. "Thank you."

"You aren't the wandering-off type when you shop, are you?"

"No, but I could stick my hand in your back pocket if you really want me close," she told him.

"Then we'd have the same problem we had when you put your hand someplace else."

She looked up at him through a sweep of her lashes. "I'll just have to wait until we're not planning on going out."

"There's your meat."

She lifted herself on tiptoe and whispered in his ear, "Just wait until I get you home." Humming, she went to the view the selection.

A few seconds later a man walked up beside her. "Planning to do some cooking?"

She glanced up. He was in his early thirties, clean-shaven, with an expensive watch and clothes. "Yes," she answered, picking up several packages of beef franks and hoping he'd heard the disinterest in her voice and would move on.

"You need any help?"

"No, thank you." Why were some men so dense? Or was it that they thought they were irresistible.

He lifted his hand. "Please, I insist."

"My husband is the only help I need. Isn't that right, darling?"

The man whirled around and almost bumped into Rio. He backed up and swallowed. "I—I didn't see you."

"You see me now," Rio said.

"Yes. Good-bye." The man took off.

Skylar laughed, put the franks in the cart, then picked up six pounds of beef sausages. "The poor man left his basket. Chuck for the burgers next."

Rio retrieved their cart. "Does that happen often?"

Skylar shrugged and went to the meat counter. "Forty chuck patties, please."

"Coming up." The man tore off a section of butcher paper and placed it on the scale.

"I don't like asking a question twice."

She went to stand beside Rio and whispered, "Grocery stores are supposed to be a good place to pick up a date. So, yes, it happens. Mentioning my husband in the next aisle looking at whatever usually does the trick. This is the first time there's actually been a man with me." She smothered a grin. "It's awful of me to laugh, but I thought he'd faint. Maybe the next time he'll take the hint and leave the woman alone."

"Here you go, miss."

"Thanks." Rio took the meat and placed it in the cart. "You ready to go?"

"We need drinks, vegetables, condiments, plasticware, dessert, chips," she rattled off.

"Then we're finished." Rio headed for the front of the store. "We have all that at the castle."

"But I wanted to do this on my own," she said, catching up with him to grab his arm. "I'll be fast. There's an employee. I can ask where everything is and we can be in line in thirty minutes."

"Thirty minutes." Rio spoke the words as if she'd said *Thirty hours.*

"Maybe twenty." She bit her lower lip, her hazel eyes beseeching him.

"Twenty minutes. Go ask."

They made it out of the store forty-five minutes later with a cart of groceries, and Skylar carrying a tray each of assorted cookies and assorted brownies. Another minute and he might have grabbed her and left.

"I'm sorry it took so long."

"Just get in." He placed the last bag in the back and started to return the cart.

"You finished with it?" a young woman with two small children asked.

"Yes." Rio held the end while she placed both children inside.

"Thanks." She hurried toward the store.

Rio got into the Jeep. Two cars heading in the opposite direction were already waiting to take his spot. Madness, he thought. Just as quickly he realized that someone had to do the grocery shopping. He was just glad it wasn't him.

He pulled out in such a way that the driver driving correctly was able to take his spot. He was more than ready to get back.

"I really am sorry."

Skylar had apologized several times already. "This had better be the best hot dog I've ever tasted."

She lifted her arms to hug him. "Driving."

"Just you wait," she promised.

After Skylar fired up the grill near the kitchen, she went to prepare the meat. When she came back outside, Rio had a large ice chest and was putting soft drinks, lemonade, and tea inside.

"Thanks for helping." She placed the patties on the front burner, the franks and Polish sausage on the back burner, and closed the lid. "I'm going inside to get trays and bowls for the buns and chips."

"Not necessary." Rio closed the lid of the ice chest and began to pull out condiments, napkins, and plates. "They don't want fancy. They just want good food and lots of it."

"All right. I'll get something for the meat when it's cooked and be right back." She hurried inside and came back with a roasting pan big enough for a thirty-pound turkey. Placing it on the table, she opened the tray of brownies, took one, and went to Rio. He had a bag of chips in each hand. "Open?" she asked with a smile.

He stared at her. "Come on. I don't want your franks to burn."

His strong white teeth bit the sweet in half. Skylar popped the other half in her mouth. "Delicious. Better check the meat." Humming, she opened the large grill top. Hickory-scented smoke wafted up. Some of the franks were ready, their skin glistening. Pleased, she grabbed the pan, placed them inside, and went to the table to prepare Rio a plate. "Mustard, ketchup, relish?"

"Where's your plate?"

"I thought we'd share." She glanced at the grill. "I'll be running back and forth until the meat is ready. It just makes sense."

Rio took the plate. "What do you want?"

"Besides you?"

His expression didn't change. "Mustard, ketchup, relish?"

"Ketchup, lots of relish, potato chips, sugar cookie, Pepsi. Since I can't have my original request." She went to the grill, checked the meat, then took a seat on a cushioned bench and patted the place next to her. "I won't bite—at least not until later."

Rio sat and slid the plate in front of her. "Eat while you have a chance. And I can feed myself."

Skylar quickly said grace and picked up the hot dog. It was just the way she liked it. She took a bite. "Good." She held it out to him. "Humor me. We went through a lot today for this moment."

He picked up his own hot dog and took a bite. She grunted and slid the plate over with the other hot dogs. "Suit yourself, but I bet mine tastes better." She took a sizable bite and went to check the meat. Satisfied that the food was cooking well, she prepared Rio a hamburger, wishing she had thought to get cheese.

She took a seat beside him and placed the burger on his plate. He was on his second hot dog. He probably hadn't eaten since breakfast.

"Thanks."

She picked up her cookie, glad to see that Rio was eating. "How did you, Blade, and Shane meet?"

He was silent so long she didn't think he'd answer. "Army."

"And?"

"We became friends." He popped the top of a Pepsi for both of them.

"I'm sure there's more to it than that."

"Not really." Rio polished off his hamburger. "Sometimes you meet a person and just know they're going to be an important part of your life."

"That we agree on." She stood. "The last of the meat should be ready. You can call your men. Do you mind taking food to the quarters for the ones on duty?"

"Why are you doing this?" he asked, coming to stand by her.

"Because they're your men. I see the respect you have for each other. Sierra said they helped move the things out of the room we're using for the auction. All of this activity must make your and their job more difficult but, unlike the rude delivery driver the first day, they've never shown it." She lifted the last burger from the grill. "My situation isn't helping. I just want to thank them."

He turned her to him and palmed her face. "Nothing is going to happen to you."

Her hands tried to circle his strong wrists. "I know. Now, call your men so they can rave about my cooking."

Rio thought his men were like a polite pack of hungry wolves. The food disappeared with alarming speed. They raved about the meal and thanked Skylar profusely. Conner offered to take food to the command center and to their quarters for the men on duty. By the time he left thirty minutes later, all the food was gone, the area clean, and two kitchen bags held refuse and recyclables.

"I'd say that went very well." Skylar turned to Rio with a smile.

"You didn't finish your hot dog." Although he told her it wasn't necessary, she'd played the perfect hostess, getting the men seconds or condiments.

With a gleam in her eyes, she opened the warming

drawer of the grill and pulled out a foiled-wrapped plate. "Guess what I have?"

Rio stepped beside her and opened the drawer beneath, lifting out a plate with an assortment of cookies and brownies. "Since I saw you stash the hot dogs and hamburger, I thought I should get the dessert."

"Like minds." She placed the plate on the table. "I'll get the drinks."

"Sit." He pointed to the cushioned love seat. "You've run around enough." He grabbed two soft drinks and sat down beside her.

She leaned her shoulder against his and looked up at the clear sky. "The night is so quiet here and so peaceful. The moon looks close enough to touch."

"You need to eat."

She straightened. "Some romantic you are. What if I said I was too tired to even lift my hands?"

He stared at her, picked up the hot dog. She'd worked hard; it wouldn't hurt this one time to humor her.

Her white teeth bit into the hot dog, her eyes on his, her tongue flicking out for the errant dot of mustard at the curve of her sensual mouth.

Rio shifted. His blood headed south. She grabbed his wrist, leaning forward for another bite, her full breast brushing against his arm. He almost shot out of his seat. He put the hot dog on the plate. "I think you'd better feed yourself."

"I like it better when you do it."

Skylar was sexy, sophisticated, and stubborn. An intriguing combination if he hadn't been trying to keep things more or less on a professional level. He'd crossed the line a time or two, but he was trying not to make that mistake again. Skylar was trying just as hard to get him to forget the line entirely. "The problem is, we both like it."

She put her arms around his neck, her lips inches from his. "Wanna see what else we both like?"

He already knew the answer to that. He picked up a sugar cookie. "You didn't get to finish yours."

"If I was sure one of your men wouldn't pop back around that corner, you'd have your hands full and it wouldn't be with food." She took the cookie and munched.

Rio was thinking another strategic retreat might be in order. He was fighting his body *and* Skylar.

"Why don't we go watch a movie?" Skylar was already standing with both plates. "It's an action movie so it won't make your teeth ache. Grab the soft drinks. I can leave this in the kitchen."

Being alone in the house wasn't wise, but there didn't seem much choice. They couldn't stay out here all night. Rio picked up the drinks to follow, well aware that Skylar wasn't through tempting him.

Chapter 8

In the seating area of the great room, Skylar picked up the controls and activated the fifty-seven-inch TV lift in the cabinet. She put the movie in the Blu-ray DVD player and took a seat on the leather sofa. Rio sat as far away from her as possible.

Skylar didn't watch the opening of *Mission: Impossible—Ghost Protocol*; she watched Rio. His feet flat on the floor, his posture erect, he watched the screen.

"You have a choice." Skylar stopped the movie. "I can sit in your lap and we watch the movie, or you can slide over here next to me."

His head slowly turned to her. His eyes were devoid of emotion.

"I know I wouldn't get within a foot of you if you didn't want me to, but we both know you won't hurt me and I won't make it easy for you," she told him.

He didn't move. She wrinkled her nose. "Good thing I have patience and I sort of like you." Getting up, she sat as close to him as possible. She felt the heat of his muscular thighs seep through his jeans. "We'll call this a draw since you let me get the food and helped, but I wouldn't mind an arm around my shoulder." Their shoulders touching, she punched the control to dim the lights and started the movie.

"You know this isn't wise," his deep voice rumbled.

She looked up at him. "This is the wisest, bravest thing I've ever done. Two years is a long time to look at a man who's just out of reach, a man who looks through you instead of at you." She ran her fingertips across his lower lip. "For the time being, you're looking back. At least sometimes. I'd begun to think it wouldn't happen. I told you, regardless of what happens afterward, I would have the remembered pleasure of your smile, your lips on mine, your hands—"

"Skylar." His voice was rough, thick. "Watch the movie."

"I'd enjoy it better if your arm was around me," she said, her breath fanning his lips.

His black eyes narrowed. He put his arm around her shoulders. "You like having your way."

She snuggled closer. "But we both know, you never do anything you don't want to. I'm just offering suggestions."

Rio grunted.

Skylar lifted to kiss his chin and settled back against him. Instead of watching Ethan Hunt save the world again, she was trying to decide how Rio would react if she straddled his lap for a long, hot kiss. All she had to do was throw . . . Her phone rang. Perhaps it was a sign that what she'd been thinking wasn't a good idea.

She leaned against Rio and pulled her cell phone out of the pocket of her jeans. "Hello, Mrs. Grayson. How are you?

Rio took the control and muted the sound.

"Fine," Mrs. Grayson answered. "I wanted to invite you to church with me in the morning, if you have no other plans."

"One moment." Skylar looked at Rio. "Mrs. Grayson has invited me to church with her. I'd like to go. You can send one of your men with me."

"What time does she want you to meet her?"

She'd hoped he'd go with her, but she hid her disappointment and spoke into the phone. "Thank you, Mrs. Grayson. I'd very much like to go. What time shall I meet you?"

"Eleven o'clock, and afterward you can come home with me for dinner," she said.

Rio hadn't said anything about spending the day with her. Perhaps being away would help him miss her. "That sounds wonderful."

"Good. I'll see you tomorrow at eleven. Rio knows the address. Good night, Skylar."

"Good night." Skylar disconnected the phone. "She said you'd know the address of the church. What time should I meet the man you're going to assign to me so we won't be late?"

"Ten twenty if you want to find a parking space where you don't have to walk a mile." He started the movie.

"Told you, I can take or leave exercise." Skylar settled back against him.

Rio sat up and stopped the movie. "Mrs. Grayson doesn't do anything last-minute."

"What's that supposed to mean?"

Rio hit the PLAY button. Skylar promptly hit PAUSE. "If we mess up Blade and Sierra's control, they won't be happy."

"I can fix anything electronic," was his answer. He hit PLAY.

She reached for the control.

He held it out of reach. "I thought you wanted to see this."

"I'm more interested in hearing why you made that comment about Mrs. Grayson. It almost sounded as if you thought she had an ulterior motive."

"I didn't say that."

Skylar rolled her eyes. "Rio, I'm not an idiot. So talk."

He stared at her and she stared right back. He leaned back on the sofa to watch the movie. "Mrs. Grayson has a habit of trying to marry off people she likes," he said tightly.

Skylar's heart lurched. "You?"

"It will be a cold day—" He stopped abruptly. "You're missing the movie."

The movie was the farthest thing from Skylar's mind as she leaned back against Rio. She recalled Mrs. Grayson's comment, *No man should walk alone,* and all her help, but that didn't mean she was trying to help Skylar with Rio. She could be trying to find another woman for Rio. Abruptly, Skylar sat up. "How successful has she been?"

"Very."

She didn't like the sound of that. Mrs. Grayson had specifically mentioned that Rio knew the address, indicating she expected him to bring her. Rio was hers! "Maybe you're wrong. She probably intended to invite me and just forgot."

"She's as sharp as they come," Rio told her.

Skylar's brow furrowed, and not because a building had just blown up in the movie. Suddenly she was glad Rio wasn't going with her. She liked Mrs. Grayson, but no woman was taking Rio from Skylar.

* * *

Rio walked Skylar to her room once the movie was over, but she didn't get the good-night kiss she'd expected. She was preoccupied with thoughts of some woman trying to get her hooks into Rio. That was not happening. "I'll be ready to go at ten twenty."

"'Night."

"'Night."

She went into her room and activated the lock. It might do Rio some good to have to work to get her, she thought, then quickly discarded the idea. The man was gorgeous, with a dangerous charisma that drew women like bees to honey. All he had to do was show up, and that was before he said anything. When he was aroused, his voice was a sexy growl that made her shiver and hunger for his mouth and his hands on her.

Which wasn't going to happen tonight, but there was always tomorrow.

Skylar went to her closet to look for a dress designed to keep a man's eyes on her. She didn't think Rio was going to church with her, but no doubt she'd see him before she left. She was going to make sure he remembered.

Seventeen minutes after ten Sunday morning, Skylar went downstairs to wait for her driver/bodyguard. Her long black hair was in a sleek bun. Pearls graced her ears and throat. A scoop-neck black jersey dress sculpted her body. On her feet were black five-inch heels with the toes in and one thin strap high above the ankle. Her black python-leather clutch purse was the perfect choice.

At the bottom of the steps, she wasn't sure if she should wait inside or out. She headed for the door on the chance that Rio would be around and they could talk for a bit. As usual, he hadn't eaten breakfast with her. If she hadn't been a strong woman, she might have been discouraged.

Outside, she saw a titanium Maserati coupe and wondered who it belonged to. The door opened and Rio stepped out, staring at her on the top step. He had on a black expertly tailored suit and looked dangerously handsome. Any woman breathing would want him. That wasn't happening if she could help it.

She continued down the steps. He rounded the car and opened the passenger door. "Good morning."

"Good morning." Her hands clamped on her purse. "You don't have to take me. I know how busy mornings are for you."

He didn't move a muscle. "Nice of you to be concerned."

"I don't want to impose."

"Since when?"

Her eyes glinted. True, but he didn't have to remind her. She opened her mouth, but he cut her off.

"You're going to be late and, since Mrs. Grayson knows the parking situation, more than likely she'll arrive early and be waiting for you," he told her.

Telling Rio he'd better not be eyeballing another woman didn't seem the thing to do. She got into the car and fastened her seat belt.

He got inside, the car accommodating his long legs. The car rumbled to life. He shifted it into gear and pulled off.

She tossed him a glance. The nine garages all had individual doors, and they were always down. "Is this your car?"

"Blade's, but Sierra mostly drives it when they go out

together." He passed the entry gate and hit the highway with a burst of speed.

She frowned. Rio wasn't the type of man to try to impress a woman. "Then why are you driving it?"

He glanced at the slim-fitting skirt of her dress, then back at the road as he passed a truck. "I didn't want you struggling in and out of the Jeep."

Nothing he could have said would have put her more at ease. Rio wasn't easily led—if at all. She knew that. No matter what woman Mrs. Grayson paraded in front of him, it wouldn't matter. "Thank you, Rio."

He didn't say anything, just continued to drive. Skylar crossed her legs and relaxed back into her seat. She could enjoy church services with a clear conscience and without malice toward the woman waiting for Rio.

Rio spotted Mrs. Grayson before Skylar did. She stood near the bottom step of the church alone. She wore a stylish magenta suit that Sierra referred to as her mother's "power clothes." Rio felt an itch in the back of his neck. She was up to something all right. At least they'd found a parking space in the church's parking lot, but from the long line of cars behind him, it would fill up quickly.

"This way," Rio said, steering Skylar around a group of men who were staring at her with open admiration. It was worse when all the Graysons and their spouses went to church together. When Brandon Grayson's wife's two brothers were in town with their wives, men seem to lose their minds over the beautiful women.

He'd never be that pitiful.

"Good thing you have height and great vision," Skylar said. "I don't see her."

Rio kept walking. Skylar was apparently oblivious to

the sudden cessation of conversation when she passed some of the men. He wasn't.

"I see her." Skylar waved her arm and hurried to embrace Ruth. "Good morning. Thanks again for inviting me."

"Good morning, Skylar. Rio," Mrs. Grayson greeted. "It's good seeing both of you again." She glanced beyond them. "We're waiting for another person."

Being right was no consolation to Rio. The real questions were: Was it a man or a woman? And was it a ruse to make one or the other jealous, or a real attempt at matchmaking? That's what made Ruth Grayson so dangerous. She had a tactical mind that saw a person's weakness, his desire, and then she set it before him and waited for nature to take its course.

"Over here." Ruth waved her hand.

Rio saw Skylar tense, then relax as a nice-looking, well-dressed man in his midthirties came into view. Rio recognized him immediately.

"Hello, Jonathan. I'm glad you could make it," Ruth greeted.

Jonathan dragged his wide-eyed gaze from Skylar and clasped Mrs. Grayson's hand. "Thank you, Professor Grayson. I'm sorry to be a bit late."

Mrs. Grayson waved his words aside. "Nonsense. You're right on time." She took Skylar's arm and drew her closer to the new arrival. "Skylar Dupree, I'd like you to meet Jonathan Douglas, a professor in my music department. You already know Rio."

Jonathan nodded briefly to Rio and extended his hand to Skylar. "Ms. Dupree, it's a pleasure to finally meet you. I was unavoidably delayed the day you were on campus."

Smiling, Skylar shook the man's hand. "Then I'm glad we're finally meeting."

"I couldn't have said it better myself," he said, still holding her hand.

"Why don't we go in?" Mrs. Grayson suggested. "Rio, please walk with me, and Jonathan and Skylar can become better acquainted."

For a moment, he didn't move. Mrs. Grayson had that warm, patient look, but Rio knew her brain was busy. He didn't like to call a woman he respected—and sometimes feared—devious, but she was.

"Rio, are you all right?" Skylar asked, reaching toward him.

"Fine." He took Mrs. Grayson's arm and started up the steps. Not by the blink of an eyelash had she reacted to Skylar's concern. She was too intuitive not to have heard the anxiety in Skylar's voice. He just had to figure out if she was trying to nudge him in Skylar's direction or Skylar's into the professor's. Rio stopped beside the pew Mrs. Grayson and her children always occupied.

"Please, Rio, go in first. I want to sit beside Skylar, since I invited her." As if it was settled, she turned and waited for Skylar and Jonathan, who were walking slowly behind an elderly couple.

Jonathan had his hand on the small of her back. She laughed softly, but Rio heard.

He was unaware of his eyes going cold, his facial features deadly until Skylar looked at him. She stopped abruptly.

Rio turned to take a seat. Skylar was free to do what she wanted. He glanced around as Mrs. Grayson lightly touched his arm. "I haven't forgotten."

Rio took his seat and stared straight ahead as Mrs. Grayson sat beside him and Skylar and the professor took their seats. She was at it again, but if she thought she could manipulate him, she had better think again. As for Skylar, if she was that easily swayed, she wasn't the woman he thought she was.

Skylar had never known a person could seethe with anger while his face remained emotionless. Rio hadn't said one word to her since they'd entered the church, and very few to Mrs. Grayson or Jonathan.

A block away from the church, she could no longer stand the tense silence. "All right. What is it?"

He stopped at a signal light. "Nothing."

She wouldn't call him a liar, but it was on the tip of her tongue. "Ever since Mrs. Grayson's phone call you've been in a crummy mood. Are you disappointed she didn't have a woman waiting for you?"

"You wouldn't have noticed," he bit out.

It only took a second to process his retort. He was jealous! She trembled. "P-please pull over."

He threw a quick look at her, then whipped into a strip shopping center. The car had barely come to a halt before he was around the car opening her door and unbuckling her seat belt. "What's the matter? You feel sick?"

She curved her arms around his neck. He didn't hesitate to pick her up and sit in the seat she'd vacated. "Skylar, what's the matter?"

She looked up at his strong features, the fierceness in his eyes now tempered with tenderness. "I just needed a hug. Nobody gives hugs like you."

He opened his mouth, snapped it shut, and pulled her closer. "Why do you insist on giving me gray hair?"

She angled her head and kissed his chin. "You'd look even more handsome with a couple strands of gray."

Standing again, he placed her in her seat. "You sure you're all right?"

"With you, always." He still stared at her. "Jonathan wanted me to go out with him. I told him I was already interested in another man. I just thought you should know."

He looked away, then back at her. "Maybe you shouldn't have."

"If I thought you meant that, I'd drive off and leave you stranded," she told him, her lips pursed.

His face morphed into a smile. "You would, too, wouldn't you?"

"In a heartbeat." She buckled her seat belt. "Come on, Mrs. Grayson is probably wondering where we are."

The smile vanished. "I wonder."

"Wonder what?"

"Nothing." He got into the car and drove off.

"Looks like Mrs. Grayson has company." Skylar unbuckled her seat belt as he stopped behind a big black truck.

"Her sons and their wives." He switched off the motor. "If her children are in town they'll eventually show up on Sunday." Since church was usually over in the early afternoon, Blade and Sierra came without him or with her bodyguards. He'd been invited, but always declined. He didn't like the way Mrs. Grayson watched him.

"Are we going in?" Skylar teased.

Rio opened his door and came around the car. As usual, she was already out. She curved her arm though his. He paused and glanced at their entwined arms.

"What?"

He wasn't about to admit that he was concerned that Mrs. Grayson would jump to the correct conclusion—if she hadn't already. If she'd picked out Jonathan for Skylar, she wouldn't change her mind. Once she set her mind on a course of action, she was relentless.

"Rio?" There was impatience in Skylar's voice.

"Just thinking." He started up the walkway. If Mrs. Grayson had tried to pull a fast one and he and Skylar were her targets, she was doomed to experience her first failure. He rang the doorbell.

Mrs. Grayson opened the door and warmly greeted them as Skylar then Rio entered the house. "I was beginning to worry. Please come in."

Skylar smiled up at Rio. "My fault. I'm sorry."

"You're here." She linked her arms with both of them. "Rio knows everyone, but I want you to meet my sons and their wonderful wives." Ruth led them into the kitchen. "Everyone, this is Skylar Dupree, the brilliant event planner that I've been telling you about. You've met Brandon, my third son. On his right is his wife, Faith. Next to her is my oldest, Luke, and his wife, Catherine. On Brandon's left is Morgan, my second son, and his wife, Phoenix."

"Hi, Skylar, Rio," they greeted.

"Hi," Rio greeted. He noted that the professor wasn't there. If he had been the one Mrs. Grayson wanted for Skylar, she wouldn't have missed this opportunity to further advance a relationship between them. Or was she trying to pull a fast one and spring the professor later?

Skylar smiled warmly. "Hello. I feel as if I know you. Mrs. Grayson talks so much about you."

"Bored you, huh?" Brandon said, stirring something in a pot on the stove.

Chuckles came from around the room. "Hardly. I want to thank you for your donations to the auction." She went to Phoenix. "*Pure Bliss* came Friday. It's one of the most sensual works of art I've ever seen."

"Thank you." Phoenix looked up at Morgan. "I have inspiration."

"Always willing to help the art world." Morgan kissed her on the lips.

"Catherine, your offer to use the name of a child under twelve for the main character in your next book series has gotten a phenomenal response." Skylar turned to Faith. "So has four nights in the honeymoon suite of your hotel. All of your generosity has been absolutely amazing. Thank you."

"Thank you for helping Mrs. Grayson and her Music Department." Catherine looked at her husband, Luke. "I get to benefit from her talent when Luke plays the guitar for me."

Faith blinked. "Brandon played the trumpet for me, then proposed."

"Music can communicate in ways that transcend race and language," Ruth said. "I wanted each of my children to have that talent."

"I just wish Pierce hadn't chosen the drums," Morgan quipped. "The only reason he practiced was to irritate us."

More laughter around the room.

"How are things going, Rio?" Luke asked.

"Fine."

"Probably a lot better since you don't have to deal with Sierra trying to have her way," Brandon said.

Rio glanced at Skylar. "You'd think."

Skylar blushed.

"It takes a strong woman to walk in today's world," Mrs. Grayson said. "I'm blessed to have five in my family, and I'm looking at another."

Skylar hugged Mrs. Grayson and high-fived Catherine, Phoenix, and Paige.

"Green beans are ready. Everyone take a seat." Brandon drained the fresh green beans and put them in a serving dish.

"Skylar, please sit here next to me. Rio, you can sit by Skylar." Ruth took her seat while Brandon and Faith set down beautifully prepared plates of Cornish hens, dressing, green beans, and yams glistening with brown sugar and cinnamon.

"Can I help?" Skylar asked.

There was a chorus of "no," the loudest from Brandon. Mrs. Grayson explained, "Brandon is a rather temperamental cook. He only allows Faith to help him."

"That's because she understands what a true genius I am in the kitchen." Brandon placed the last plate on the table, then held Faith's chair for her to sit down. He took the seat next to her.

Mrs. Grayson bowed her head. "Master of Breath and God, thank you for this day, for family and friends. May we be in your perfect will. Lead and guide us as we help those we see in need of our help. Amen."

Rio heard Brandon's groan. Mrs. Grayson was definitely on another mission to marry someone off. He lifted his head and stared straight into Mrs. Grayson's unblinking eyes.

"Mama, please," Brandon said. "Not again."

"Save your breath, Brandon." Morgan picked up his knife and fork. "She'll only remind you of how happy we all are."

"Which is the truth." Luke looked at Catherine with complete love.

Brandon cut into his Cornish hen, cooked to a perfect golden brown. "Who is it this time?"

Mrs. Grayson forked in a bite of meat and smiled. "Delicious as always, Brandon and Faith."

"Forgive me if I'm being nosy, but what are you talking about?" Skylar asked.

Brandon opened his mouth, but closed it when Faith put her hand on his arm. "Not your call."

Mrs. Grayson placed her knife on her plate. "Skylar, forgive us. Don't think us rude for bringing up a subject you know nothing about. Rio is already a part of this family and I feel as if you are as well, therefore we all speak freely around you."

Skylar nodded, but lines still furrowed her forehead.

"I had a small hand in helping my children find their special someone. Although they're all happy, they'd rather not, shall we say, 'help' anyone else." Ruth picked up her glass of iced tea and looked at her middle son. "Right, Brandon?"

He grinned and kissed Faith on the cheek. "Right. No sense ruining your perfect record."

"That's what makes her so formidable," Luke said. "She's never failed at anything she set her mind to, and I'll forever be thankful."

"So will I, although we didn't think that way when we first met," Catherine said. "But look at us now."

Faith grinned. "I was floored, but over the moon."

Phoenix looked at Morgan through a sweep of her lashes. "I had to outbid another woman at the auction for Morgan. Good thing Sierra was there to give her an incentive to sit down."

Mrs. Grayson's lips twitched. "Sierra definitely has her moments."

"Wow," Skylar said, glancing around the table. "Someday, I hope you'll tell me more."

"Who knows, one day you might know someone close to you with their own story to tell," Mrs. Grayson said with a smile.

Skylar blinked. Brandon shook his head. Morgan and Luke just stared. Their wives smiled.

"Just seeing if you were listening." Mrs. Grayson picked up her utensils. "Now, Skylar, tell me about the latest pieces you've received."

While Skylar quickly composed herself and told Mrs. Grayson about the shipments, Rio watched the older woman. Luke was right: She was intelligent and determined. She was so confident in her victory that she'd announced it. *I'm on to you,* he thought, and hoped she got the message and gave up.

As if aware he was watching her, her gaze momentarily caught his. She wasn't intimidated by him or anyone else. She was going to do as she pleased. It wouldn't do her any good. This time she was doomed to failure.

He'd accepted long ago that he'd never marry, never have a family. It was foolish to start something that was doomed to end badly. Her perfect record was about to end.

Chapter 9

It was nearly six when Rio pulled up in front of the castle. After dinner the men had watched a ball game while Mrs. Grayson showed her prized flower garden to the women before they returned inside. He'd been on the small sofa with Brandon, but he'd immediately gotten up and given Skylar his seat.

He wouldn't have dared look at Mrs. Grayson as the men shifted to make room for their wives. Brandon pulled Faith down in his lap. She squealed, admonished him, then leaned back against his wide shoulders. Rio kept his gaze on the wide screen of the television. Thankfully, Skylar wasn't in one of her playful moods and kept her hands and lips to herself.

The problem was, she had remained quiet. He glanced at her, but she was already getting out of the car. She hadn't said one word since they'd left the Graysons. Closing his door, he followed her inside the castle.

Wordlessly, she started toward the stairs. He should let her go. She'd finally stopped hugging, kissing, tempting him. Even as the thought came, he remembered the softness of her touch, the alluring sweetness of her mouth, her scent that he'd remember a lifetime.

"What's wrong?"

"Nothing. 'Night."

Rio put his hands on his hips, watching the easy, enticing sway of hers in the black dress that he'd wanted to peel from her trim body ever since his first glimpse of her that morning. The shoes were as wickedly sexy as she'd intended, the one strap taunting him to slip it and the thin black hose off. His body hardened. He cursed under his breath and bounded up the stairs after her.

Her door closed seconds before he reached it. The red light blinked.

He ran his hand through his hair, encountered the silver hair clasp he always wore. He was relatively certain she wasn't sick. He should just leave well enough alone.

He went to his room, jerked off his jacket and hung it up. No matter how irritated he was, his military training and his own penchant for neatness wouldn't let him throw his clothes down. His scalp felt tight. He reached for the buttons of his shirt.

Muttering, he yanked open his door and went down the hallway to Skylar's room. He rapped on the door. Hard.

"Who is it?"

Who did she think it was? "Rio."

There was a long pause. "I'm resting."

His eyes narrowed in irritation that just as quickly disappeared as concern took its place. "Skylar, are you sick?"

"No. I—I just want to rest."

Were there tears in her voice? "Open this door."

"Rio—"

"I know the code, remember, but I'd rather you open it voluntarily," he said, aware he was splitting hairs.

Several seconds passed before the light went off. The door opened a fraction. Misery stared back at him. She'd pulled off her shoes, but she still wore the black dress. "I really am tired."

"I'm coming in." He didn't give her a chance to argue. He gently pushed open the door so it wouldn't hit her. He'd seen her scared, angry, pissed, playful, but only one other time had he seen her miserable. He closed the door behind him, curling his hands into fists to keep from pulling her into his arms.

A tear formed on her lash. He felt panic for the first time in his life. He grabbed her. "Are you sick? Do we need to call a doctor?" He picked her up and put her on the bed, kneeling down and holding her hand. "Why didn't you—"

"I'm not sick." She gulped.

His heart slowed from a gallop to a fast walk. "Then why are you crying?"

"Because Mrs. Grayson has some big-chested woman all picked out for you," she sniffed. "You heard her— someone close to me will have their own story." She swallowed hard. "And I thought she liked me."

Rio's heart finally settled to a normal pace. "So you're going to hand me over to some big-chested woman who'd bore me in two seconds?"

Skylar's head came up and with it the most beautiful smile he'd ever seen. "No way!" She launched herself at him.

Laughing, he caught her and let himself fall backward, keeping her on top. He stopped laughing when he felt her breasts against his chest, her thighs against his, her hungry mouth on his.

A second later he was lost in the sensation of the kiss, her tongue dancing with his, this woman in his arms, the thrill of her body pressed against his. He felt protective and carnal at the same time. Strange new emotions shook him.

His hands threaded though her thick, silky hair to lift her head. He'd often thought of her hair on his pillow, gliding over his body. "Don't scare me like that again."

She frowned down at him, her fingers worrying the button of his shirt. "I'm going back to Tucson next Monday. Blade and Sierra plan to be here, and that means you'll be here." Her beautiful hazel eyes flashed. "And that woman, whoever she is!"

"And I'm so gullible, I'll fall into her and Mrs. Grayson's plans?"

She finally smiled. "Nope. You're as slippery as an eel. I should know." She sighed and rested her head on his chest. "I guess the prospect of losing you before we really got to know each other better scared me so much, I couldn't think clearly."

His arms tightened. Yet she'd been followed in her car and had remained calm. No matter what she said about a no-strings affair, he knew that wasn't all she wanted. He could tell by the way she looked at him, smiled at him, that it went much deeper. So why wasn't he running? His mind and his feet couldn't agree.

He wondered if she'd feel better or worse if he told her of his suspicion about Mrs. Grayson trying to match them up. For them, there would be no marriage. "Do you know Felicia Falcon?"

"No."

He'd been so sure.

Her head lifted. "Not personally, but I've met her several times. She's a sorority sister of my mother's. Mother and Father went to Daniel and Madelyn's wedding, and Trent and Dominique's, too. Why?"

The hairs on the back of Rio's neck stood up. "It's a long way from Boston to Tucson. Any particular reason?"

She placed her folded arms on his chest and put her chin on top. "Like I said in the application, I wanted to work for a Fortune 500 company, and I thought I had the experience, connections, and drive to plan the best events in the country."

"But why Navarone?" he persisted.

She arched a brow. "Is this going anyplace?"

He gently tugged on a curl, glad she was back to her outspoken self. "Yes."

"Mrs. Falcon was in town for a sorority event and picked up Mother. I'd dropped by. When Mother went to answer the phone, Mrs. Falcon mentioned she'd heard I wasn't going back to law school, asked about my plans. I told her I was looking for something that might interest me. They left.

"A month later she called and told me about the position at Navarone. Of course I'd heard a lot about Blade, and thought it might be exciting. And it would be far enough away from Mother and Father that I wouldn't feel guilty about talking to one or the other of them." She traced his lower lip. "Looks like I was right."

Two years. Coincidence. Rio didn't believe in them. Even then Mrs. Grayson had been planning to marry her children off, and Felicia was her willing accomplice.

"So talk."

If he told her, she'd start thinking about marriage. It wasn't going to happen. "Just trying to figure out something in my head." He kissed her, then got to his feet with her in his arms. "You want to go for a walk?"

"If you make it worth my while." Her head lowered, her mouth teased his, nipping, sucking, until he palmed the back of her head and kept her mouth on his. Then, with his other arm, he slowly let her slide down the front of his body, the friction highly charged and erotic.

He gathered the dress in his hands, the urge to peel it off her body throbbing with every beat of his heart. If he did, if he saw her in her lingerie, he wasn't sure he'd be able to leave without making her his. Once he took that irrevocable step, he somehow knew it would change everything for him.

His hands unclamped, his mouth nuzzled her neck, kissed her fragrant skin, skin that was softer than velvet. Skylar might be the one thing in his life that made him second-guess himself.

His head lifted. "I'll be back in an hour."

"I'll be waiting."

Resisting the urge to kiss her again, he left. He'd willingly crossed another line. Skylar Dupree pulled at emotions he'd thought long buried. The need to see her happy overruled his own credo of self-preservation. She was important to him. He was in danger of losing something more important than his life . . . his heart.

Skylar was waiting on the bottom stair when Rio returned. She'd been too excited to wait in her room. She jumped up and hurried to him. "I promise to be good until we're out of sight."

"There are cameras everywhere."

"And you know exactly where they are to avoid them." She batted her eyelashes at him. "Don't you?"

Rio opened the door. "Let's go."

Her hands behind her back to keep them out of trouble, she walked through the door and waited for Rio. She practically skipped down the steps, waving and speaking to his men as they passed. None of the men she'd seen was under five foot eleven. Some were broad, some lean, but she knew each was skilled or Rio wouldn't have had him on his team.

"Everything all right?"

"Yes." He headed down a paved path past the compound.

She glanced over. "You know you're tempting me."

He kept walking. The path widened.

"Oh, my!" Skylar palmed her face, then grabbed Rio's hand and pulled him toward the small lake. Two swans and their goslings swam on the placid water. She leaned against Rio. "Did you know swans mate for life?" She didn't expect an answer. "If only people could be that same way."

His arm went around her. "Your parents?"

She nodded. "I always thought their love was forever. I . . . I think—" She hesitated.

"What?"

She straightened and gazed up at him. "That they might still love each other, but each is too proud and too stubborn to admit it. They'd rather be miserable than risk being vulnerable."

"So what makes you so courageous?"

She glanced toward the swans. She wasn't sure how he'd react.

His finger and thumb turned her face toward his. "I'm waiting."

And he didn't like waiting or asking a question twice. "You. It was you."

Lines she'd never seen before formed across his smooth forehead. His hand lowered. "How?"

He certainly liked answers. She just hoped he liked hers. "I thought you needed me. I saw you with Blade and

Shane and their wives. You were walking by yourself. You seemed not to need anyone or anything."

"You felt sorry for me," he said, words devoid of warmth.

"Only a fool would feel sorry for you, and I'm not one," she came back. "Seeing you gave me the courage to finally stop looking and test the waters, so to speak. I had some bad moments because, if you weren't interested, not only would I make a fool of myself, but you'd have every right to have Blade fire me for sexual harassment. And I really like my job."

"Yet you went after me anyway," he said as if trying to understand.

She curved her arms around his neck. "You snapped out *Ms. Dupree* once too often and it ticked me off. I was determined you'd call me Skylar."

"You risked a lot."

"But look what I gained."

"Skylar." His mouth took hers. He savored her taste, the swipe of her tongue against his, the little sounds in the back of her throat. Each time they kissed was more exciting than the last. Each time tempting him to strip them both naked and make love to her until time faded away.

His head lifted.

"No," Skylar protested, trying to pull his mouth back to hers.

He grabbed her hand. "Let's go."

She stepped back. "Why?"

"It's going to rain," he answered and watched her face light up.

"Really?" She looked up at the clear sky.

"Really. Come on." He started walking and felt her resistance. She was still looking upward with her free hand cupped as if waiting to catch raindrops. "You're going to get wet."

She threw her free arm around his neck and grinned up at him. "Haven't you ever wanted to walk in the rain with someone special?"

He lifted a brow at the silliness of the question.

She wrinkled her nose. "I forgot. Well, I have, and you can't tell me that you haven't seen other couples walking in the rain and enjoying it."

"They had umbrellas."

Her eyes narrowed. "We're really are going to have to work on your romantic side."

Overhead, blue sky had turned to gray. "You have two more days of deliveries. You don't want to be sick."

She looked up at the sky again. "I'm stronger and healthier than that. I'm from Boston, remember, and I know you've been in the rain, probably with little more than what you have on now."

He had. "Why do you say that?"

She sent him a droll look. "Rio." She said his name with a mixture of annoyance and affection. "You said you were in the army. I'm thinking Army Rangers. Your men are military, too."

Thunder rumbled in the distance. "You think?"

"I know. It stands to reason Shane and Blade were in the same unit. My uncle said bonds are formed for life in combat." She briefly scanned the sky. "You'd want men as quick thinking, as skilled, and as resourceful as you. Although I'm not sure that's possible. There's only one you. In any case, when you stopped the Jeep the other day, they didn't hesitate to come out with guns drawn."

He'd always known she was smart. "You're going to get soaked. Jeans are a bear to get off when they're wet."

She pressed against him. "You could always help."

His heart pounded. He'd liked the idea more than he wanted to admit of sliding those jeans down her long legs, his lips following. "You'll track water from the front door to your room."

"I'll mop it up."

"That's a lot to mop."

"It will be wor—" She laughed as the first raindrops hit her, then lifted both hands and smiled at him. "It's raining."

Skylar embraced life. He realized that at times, he had just gone through the motions.

She caught his hand, then rose onto her tiptoes to kiss him as the rain began to come down harder. "Thank you."

"You didn't give me a choice."

"We both know that's not completely true." She leaned her head back for a moment. "Kiss me, Rio."

He pulled her closer with the first word she uttered. By the time *Rio* came out, his tongue was searching the sweet recesses of her mouth. She wrapped her long legs around him and kissed him until he wasn't quite steady. With the rain beating down on them, her wrapped around him, his mind was centered only on one thing—pleasing his woman.

His woman. The thought caught him off guard, shocked him, but not enough to release the woman who had come to mean so much to him.

Thunder rumbled again. He lifted his head. Her eyes slowly opened. She looked a little dazed with the rain running over her face. It didn't seem to matter to her. He knew why—because she was with him. Just as it didn't matter to him because he was with her. He swung her up in his arms and began to walk slowly back to the castle.

She kissed the side of his neck and snuggled closer. "Nice."

They hadn't made it to the cameras yet. Sierra had wanted some privacy for her and Blade. Rio kept walking. The men who had met Skylar liked her even before she started feeding them. In the military, you learned to size people up quickly or you suffered the consequences.

"Please put me down."

He set her on her feet. As soon as he did, she took his hand and stared up at him, rain drizzling over her face. "How much farther before your men can see us?"

"About ten yards."

"Since I'm not as good as you, just give my hand a little squeeze and I'll let it go." She started walking before he could answer.

Despite the rain, he felt the warmth of her small hand in his, the trust. Walking in the rain wasn't so bad after all.

Rio was a resourceful man, Skylar thought as she stepped out of the shower twenty minutes later. When they'd walked in the front door, there had been large bath towels waiting for them to dry off. He'd radioed ahead.

Skylar grinned wickedly as she slipped on her gossamer-thin lingerie. Although he'd declined to help her pull off her jeans, he had agreed to meet her for dinner later on that evening.

Skylar quickly dressed and went to the kitchen, thinking she'd like to nibble on Rio. The refrigerator and freezer were as well stocked as she'd imagined. She decided on shrimp and chicken quesadillas, mini peach trifles, and nonalcoholic sangria. Finished preparing, she placed everything on the cart and rolled it into the great room by the fireplace.

She stared at the rug in front and decided it wouldn't be right for her and Rio to roll around on Blade and Sierra's rug or pull the cushions off the sofa. But they could sit on the floor with their backs to the sofa so they faced the fireplace. With the lights dimmed, it would be just as romantic.

She heard the front door open and felt her heart leap. In seconds, Rio was walking in, his intense eyes on her. "If I kiss you, the food will get cold." Her voice trembled. There was no sense hoping he hadn't heard it. She just hoped he didn't guess how deeply she loved him. "I thought we'd sit on the floor with our backs to the sofa and enjoy the fire and each other."

"The floor?"

"Do you mind?" It had sounded like a good idea to her, but with Rio looking at her she wasn't sure.

He glanced from the floor to her. "You need a pillow or something?"

She relaxed. He'd been concerned about her. "Told you I'm tough. Have a seat and I'll fix our plates."

He sank gracefully to the floor and stretched out his long legs.

Skylar quickly put their food and drinks on a tray and handed it to Rio. She picked up the control to start the fireplace and dimmed the lights. Finished, she sat as close to him as possible, took the tray, and placed it in her lap. "You get everything done?"

"Yes."

She gave him his glass. "Chicken and shrimp quesadillas, and a surprise dessert."

He picked up a quesadilla and offered her a bite. "First and last."

Smiling, she bit into his quesadilla, then picked up her own. He was learning.

"Where did you learn to cook?" he asked once he'd swallowed.

"My mother and my grandmothers." She sipped her drink. "Being a good hostess meant also being a great cook, knowing how to arrange flowers, proper etiquette, and too many other things to count."

He placed his food on his plate. "Sounds as if they wanted you to marry in their circle."

She looked him in the eyes. "They also wanted me to be a lawyer and stay in Boston. I did neither. I'm my own woman and I make my own decisions. You should know that."

"You can trace your family on both sides to before Lincoln was president," he persisted.

And he was an orphan. "And some of them we'd rather forget. Like Grandfather Carrington always said, every man or woman has to make his or her own mark, stand on his or her own two feet. Family can be a help or a hindrance." She nodded toward his plate. "You need me to feed you?"

He picked up his quesadilla. They ate in silence. Skylar sensed there had been a shift in their relationship, but she wasn't sure if it was good or bad.

She didn't try to fill the silence as they finished their meal and ate dessert. She placed everything back on the cart. If he was thinking of dumping her, she might as well do something she had longed to do almost from the first.

She sat in his lap, put her arms around his neck, and rested her head against his broad shoulder. A second later his arms closed around her. She was so relieved she trembled.

"You all right?"

She didn't even think of evading. "You were thinking of dumping me."

His hand tunneled though her hair. "Most people can't read me."

I love you. "I've been watching and studying you for two years. Remember."

"Still."

"Don't worry. It's not all the time," she admitted truthfully. "You can be pretty intimidating."

His lips brushed against her hair. "Apparently not intimidating enough."

"You shouldn't be so tempting. I've seen you send woman after woman running."

"Not you."

Her head angled up, she kissed him. "Told you, Boston-tough. Plus, as I said, I was ready to do a little touching."

"So you did." His head angled down and their lips met. His phone rang. Quickly he sat her up and answered. "Rio."

"Intruder. Section four."

"I'm on my way. Yellow alert. Code Red Sky." He came to his feet with her. "Someone is coming to stay with you. I need to go."

She clutched his hand, then released it. "Be careful."

Touching her face, he was gone.

Chapter 10

One of Rio's men was there before he reached the front door. Rio jumped in the golf cart waiting for him, and the driver took off.

"Skylar, we should go back inside," Jason suggested.

Skylar continued to stare at the fading lights of the golf cart until Jason stepped in front of her and gently urged her back inside, then closed the door. Her gaze shot to the man in his early thirties dressed completely in black, with broad shoulders, a square jaw, and light eyes. Beneath his lightweight jacket was a .45 pistol in a shoulder holster.

His expression didn't change. "Boss won't be happy to learn I didn't take good care of you."

She tunneled her hand though her hair. If anyone was seriously after her or the auction pieces, standing with the front door wide open in bright light wasn't smart. But she was worried about Rio. What if there was someone else out there his men hadn't detected?

"The boss can take care of himself," Jason said as if reading her mind, his Georgian drawl thick. "Why don't we go into the kitchen. I'll fix you a cup of coffee."

He was trying, but nothing would help until she knew if there was real danger or just someone trying to sneak onto the property. "I'm fine, thank you. How long does it take to get to section four?"

"Four minutes. Conner would have already run his ID if he had any on. He's also sent someone to the road to see if he had a vehicle or motorbike. Or someone could have dropped him off."

Skylar glanced at her watch. She was usually patient. But not with Rio possibly being in harm's way. Instinctively, she was aware he'd put himself in front of his men if there was any real danger.

And he'd want her safe when he did. She had to be as brave as he was. "How about I make the coffee?"

"I'd appreciate it."

In the kitchen, Skylar made coffee she had no intention of drinking, but she needed to keep busy. Jason had probably accepted for the same reason. She handed him a steaming mug just as his radio went off.

Her eyes widened.

"All clear. Yellow alert canceled." Rio's voice came through loud and clear.

Skylar's cell phone rang seconds later. "Rio."

"It was a reporter. Back in twenty. Bye."

She almost sagged with relief. "Jason, how about some food to go with that coffee."

"You cooking?"

Skylar playfully held up her hands. "With my own two."

"Thanks. Don't mind if I do." Jason took a seat at the table, but his back was to the wall and he could see the back kitchen door and the hallway. The alert might be over, but clearly Jason wasn't letting his guard down.

Rio was two minutes later than he'd expected when he stepped out of the converted golf cart; it had halogen headlights and four-wheel drive, and was capable of reaching sixty miles an hour. He bounded up the steps, punched in the code, and opened the front door.

Jason stood slightly in front of Skylar, but she quickly stepped around him. She was smiling. Her hands were clasped to keep her out of trouble, her hazel eyes twinkling. Rio felt the warmth of her smile all the way to his soul.

"I'll be going. 'Night, boss. 'Night, Skylar, and thanks for the coffee and food." Jason closed the door behind him.

Skylar was running the instant the door closed. Rio caught her to him, taking the lips she offered.

"You all right?" he asked, his arms still wrapped around her trim waist.

"I am now." She sighed and rested her head against his chest briefly before lifting her head again. "I admit I wasn't too steady until you called."

He palmed her face. "There was never any danger and, if there had been, I would have taken care of it."

"And I know that here." She pointed to her head. "But here . . ." She touched her heart. ". . . is a different matter altogether."

He didn't want her worried every time he had to check out an intruder. His eyes narrowed. *Every time.* Had he started thinking about them being together after the auction?

"What is it?" she asked.

"Just thinking." Pulling her arms from around his neck, he started for the stairs. "The first delivery is at eight thirty in the morning. You better get some rest."

She rolled her eyes. "It's barely nine thirty."

"You can check on the bids and other things." He continued up the stairs. He needed to do a lot of thinking.

"Are you going to tuck me in?" She glanced up at him through a sweep of thick, dark eyelashes.

His manhood leaped at the prospect. "I think you can do that by yourself."

She stopped in front of her door and circled his waist with her arms. "One day you won't be able to say no."

Staring down into her stunning face, her soft lips curved temptingly, inhaling her fragrance, he felt as if she might be right. "Skylar, I'm not a home-and-hearth type of man. Eventually, I'll move on. I don't want to hurt you."

Her hands moved to flatten against his chest. He knew his heartbeat was unsteady. "The only way to hurt me is to walk away. I told you, I'm my own woman. I want to be your woman."

Her softly spoken words sank deep into him. They were so much like what he had thought earlier. He couldn't remember a time someone had been just for him. His two best friends, Blade and Shane, had wives. Even the Man With No Name had helped others before and after him. "We'll talk tomorrow."

Skylar looked at him with suspicion. "You better not dump me."

"After we talk, you might want to dump me." He'd intended the words to come out flat; they hadn't. They'd held a bit of uncertainty laced with longing.

"Not happening." Gathering fistfuls of his shirt, she rose to her tiptoes and kissed him long and hard. "That should last until in the morning."

It wouldn't, but it would have to do. "I won't make it to breakfast."

"Lunch? I think I can last that long without another kiss."

She made him smile. She was outspoken, gutsy, incredibly beautiful, and caring. "All right."

She kissed him again. "You taste better each time. Good night."

"Good night, Skylar."

Opening her door, she went inside and slowly inched the door closed as if wanting to look at him for as long as possible. He heard the lock engage.

He stood there a few moments longer, then headed for the command center. He had work to do. Going up the stairs, for better or for worse, he carried Skylar's smile with him.

Skylar woke up in a fabulous mood. Things were coming along nicely with Rio, if a bit slower than she'd like. She threw back the covers, grabbed her lingerie, and went to the bathroom. She wanted to know they were a couple before she left for Tucson. Once he was committed to her, he'd stick. Until then, he might walk away.

She needed the words.

Too keyed up to bother with running a bath, she showered and quickly dressed in a long-sleeved emerald-green mid calf sheath, black tights, a chunky gold-and-emerald bracelet, necklace, and drop earrings. After she combed her hair over her shoulders, she stepped into emerald-green suede platform shoes.

She snagged her iPad on the way out the door to breakfast. She wasn't that hungry, but she wanted to tell Mary there would be two for lunch. Hopefully, Rio wouldn't cancel on her.

In the hall leading to the small dining room, she met Mr. Patterson, the house manager. Sadly he looked more haggard than he had last week. Worry was in the deep lines of his forehead, the droop of his mouth, the dark circles beneath his eyes. Whatever problem he had, it clearly hadn't gone away.

"Good morning, Mr. Patterson. I hope you had a restful day off yesterday," Skylar greeted.

He nodded, not quite able to hold his smile or her gaze. "Thank you. I had a very restful day, but it's always nice to come back here."

"I'm sure." She was not going to embarrass him again. "This is a wonderful home. I can clearly see why you like coming to work."

"Yes. If you'll excuse me. I want to check all the rooms to ensure that everything is as it should be."

He was as conscientious and as dedicated as Rio. "Of course."

With another nod, he continued down the hall. Skylar stared after him for a couple of seconds, then continued to breakfast, wishing he felt comfortable enough to talk to her about his problems.

Skylar walked out the front door of the castle to the tent at eight twenty-four. The weather had turned cooler, as Mary had said at breakfast. Blessing her mother for packing her black cashmere serape, Skylar went down the steps, the ends of the oversized shawl lifting with each bouncing step, her gaze searching for Rio.

Her spirits sagged a bit when she only saw Conner and Henderson. "Good morning," she greeted.

"'Morning, Skylar," the men responded in unison.

She took her seat and turned on her iPad, surreptitiously trying to watch for Rio. Moments later, when she saw him coming from the direction of the men's quarters, her heart thumped and her pulse raced. Tall, broad-shouldered, he walked with confidence, his steps quickly eating up the distance between them. This morning he wore a black jean jacket, white shirt, and black jeans.

Her mouth dried just looking at him. His curly black hair was pulled back as usual, exposing his razor-sharp cheekbones, thick lashes over midnight-black eyes, sensual lips, and a slightly crooked nose that gave a dangerous, rakish quality to his heart-stopping face. Despite his hard stare, he was gorgeous.

"Good morning." He stopped in front of Skylar's table.

She suddenly felt a bit unsteady with him staring down at her. "Good morning."

His eyes narrowed. He'd heard the quivering in her voice. "It's going to be a bit cool early this morning until the sun comes out. Go back inside. I'll call you when the packages are unwrapped."

She stood and held out the serape. "Boston, remember. I've gone swimming in weather colder than this. But thanks." Rewrapping the serape, she retook her seat and picked up her iPad.

She was acutely aware of Rio still standing in front of her. No one, besides Blade and Sierra, went against his orders. Especially in front of other employees.

"Skylar." There was the tiniest bit of warning in his otherwise flat voice.

She finally looked up. His face wasn't hard and neither were his eyes, but they weren't warm, either. "Rio, I'd like to stay. The first time I sneeze or cough or reach for a tissue, I'll go inside. Girl Scout's honor."

"The first truck is coming," Conner said.

Please, she mouthed. *I want to stay with you.*

"One sniffle and you're in the house."

"Thank you." She grinned. "You'll see. I'm stronger than I look."

Wordlessly, Rio turned and walked to the delivery truck.

Rio kept an eye on Skylar. At the first sign that she was getting sick, she was going inside if he had to carry her.

I want to stay with you.

She looked so damn beautiful. When she'd held the serape with her arms outstretched, the material of her dress had pulled tightly over her breasts. It had been all he could do not to let his gaze linger there. He'd let her ignore his order because, heaven help him, he wanted her to stay as well.

As always, she'd proven she was up to the challenge of the colder weather. Less than two hours later she had thrown off the serape. While he was glad to see the weather warming, the long dress skimming over her sleek body gave him a lot of bad moments. It didn't help that she always stood next to him while he opened packages. She was quietly driving him to the edge of wanting her.

Finally, he'd reached his limit. "Skylar, why don't you call and double-check the guest list to ensure they still plan to come, and politely remind them that only those on the guest list will be allowed past the guardhouse?"

"I did that last week," she replied as another delivery truck pulled away. "I don't want to make a nuisance of myself."

She was efficient and methodical. "How are the bids going?" he asked.

Her face lit up. "Wonderful. Mrs. Grayson will be so pleased. The guests on the premises can take their purchases or have them shipped directly to their homes. They can watch the item being packaged for shipment if they desire. Sierra said I could use the gift-wrapping room."

"You seem to have thought of everything."

"Not everything." She reached across him to pick up a pair of scissors, her breasts brushing against his arm. "But I'm working on it."

He was about to blow. "Behave. Remember the Jeep."

Her eyes grew wide, then cut to him, then downward. Her face flushed. She looked contrite. "Rio, I need to show you one of the auction pieces inside. If you have a moment."

Because he needed a few moments to cool down, he followed her inside to the room where the auction pieces were being held. That she had known and given him an excuse to leave only marginally worked in her favor. He was ready to chew nails—or better yet, grab her and run to her bedroom.

"I'm sorry." Her shoulders were hunched.

She looked miserable. How could she not know how all the touching, teasing, and double meaning bothered him? Unless. He closed his eyes. This could not be happening to him. No way was what he was thinking the truth. Skylar acted as if she knew what she was doing. "How many boyfriends have you had?"

She blinked, startled by the question. "Enough."

"Define *enough*." He crossed his arms.

Her gaze bounced off his. "Three."

"What!" He snatched his arms to his sides "When?"

"Two in high school, and one in college." She clasped her hands. "I never was that interested in boys except as friends. You know my cousin Tracy has an older brother,

Carson. Boys were always hanging around their house, and since they lived next door and I was an only child, I was over there a lot."

"Go on," he urged when she stopped talking.

She swallowed. "As we grew older, Carson and his friends put the word out that if any boy got out of line, they wouldn't like the consequences. Since Carson was BMOC, six-feet-plus, captain of the state football team, boys listened, out of either fear or respect. He was just as much of a huge figure on the college campus."

"Freddy Haines didn't seem afraid," Rio said, his voice hard. He'd like to kick the twerp's butt.

Her head lifted, the corners of her mouth tilting upward. "And suffered the consequences and embarrassment when he had to walk into his dorm bent over. Carson had graduated but, before the night was over, two guys from his frat house paid Freddy a little visit."

So she'd been protected, probably sheltered all of her life. To her credit, she hadn't let it make her weak. Just the opposite. She fought for what she wanted and stood up for herself—which made his task of brushing her off more difficult. But was he really trying all that hard?

He started to ask about her experience, but he already knew from the flush on her cheeks. Little to none. "So the touching, sitting in my lap?"

The corners of her sensual mouth turned downward. "Movies, romance books, and my friends talking."

Rio looked skyward as if seeking help. He'd never expected this. She set him on fire and she was inexperienced.

"Sky—"

"No, you're not dumping me because I haven't had a lot of boyfriends." Her face mutinous, she stood toe-to-toe with him. "You haven't complained so far."

She had him there. "I don't want you to get hurt."

"I won't, as long as you give us a chance." She reached out to touch him, then withdrew her hand. "Don't push me away."

"I'm not sure I can," he answered before he thought. Something he never did.

She didn't gloat, just gave him a trembling smile. "It will be all right, I promise."

Lord help him. She was trying to reassure him. "Come on, the next delivery should be pulling up." What had he gotten himself into?

She'd almost messed up. Every time she thought of her and Rio's conversation about her experience with men, she got cold chills. He might still dump her. They were finished for the day and he was waiting for her downstairs for their "talk." He'd picked at his lunch instead of eating. So had she. He'd declined her dinner invitation. Since she knew she wouldn't eat, she'd let Mary leave early.

She desperately clung to the fact that he still wanted to talk and had told her to dress warmly since the temperature would drop. He could just as easily dump her over their next lunch or when they'd placed the last item for the day in the auction room.

Blade and Shane might talk a lot, but Rio was a man of few words. He didn't need them. His flat black eyes, bone-chilling voice, and dangerous body language spoke very eloquently.

To give herself a little boost, she'd dressed in a red shearling hip-length coat, black cashmere sweater, black jeans, and short red boots. Around her neck was a red scarf. The matching gloves were stuffed in the pockets of her jeans. Remembering the feel of his hand in her unbound hair, she'd left it loose. She certainly liked running her fingers through his.

Plus a lot of other things, and she wasn't going to give them up!

Her chin lifted, determination glinting in her eyes. She hadn't come this far to fail. Rio cared about her. She was sure of it. If he had some misguided thought of trying to protect her from him or push her away because he didn't know his family lineage, he'd better think again.

She'd fight dirty if she had to now that she knew how she affected him. She smiled into the mirror. Rio was not getting away from her!

Rio watched Skylar bound down the stairs toward him, a determined smile on her striking face. He much preferred that to the despondent one after the last delivery. He knew nothing about romance, had never bothered to learn since he figured he'd always walk alone.

Now there was Skylar, pushing her way into his life, his heart.

She stopped with their boots almost touching. "On time and dressed warmly."

He stared hard at her. She didn't blink or move. He intimidated her only so much. "Where are your gloves?"

She wrinkled her nose, pulled them out of her pocket, and put them on. "Satisfied?"

Far from it. "Let's go."

Skylar lifted her arm for him to take. "I'd love to."

He could keep going or wait her out. He made the decision that gave him the most pleasure and took her arm. He was twice her size, outweighed her by ninety pounds, and yet she managed to entice him to do things when no other woman had even come close.

He opened the front door. She stepped through and waited for him to take her arm again.

A few of his men passed, and Skylar waved and spoke. They waved back and kept going. Since they were observant, they knew something was going on, but they wouldn't discuss it among themselves. Neither Rio nor Blade would tolerate men who had loose lips or didn't respect another person's privacy.

"It's so peaceful here. I like the woods."

He was surprised by her comment. He'd always been drawn to the outdoors, even before the Man With No Name found him.

The sun had gone down and the sky was a beautiful mauve-blue. Tonight there'd be a full moon. He'd always thought of the moon in terms of hunting or war. Neither would ever enter Skylar's mind. She had no idea of the kind of man he was. But he was going to tell her. Once he did, she'd never want to touch him again.

Chapter 11

Rio followed the winding path in the flower garden until he came to a stone bench beneath an arbor of wisteria. He'd wanted a pretty spot for her, and hopefully one day its memories would overshadow the bad.

"Please have a seat."

As he expected, she sat on the end to give him room to sit beside her. When he didn't, she patted the bench. "You're been standing all day. Sit down."

"I'd rather stand." There was no reason for him to be nervous, yet he found himself wanting to pace, to stick his hands in his pockets. He did neither. He'd mastered his body long ago.

"All right." She lifted her face. "But I feel I should say that whatever it is you want to talk about is not going to change how I feel about you. Even with the ups and downs and uncertainty, I've never been as happy or as contented as the times I've been in your arms. Just being held by you is one of the best things that has ever happened to me. Don't get me started about the way your kiss makes me feel—giddy, powerful, and lustful. Your turn."

Skylar. She just had to have the first words, words that

arrowed straight to his heart. She moved him in ways he'd never imagined.

Arms crossed, he leaned against the weathered post of the arbor. "I'll talk, but I don't want any interruptions."

"I'll try, but I'm not making any promises."

He'd initially thought she defied him because she liked having her way. Now he knew she did it because she cared about him and fought to be with him. No woman had ever put him first or fought for him. "Try extremely hard."

She gave him a curt nod and pulled off her gloves. "You have the floor."

Rio accepted that she'd go word for word with him. She was in her fighting-for-them mode, and she wasn't going to make it easy.

"I was found wandering along the banks of the Rio Grande on the American side by a Catholic priest, Father Sanchez. The doctor who examined me estimated I was around two years old because of my teeth development, but cognitively and developmentally much older. I was healthy and had been well cared for. They thought from my features and hair that I had Native American, African American, and Mexican blood. I had an extensive vocabulary for my age, I'm told. I spoke English, but with an unknown accent. My clothes had expensive labels and were relatively clean. There was a news story on me, but when no one came to claim me, I remained in the orphanage where Father Sanchez placed me and became Rio Sanchez. I'm sure you can see why."

Sky brushed away tears, but remained quiet.

He looked out in the distance. "I never felt I belonged there. I never fit in, so I stayed by myself and read. I was six when I first ran away to the woods behind the orphanage. I was gone two days before I came back on my own because I was hungry."

Skylar gasped and put her closed fist into her mouth.

"The next time I was smart enough to take food and water. That ran out in three days. There was something out there that I felt I needed to do. The nuns finally gave up trying to stop me from leaving since I always came back unharmed. I finally found a partial answer when I was twelve and saw a gray-haired Native American man wearing buckskins and moccasins in the woods. In his right hand was a staff six feet long. He was at least five inches taller.

"He said two words: *It's time.* In the years that followed, when I ran away, he was always there, and I never had to worry about taking food or water. He showed me where to look for water, how to hunt and survive off the land. He taught me how to be at peace with solitude. He never told me his name so I called him the Man With No Name."

"I'm glad he was there for you."

Rio's eyes narrowed. That wasn't the response he expected. He'd never told anyone about the man except Blade and Shane. Even at twelve he knew to keep his mouth shut because people would have thought him crazy. Yet Skylar believed him without a moment's hesitation.

"Even with disappearing for days at a time, I excelled academically and tested high enough on my SAT scores to get a college scholarship. I went to tell him but he wasn't there. I never saw him again." He'd felt a deep loneliness at the time. Tears had welled in his eyes as he'd knelt on the earth in the woods.

Arms went around him now. Skylar placed her cheek

against his chest. "That must have been like losing a part of yourself."

It was. He'd felt adrift until he met Blade and Shane in the Army Rangers.

"But he'd made it easier for you at the orphanage and prepared you for what was to come," she said, still holding him tightly.

His arms rose to hold her as his head rested against hers. "It was difficult."

"How long was it before you met Blade and Shane?"

"Six years."

"As you know, my uncle was a Navy SEAL. He said they send special forces on the most dangerous, most secretive missions in some of the most remote and hostile places in the world." She shivered. "Even before your specialized training, you had someone to prepare you to survive and help your unit. I'm so thankful he was there for you."

Numerous times he'd had nothing but instinct to lead his unit to safety, to recognize a trap, to track over rocky ground or thick vegetation. She was right. If it was tough and dangerous, the odds of returning low, their unit was picked to do the job. They always completed their mission.

"I've done things . . ." He lifted his head, dropped his arms, stepped away, and stared at her with cold, unblinking eyes. "I'm not the kind of man your wealthy and influential family would want you to associate with, let alone anything more. I'd have to agree with them. I know nothing about my heritage, not my real name, not my birthday. You need to move on and find someone your equal, someone you and your family will be proud to introduce to your circle of friends. I'll walk you back to the castle."

She batted his hand away. Her hazel eyes fired. "You're

not the tucking-head, shuffling-feet kind of man, so don't pull that crap on me." She jabbed him in the chest with her finger.

"Anyone who can accomplish what you have is to be commended, not looked down upon. You've been in the presence of some of the wealthiest and most influential men in the world—governors, our president—and carried it off with aplomb. You won't bow to any man, and that includes Blade. He might have more money, but you see him as an equal, the same way he sees you."

She spun away, then whirled back. "You're stuck with me. You care or you never would have kissed me or told me about your childhood." She narrowed her eyes at him. "Learning about your childhood made me care more, not less. Some people might think the Man With No Name isn't out there, but if you said it, I believe it. What I don't believe is that you-deserve-better nonsense or blaming yourself for what you did in the military. I have family in the armed services, and thank God for them. They protect this country while we sleep and enjoy life."

"Are you finished?" he asked.

"No. Not by a long shot! You're not my equal. No man or woman could be *your* equal, because I don't think that's possible. There's only one Rio Sanchez, and when my parents and grandparents get here Friday evening, I'm going to proudly introduce you to them." Her chin lifted. "Now this talk *is* over. I'm going to go fix our dinner and you can thank me by letting me sit in your lap since the house staff is gone except for Patterson, and he stays in his room after six."

"What if I say no?"

She threw her arms around his neck. "I'll just have to kiss you until you say yes. You dump me and I'll put a prickly pear in your boots," she warned, her voice and body trembling.

Rio gazed into eyes that were frightened and determined and filled with heart-wrenching tenderness. He'd never seen eyes as beautiful. Instead of running, she'd challenged him. "Little warrior." His head lowered, taking her mouth, finally yielding to the need for this one special woman. "I'm not dumping you." He couldn't.

She beamed up at him. "I was really going to be mad at you if you had."

His mouth quirked. "Cactus in my boots, huh?"

"For a start." She swallowed. "Just so we understand each other, and because I'd sort of like to hear the words. Does this mean we are officially dating, a couple?"

He didn't have a ready answer for her. "A couple, I guess. My record is worse than yours."

"Really?" She was beaming again. "Oh, Rio." She was back to kissing him again and slowly driving him near the edge as the full length of her sleek tempting body pressed against his, her tongue sliding across his. "I'm so happy."

He felt his own smile. It was impossible not to smile around Skylar. He'd tried. He bent to pick up her gloves. "Put these on. I don't want you getting sick."

For once she didn't argue. "Neither do I. I have too much to look forward to."

His fingers lightly tunneled through her hair. Skylar was going to be a handful, but he was looking forward to every moment.

Skylar didn't even try to keep the huge grin off her face on the way back to the castle. She could have happily turned backflips. Once there, she went straight to the kitchen with Rio beside her. To her surprised delight, he wasn't lost in the kitchen. In less than thirty minutes, they had pan-seared salmon, red-skinned potatoes, and broccoli on two plates. True to her word, she sat in his lap.

"You do like pushing the limits," Rio said.

Skylar felt the hard bulge beneath her hips. "I won't embarrass you when we're around other people, but when we're alone is an entirely different matter. I just like being close to you."

"That wasn't a complaint," he said, his eyes pinpoints of desire.

She shivered from the searing gaze. She still found it hard to believe that there had never been a special girl or woman in his life. She wished there had been someone to love him until they found each other. She wasn't so selfish that she was glad she was the first woman to matter to him. No one should be that alone.

His callused thumb wiped away the tears on her lashes. "Don't cry for me."

She shook her head, afraid if she opened her mouth she'd cry. Instead she placed her head on his broad shoulder.

"Being alone is not the same as being lonely." His wide hand swept up and down her back. "Some people need people or things going on around them to be happy. I never have. I'm content to be by myself. Or I was until I noticed you watching me."

She lifted her head. "I've never done anything like this before. Nothing was ever as important to me as being yours. No risk was too great. You certainly weren't going to make the first move."

He looked thoughtful. "Somehow I knew that if I took you up on the signals you were sending, my life would never be the same."

"How do you feel now?" she asked, her hands clamped in her lap. She wanted him to be as happy as she was.

"Truthfully?"

She swallowed. Nodded.

He smiled. "I'm a bit surprised you overcame every one of my defenses. I thought I was winning for a while, but even before the night you gave me the ultimatum, I think I was a goner. You're a hard woman to resist, Skylar Dupree, and I'm glad I don't have to try."

"Rio." She melted in his arms.

His head lifted. "I need to check in with the other security teams."

"Are you coming back?"

"Not tonight."

Her shoulders sagged. She stood.

He came to his feet. "I'll make sure after the last delivery tomorrow that I'm free for the rest of the evening. How about that? We can go anywhere you want."

"I'd rather stay here."

"Ask Mary to cook," he told her. "Tomorrow is the last delivery day, and it's going to be hectic."

"I know." And she was going to cook for them. "Give me a kiss and go take care of things."

"Ordering me around already." He dragged her into his arms for a long, hot kiss. "I won't make breakfast, and tomorrow don't wear anything distracting."

"I'll save that for tomorrow night."

"See that you do." He dropped a kiss on her nose and he was gone.

The next morning, when Rio saw Skylar in a gray cashmere cowl-neck poncho that reached below her knees and matching pants, it confirmed what he'd already suspected.

Regardless of what Skylar wore, the wanting was just as sharp and intense.

She spoke, flashed him a sultry smile, then went back to working on her iPad. She'd said hello to Conner and Henderson and waited for the first delivery.

Fifteen minutes later, the first of thirteen delivery trucks pulled up. While Henderson and Conner helped the driver unload, Rio began opening the packages. Unlike the day before, Skylar didn't hover and make his body ache with need. She was going to behave, but as the day progressed he knew that would quickly change when they were alone that night.

He hoped he was up to the challenge.

It was almost seven when the last delivery truck crossed the drawbridge. With her iPad beneath her arm, Skylar said good night and thanks, then headed inside with the last item, an autographed baseball from the World Series champions, and placed the prize in the waiting glass case.

She took a moment to turn in a full circle to view all the fantastic donations that had been sent. Bids were steadily inching higher. The auction was going to be a success. She pulled out her cell phone to call Mrs. Grayson to ask if she wanted to come—preferably now—just as it rang. "Hello."

"Hello, Skylar. I can't make it tonight. I'm sorry," Mrs. Grayson said.

"That's all right," Skylar said, a bit concerned. "Is everything all right?"

"Yes. Something unexpected came up. Did everything arrive?"

"Yes. It looks fabulous," Skylar told her.

"I never doubted. We'll talk tomorrow. Good night."

"Good night." Skylar disconnected the call. Her smile slowly grew. She and Rio would have more time together. She hugged the iPad to her chest. She still couldn't believe that they were a couple. She giggled and went to the kitchen to turn the marinating porterhouse steak, wash the vegetables, and check on the potatoes baking in the convection oven.

Satisfied, she showered and changed into an off-the-shoulder, banded spandex dress that fit her body like a second skin. Finally, she stepped into backless heels. She pulled her hair up loosely on top of her head and let tendrils fall, giving the appearance that one tug and her hair would fall.

She bit her lip and stared at the bed. Deciding there was no sense being coy or pretending that the night might not end in her bed, she pulled the covers down, fluffed the pillows, and left the table lamp on dim. If anyone had told her she'd be doing this even a month ago, she would have denied it with her last breath.

But she hadn't kissed Rio then, hadn't felt the pull of his heated gaze, the touch of his callused hand on her bare skin. She was gambling that Rio would be her first and her last lover. She'd figured out that what Rio refused to say with his mouth, he said eloquently with tender touches, hot kisses, and on rare occasions his eyes. He cared about her.

"Here goes." She opened her door and went downstairs to put the steak on the grill and set the table in the small dining room. After breakfast, Mary had helped Skylar take out the two leaves in the rectangular table so it now seated four. Much cozier.

Rio had said he'd be back in thirty minutes, and she wanted everything ready.

* * *

Rio wasn't exactly nervous when he came back inside the castle for the second time. He'd been in earlier, heard Skylar humming in the kitchen on his way to his room to shower and change clothes. He tried not to think of the implication of that. It was on his way back downstairs when it hit him. He wasn't sure where the idea had come from, but he went back outside to get what he wanted.

Finished, he went back inside. He saw Skylar leaning against the door frame of the dining room. Arms folded, long legs crossed in a dress that hugged every luscious curve of her body.

His body tightened. His breathing altered.

He was a foot away from her when her arms fell to her sides, and she uncrossed her legs. He didn't stop until their bodies touched. He expected the heat, but not the almost uncontrollable urge to make her his in every way possible.

Her eyes darkened. Desire stared back at him. If she kept looking at him like she wanted him for dinner, she might get her wish.

"Is that for me?"

He'd almost forgotten. For a moment he hesitated, then lifted the single long-stemmed rose. She wouldn't laugh at his first impulsive act.

She took the bloom, swallowed, and lifted it to her lips. "I love pink roses. Thank you."

"I know. Occasionally you have them on your desk in your Tucson office. You also received a huge bouquet a couple of weeks ago," he said.

She brushed the rose against his lips. "I told him before and after that he was wasting his time. I had already seen what I wanted."

His blood heated. "Skylar, maybe we better sit down and eat."

"There's something I wanted to show you first. It won't take a minute." She walked off and he followed, hoping he could hold it together better than he was doing now. His eyes caught on the enticing sway of her hips in the tight dress and he wasn't so sure.

She opened the door to her bedroom and went inside. Bad idea, he thought, but he followed her anyway. They'd only be a minute. Automatically, he closed the door and stuck his hands into the pockets of his slacks. Surely he could last that long.

She went to the bedside table, placed her rose on top, then came back to stand in front of him. Her eyes were soft. "I was thinking the porterhouse will keep. So will the vegetables and pecan pie." Her arms slid around his neck, her enticing body pressed against his.

Rio hardened. His hands lifted without thought to span her waist. Instead of pushing her away as he knew he should, he inhaled her compelling fragrance as his mind filled with erotic images of her with her beautiful hair spread on his pillow, her eyes heavy-lidded with desire, her hand reaching for him.

She stepped out of her heels. "Maybe there was something else we'd both like to do first."

Her breathless voice made every nerve in his body go on full alert, called to him. His breathing altered, became ragged. Need rushed though his heated blood, made rational thinking impossible. All that he desired was standing in front of him. Yet if he took that step, it would be irrevocable. There would be no going back.

He stared into her trusting face. He wanted this to be right for her and was shaken inside that he wouldn't be tender enough, that he'd mess this up for her. The women before her had been experienced. He'd rather walk away than hurt her or see disappointment in her eyes.

"I know you're used to more experienced woman," she said, a bit uncertain for the first time.

"Easily forgotten."

"I don't want to disappoint you," she went on to say.

Rio scoffed at the idea. "Impossible."

She undid the clip on his hair, tossed it on the bed, and ran her fingers through his hair. "I wondered what you'd look like this way." The back of her hand grazed his cheek. "Magnificent."

She said the word reverently as she stared up at him with intense eyes, eyes he'd never tire of looking into. This one courageous and outspoken woman had managed to do what he'd never imagined possible. She'd taken up residence in his heart, a heart he'd thought impenetrable.

"So are you," he said.

As if aware of the shift from resistance to acceptance, her body sank more fully against his, her mouth moved closer to his. He took the offering, his mouth gentle as it brushed across hers when he wanted to rush. He caught the soft sigh of surrender and, more than that, of trust. She deserved the words and the romance, but he wasn't familiar with either. There had been women, but they both had forgotten each other before the night was over.

His head and hands lifted. Her hold tightened. "No! Don't leave me."

He couldn't. He pulled the pins from her hair. The thick, silken mass tumbled around her shoulders and into his waiting hands. He'd thought of this moment so often and feared it.

She relaxed in an instant. Her eyes held his. "You make me ache with longing. Happier than I ever imagined."

And he'd gladly walk through hell before ruining this night for her. He didn't know how to make love to her the way she wanted, the way she deserved, gentle and sweet.

He couldn't fail her.

Her soft lips brushed across his, her breath warm as she said, "I might have watched you for two years, but I've been waiting for this moment a lot longer." The tip of her tongue glided across the seam of his parted lips. "I waited for you."

No words could have humbled him more or been more troublesome. Yet as he stared down into her face, a fierce yearning swept though him so deeply that he trembled, then just as quickly he relaxed as he remembered the fierce protectiveness of her, her uncompromising strength and courage.

He let himself go.

He pulled her more securely into his arms and fiercely fastened his mouth on hers, as if he had no intention of ever stopping. The sweet, yielding taste of her heated his blood and hardened his body. Every fear, every worry vanished from his mind. There was only this woman burning passionately in his arms.

His mouth moved to her bare shoulder, nipped. She shivered and clutched his shoulders. He would have laughed if he'd had the breath to do so. He should have known she wouldn't hide from the driving need swirling through them, but rush to meet it.

Her heart pounded so fiercely she felt light-headed and exhilarated at the same time. She felt him peeling the dress from her overheated body, his large, rough hands and lips following. She twisted, shivered, and enjoyed the twin assaults.

"I can't get enough of you," he murmured.

She felt the same glorious way. She tugged the shirt out of his pants. Too anxious to feel his naked skin, she ran her fingers under his shirt. Now he was the one trembling. Nothing at that moment could have pleased her more than knowing he was as affected by her touch as she was by his.

"Me either. More." She wanted more of everything and knew without a shred of doubt that he'd give it to her.

He swung her up in his arms and carried her to the bed. Gently, he set her down and looked his fill. All she wore was a lacy black thong with a lacy black bra that only cupped the bottom of her incredible breasts. He swallowed.

With her arms resting casually over her head, one leg flexed, she watched him watching her. His groin pulsed, moved with hunger and need.

She sat up and reached for the buttons of his shirt. "My turn."

He could have done it faster, but he wouldn't have enjoyed it as much as her soft fingers brushing against his naked skin, seeing the annoyance on her beautiful face because of a stubborn button's refusal to slip free or the triumph when it did. His hands fisted at the brush of her firm breast against his chest as she drew the shirt away and tossed it aside.

"I've got the rest." He toed off his loafers, shucked off his briefs and jeans with one smooth motion. Straightening, her gaze met his, then lowered.

She sucked in a surprised and appreciative breath, then reached an unsteady hand out to touch him. He gritted his teeth and was rewarded by the softest touch he'd ever felt as it glided over the hard length of him, the glistening tip.

He inhaled sharply. She jerked her hand back. Her eyes were huge.

"I did something wrong again?"

"Too right."

Unable to wait a second longer, he climbed on the bed and took her in his arms, once again tasting the seductive innocence of her mouth and body, his hands roaming freely. There was no place that was forbidden to him, no place that he didn't taste or touch, and with each touch, he wanted more.

She was just as greedy and insatiable. She felt cherished by the tenderness of his touch loving her so completely, his hot mouth suckling at her aching nipples. His callused hands turned to velvet on her heated skin.

He burned to possess her. His searching fingers found her hot and wet and ready. She twisted restlessly beneath him, her nails digging into his shoulder.

He rose up on his knees and sheathed himself. "Trust me."

"With all that I am." She reached for him.

He slid his hands beneath her hips and began to fill her, all the time watching her. The fit was tight, the building pleasure like nothing he'd experienced before.

Her lashes fluttered closed. She sucked in her breath. He started to stop until he heard a deep moan of pleasure, felt her hips move against his.

His hips flexed, slow and gentle against her. He withdrew slightly before increasing the depth of his penetration again and again, slowly allowing her to adjust to him. He needed all of his control to do so. He'd never felt anything so good or that he needed so much.

She began to move against him, shyly at first as if unsure, then with increased urgency and need, meeting him thrust for thrust. Her murmurs of pleasure filled his ears and tested his control.

His heart raced; his breath shuddered out.

She wrapped her legs around his waist, pressed her lips to the side of his neck—and he was lost. His pace quickened, taking both of them higher, the pleasure and ecstasy building until release caught them both up, taking them over and under together.

For a long time he just held her. Then he moved off her to his side, pulling her naked warmth against him. He'd never felt this content or this happy. "Are you all right?"

He frowned and lifted up his head when there was only silence. "Skylar?"

She crawled on top of him, crossed her arms on his wide chest, placed her chin on top, and smiled smugly. "*All right* doesn't seem to encompass what I'm feeling. If I had known it would be this good, I would have seduced you sooner."

Rio chuckled. "You have a mouth on you."

Her brow shot up. "I don't recall you complaining earlier."

"Point well taken." He kissed her bare shoulder and scooped her up. "Take a soak while I go reheat the food. I'll fix a tray and bring it back up."

"Then one of us would have to take the tray back down before morning." She bit his earlobe. "I'll meet you downstairs in ten minutes and we can eat in the dining room as planned. Then we can come back up here. I'm not finished with you."

He placed her on her feet in the bathroom and pulled her into his arms for a hot kiss. "You read my mind."

Skylar's eyes went hot with desire. "Maybe we can wait to eat later."

"Stop tempting me." Moving her gently into the bathroom, he closed the door. Smiling, he dressed and went to the kitchen.

Rio had the food on the table, the candles lit, when Skylar arrived in a loose soft blue sweater and slacks. As expected, she sat in his lap and they fed each other and talked about nothing in particular. Soon food ceased to hold either of their interest. Together they cleaned up the kitchen and then hurried back to Skylar's room.

Rio had barely closed the door before she was reaching for the buttons of his shirt, he for her sweater. He was faster getting her undressed.

She was giggling until his mouth closed over the turgid peak of her breast. She sucked in air, her hand holding his head as sensations rocked her body. "We're going to make up for lost time," she said.

"Count on it." His dark head dipped.

A noise woke Rio. Instantly alert, he tensed on hearing the lock disengage on Skylar's door. The lock had been on when he'd gone to sleep.

He covered Skylar's mouth with his hand and whispered in her ear, "Quiet. Someone's in the room."

She shivered once, then nodded. Quietly Rio got out of bed. He snapped on the bedside lamp with one hand; with the other he picked up the heavy crystal clock on the nightstand and threw it at the man. Dressed in black, he held a .45 with a silencer. The heavy clock hit the intruder squarely in the forehead.

He howled and dropped the gun to grab his head. Rio

ripped the night-vision goggles from the man's face, slammed the heel of his palm against his nose, and quickly followed with a karate chop to the man's throat. The intruder slid unconscious to the floor.

Rio turned to see a naked Skylar with a fireplace poker in her hands. "I could have handled another man. Don't you dare think of trying to help me again."

Calmly she replaced the poker and tossed him his pants. "Never said you couldn't. I just wanted to do a little payback for coming at me." She turned toward her closet and pulled out the first thing her hand touched, a loose-fitting black dress. "I contacted the command center and told them to call the police. I suggest you put on some pants before they get here. I'll take your shirt with me. I kicked your shoes under the bed."

"I heard something and came to investigate. Got it."

"He's not the man from the restaurant. I've never seen him before." She opened her bathroom door. "Thank you." The door closed.

Rio heard running footsteps and jammed his legs into his pants. Rage made his hands shake. Someone wanted Skylar dead.

Chapter 12

Four men rushed into Skylar's room with guns drawn. Two went to stand by the unconscious man. One moved to Skylar. The fourth stood by Rio for orders.

"I want this place checked from top to bottom. If there is anyone else in this house I want them found and bought to me. We're on high alert until we have some answers. Jason, stay with Skylar."

"I'm going with you," she said quietly.

She had on the black dress and flats. Her hair was a tousled mass of curls. He remembered too clearly running his fingers though it earlier. He swung toward the unconscious man and jerked him up by his shirt.

"Rio, don't!" Her hands caught his raised fist.

Rage poured though him. He kept thinking what might have happened if he hadn't been there.

"Please." Her voice and hands trembled.

Rio shoved the man back to the floor. If he hit him again, he wasn't sure if anyone could stop him. "Get his gun and take him to the room across from the command center."

Conner and Matthews dragged the unconscious man away. Rio took Skylar's arm and felt her shudder once; then she squared her shoulders.

"I'm all right, and your men are waiting," she said, her voice and gaze steady.

"Nothing is going to happen to you," he gritted out.

"I never doubted." Gently, she touched his cheek.

"Come on." They quickly reached the room. The man lay on his back with his arms outstretched. He had a rough, clean-shaven face with a two-inch scar on the left cheek. He appeared to be in his later thirties.

"No ID," Conner said.

"Stay here," Rio instructed Skylar and knelt by the man. He slapped his face. Hard. "Wake up. Wake up," he repeated, finally getting a low moan. "Who sent you?"

The man shook his head from side to side as if trying to orient himself, then lunged for Rio. A sharp jab to his nose had him howling, grabbing his nose, and trying to scoot away. He didn't get far before Rio grabbed him again.

"Conner, take Skylar outside," Rio said.

"Rio—" she began, but was cut off.

"Conner!"

"Why don't we just step out for a moment?" The door closed behind Conner.

Rio squatted before the man, his forearms on his thighs and his hands dangling down. He looked relaxed until you looked in his deadly eyes. "Who sent you?"

The man shook his head, his gaze flickering over Rio's shoulder to Matthews, standing with his hand on the butt of his Glock.

Rio leaned closer. "You've just begun to feel pain."

Matthews's radio beeped. "The big man just passed security."

Rio had minutes. He caught one of the man's hands. "There are twenty-seven bones in the hand. A snapping bone has a distinct sound." Rio caught the man's fourth finger. "Who sent you?"

The man's eyes widened. He tried to scoot back.

Rio bent the finger back. The intruder whimpered. The door behind them swung open.

"Rio, I believe you have my prisoner," Dakota said.

"All I need is five seconds." Rio's voice was deadly quiet.

"And I wish I could give them to you." Dakota walked over and squatted beside Rio to read the man his rights. "Do you understand what I just said?"

The man just stared. Dakota glanced at Rio, then back at the man. "I can always go out and come back in—I'm a generous man—let's say in ten seconds."

The man's lips curled. "Yeah, I understood. I want a lawyer."

"You'll get one—in time." Dakota got to his feet and motioned for Rio to follow him. "What happened?"

Rio was ready for the lie and looked Dakota straight in the eye. "My room is down the hall from Skylar's. I thought I heard something and went into the hallway. I saw him entering Skylar's room. He has to be a professional to bypass the lock on her door."

Dakota glanced from Rio's bare chest to his bare feet. "Good thing you're a light sleeper. She recognize him?"

"No, and he has no ID." Rio glared at the man on the floor. "He's hired. Give Dakota the gun."

Matthews stepped forward and handed the police chief the .45 in a plastic bag. Dakota's eyes hardened. He whirled back to the man. "Get up and sit on that bench."

The man struggled up and sat on the bench.

"Who hired you?"

The man glared at the policeman, then Rio, his dark eyes filled with rage and hate.

"Mr. Tough Guy." Dakota stepped behind him and cuffed the man. "We'll see how long that attitude lasts when you don't get bail."

"I'll make bail." His head swerved to Rio. "We'll meet again."

"Count on it."

Two more policemen entered the room. Dakota handed the gun to one of the officers. "Take this scum in and book him for attempted murder of Skylar Dupree."

Dakota pulled the man to his feet. His nose was bruised and bloody. He had a large knot on his forehead. "I guess you better run him by the ER before you book him. I'll be along shortly."

"Yes, sir," the one with the gun answered.

"How did you get here so fast?" Rio asked the policemen as the intruder was led from the room.

"On my way home after a long day, and it just got longer." He cocked his head. "Looks like I got here just in time. I would have had a hell of a time trying to arrest you for assault no matter the provocation."

Rio's expression didn't change. "I believe the car incident and tonight are connected. I don't like coincidences."

"Neither do I, but nothing popped." Dakota rubbed the back of his neck. "Like you said, she's as clean as a whistle, comes from a wealthy family of lawyers. And that jerk thinks he's going to walk."

"Not to mention she's here on behalf of Mrs. Grayson, and her son-in-law is Blade," Rio added.

"Some people are stupid. I just hate it landed on her doorstep."

There was a commotion outside, and Rio and Dakota went to investigate. Eli Patterson was there with two of Rio's men.

"The house manager is the only one we found," Jason reported. "He was asleep in his bed."

Patterson's thin hair was spiked over his head. His light blue silk pajama legs stuck out from under his matching silk robe. His hands trembled. "Is it true, Ms. Dupree, that someone tried to attack you?"

"I'm afraid so," Skylar answered.

He swayed. Skylar and Jason steadied the older man. "Thank God you're all right. I . . . nothing like this has ever happened."

Her arm curved around the older man's trembling shoulders. "I'm fine. Rio arrived in time."

He nodded, wiping his sweaty face with his hand. "I can't believe this is happening."

"You didn't hear or see anything?" Dakota asked.

The man jumped. "No. No. If I had, I would have sounded the alarm." He turned to Skylar again. "Are you sure you're all right? Mr. and Mrs. Navarone left their home in my care."

"You couldn't possibly be held responsible for what some crazy man did." Skylar smiled at him. "Why don't I fix you a hot toddy? I'm sure everyone will understand if you want to sleep in tomorrow."

"You're so kind."

"I'll be back." Skylar and the man left the room.

Rio signaled Jason to go with them. From now on, everywhere she went she'd have eyes on her.

"That's one gutsy woman," Dakota said.

"Too much at times." Rio shoved his hand through his unbound hair. "No one is invincible. This wasn't random.

The castle has over fifteen bedrooms—how did he find hers? He didn't drop out of the sky. No one breached security, so that meant he had to have come in with someone."

Dakota nodded. "My thinking exactly."

"My security team has been with me a long time. I know men sometimes turn, but I believe in them," Rio flatly told him.

"Staff?"

"Thoroughly vetted. The house manager has been here the longest. The castle had been on the market for four years. When Sierra snapped it up at a steal, she asked him to stay and keep things in order. Because she wanted to live here six months out of the year, they started renovations before they married."

Dakota chuckled. "Nobody wheels and deals like Sierra."

"Except perhaps Blade," Rio said.

"Here's a copy of today's log, boss." Matthews handed the sheet of paper to Rio.

Rio scanned the list then handed it to Dakota, who whistled. "Cleaning, delivery day, and a beehive of activity. Someone could have slipped in inside the trunk of a car or inside a van."

"They're always checked without fail for that very reason," Rio told him. "We've used these services before with the same people each time. My men are doing another check on them."

"Then how did he get in?"

"I don't know. If I hadn't—"

"But you were, and now that you're on the alert, Ms. Dupree will be safe," Dakota said, his hand briefly on Rio's taut shoulder.

Rio didn't say anything. If a killer was determined

enough, there were ways. "If that's all, I'm going to find Skylar."

"I have a feeling even if it wasn't, I'd be talking to thin air," Dakota said.

"Glad you understand. I'll keep you posted."

"Do that." Dakota tipped his hat, but Rio was already gone.

"I'm fine," Skylar said the moment she saw Rio approaching her and Jason. Rio had the hard look of a dangerous man.

"That's all, Jason. Thanks." Rio stopped in front of Skylar, his gaze on her.

"'Night." The man continued from the room.

Skylar curved her arms around Rio's neck, pressed her body against his. "Nice."

His arms clutched her to him. "You're taking care of Patterson when you're the one who should be taken care of."

"I have you." She rubbed her cheek against his naked chest. "You're all I need."

Sometimes even the best lose. "I'm fitting your door with a deadbolt. It won't be breached without a lot of noise."

"I have something to tell you," she said quietly.

"What?" He lifted his head, set her away from him, his heart thumping. "You all right?"

She glanced away, then took another breath. "When Conner didn't tell Dakota immediately where you were when he asked, I told him. I didn't want you getting into trouble because of me."

"Three, perhaps five seconds more, and he would have talked. He's all bluff." Rio's lips flattened into a thin line. "I would have known who's behind this."

"And you would have been in the cell next to him."

She palmed his face. "I'd do anything to keep that from happening."

Rio wouldn't have been arrested. He and his men would have sworn that the man's injuries occurred during the fight, if he had to go that far. But he didn't think so. The man was sweating and scared. He had been ready to talk.

"You'll find another way to get the information. You're too intelligent and determined not to. Now let's go to back to bed."

Rio curved his arm around her shoulders. "I need to check on a few things first."

Skylar frowned up at him. "If that coward keeps us apart the first night we should have spent together, I'm going to wish I'd gotten in a good whack with that poker."

Rio almost smiled. "I'll leave Jason outside your door."

"I don't think that's necessary, but I won't argue." She stopped in a large open area outside the dining room. "I've been trying to think of the reasons for someone trying to harm me. My parents are corporate attorneys and have won some pretty big cases for their clients, but as far as I know they've never been threatened. Even if that was the case, why would the person wait until I'm here? I've never even been here before, and I wouldn't have come now if not for the auction. Why here? Why now?"

"Damn!" *Mrs. Grayson*. Rio jerked his phone from the pocket of his jeans. Grabbing Skylar's arm, he hurried toward the front door. "Code Red on Mother Goose. Status of that location."

"Motion detectors on since nine thirty-nine. Car rolling to that location. ETA seventeen minutes."

"Bring the car around. I'm on my way there. Conner with me. Code Red Sky. I want two men with Skylar until

I return." Rio was at the door when he snapped out the last order.

"Sky—"

"I want to go with you."

He didn't have time to argue, and although he knew his men were efficient he'd feel safer with her along as well. "Cancel Red Sky. Skylar is going with me."

"Coming, boss." Conner hurried down the stairwell, a handgun strapped to his hip.

Jason opened the front door as the three rushed out of the house and down the steps. A black SUV came to a quick stop in front just as they reached the bottom step. Rio opened the back passenger door for Skylar and got into the front passenger seat. Conner got in the driver's seat. He stepped on the gas before Rio's door was closed.

Rio hit a number in his contact list. It rang twice before being answered.

"Hello."

"Luke, Rio. No time to explain. Are you in town or the cabin?"

"Cabin!" was his quick, calm answer.

"It might be nothing, but I've gone red on Mother Goose. Sierra and Blade not involved. My men are on the way. ETA fourteen minutes. I'm another five. Dakota or secondborn?"

"Morgan can be there in three. I'll meet you there."

"Call her and tell her to stay inside. Her motion detector is active. My men will check the perimeter, then position themselves at the front and back."

"Got it. Bye."

"You—you think they might try to hurt Mrs. Grayson?" Skylar asked in an unsteady voice from the backseat.

"I don't know, but I plan to make sure they don't."

* * *

Less than a minute later his phone rang. He wasn't surprised to receive the call.

"Are you positive Sierra and Blade are all right?" Mrs. Grayson asked immediately when he answered.

"Positive," Rio answered. "It's another matter. I'll explain everything when I get there. I'm just being overcautious."

"You wouldn't do this without good reason. Is everything all right?" she asked.

"Yes," he answered. At least at the moment. He heard a click. "Someone is trying to call you."

"One of my children. Bye."

Rio hung up. Minutes later he received a call from Morgan wanting information. Rio told him the same thing he'd told his mother: He'd explain when he got there.

Parents worried about their children; children worried about their parents. He looked over his shoulder at Skylar. Her hands were clamped together tightly. There was fear in her eyes. Not for herself, but for Mrs. Grayson. "She's fine. Morgan is there. Do you want to call your family?"

She shook her head. "They'd just worry, and probably demand that I come home."

Even as a part of Rio rebelled against the idea, another part thought it might be safer.

As if reading his mind, she gently touched his shoulder. "I'm staying here with you."

His phone rang. "Rio."

"We're three houses away."

"Follow protocol. Number two son is there. Number one on his way. Take care of anything that looks suspicious."

"Understood."

The line went dead.

"Four minutes," Conner said, the speedometer reaching ninety-five on the almost deserted early-morning road.

Rio's phone beeped twice, then was silent. "The house is secure. A man is stationed in the front and in the back," he explained for Skylar's benefit.

The SUV came to an abrupt stop in front of the house. Rio had barely gotten out before he heard and saw Luke's truck. They met on the sidewalk. Rio wasn't surprised to see Catherine with him. She'd always been neat and well groomed. Obviously, like Skylar, she'd grabbed the first thing she saw, a red skirt and blue blouse. Her hair was as mussed at Skylar's.

"Inside." Rio started for the front door. His man stationed at the front door stepped to one side.

Morgan opened it when they were on the porch. "Come in."

Mrs. Grayson left Morgan's wife, Phoenix, and quickly went to Rio. "Tell me."

"Someone tried to kill Skylar tonight."

There was a collective gasp from Catherine and Phoenix. Skylar found herself tightly held in Mrs. Grayson's arms. Catherine and Phoenix stood close by.

"Thank God and the Master of Breath that you are all right."

Skylar looked at Rio. "Thanks to Rio, who heard the man."

"I wondered why no shoes or shirt," Morgan said with some levity.

"A warrior must move quickly." Ruth turned to Skylar. "Another warrior, I think."

"I'm glad you're all right." Skylar took the other woman's hands. "I don't want to bring my troubles on you."

"I can handle trouble. Come sit down. I have tea and

coffee already prepared." Ruth sat with Skylar on the sofa. "Would anyone like anything?"

"Answers," Luke said.

Skylar noted he had moccasins on his feet. Morgan had on Italian loafers. Both men had on partially buttoned shirts. Phoenix wore a paint-splattered blouse, jeans, and flip-flops. They'd all come as quickly as possible to protect the woman they loved. Skylar thought again that no family would come running for Rio. But he had her now.

"I don't have them, but I'll tell you what I know," Rio said.

Skylar listened with Ruth's arm around her and Catherine's hand on hers as Rio told them everything, ending by saying, "The only connection Skylar has here is with the auction. I wanted to make sure Mrs. Grayson was safe. I didn't mean to alarm you."

Mrs. Grayson sent him a warm smile. "I trust you implicitly. You acted with reason and merit. I thank you for your concern."

"Do you still think Ruth is in danger?" Catherine asked the question her family seemed hesitant to voice.

"I can't be sure," Rio answered. "I have a hunch this might have something to do with the auction, but it's just that. This could have been planned to hit the first target, then wait and go for the second in a different way."

"Why?" Luke Grayson barked out, his eyes narrowed in rage.

Rio's eyes held the same burning rage. "That I don't know, but until I find answers that make sense to me, Skylar and Mrs. Grayson will have someone with them at all times."

"I don't—"

Luke cut his mother off. "It's settled, Mama. Cath and I will be in the guest room until this is over. Rio, if you don't mind, I'll assign my own men and trade off with them."

"Mrs. Grayson, you'll get to compare notes with Sierra," Phoenix said, trying to lighten the mood.

Mrs. Grayson's gaze swung to Rio's. "Does she know?"

"I plan a conference call with Blade in the morning at nine," Rio answered. "Your first class isn't until eleven. I thought you'd want to be there."

She nodded, smiled. "Blade chose well."

"I realize you need to tell Brandon and Pierce and they'll tell their wives, but I'd like for this not to go any farther," Rio said. "Not even Daniel and his family or Felicia and John Henry. They'd all rush here, making things more difficult."

"This doesn't go farther than the immediate family," Luke assured him.

"I'll see you in the morning at nine," Rio said. "Until you get your team assembled, my men will be here through the night."

Luke stuck out his hand. "Twice you've protected my family. *Thank you* doesn't say it strongly enough. I'm glad we have you on our side."

As soon as Rio finished shaking Luke's hand, Morgan was there. "Same goes for me."

"We protect our own." Rio looked at Skylar. "Are you ready?"

She gave Mrs. Grayson one last hug, then joined him. She hoped she hadn't brought danger to Mrs. Grayson, and that her family didn't blame her.

Mrs. Grayson went to them. "You're well matched."

Skylar blinked. Mrs. Grayson had spoken softly, but she couldn't be sure that no one else had heard her. She didn't dare look at Rio. Conner was just inside the door.

"Good night." Skylar swallowed and hurried out the door, Rio close behind her.

Chapter 13

It was almost one in the morning when Rio walked Skylar to her door at the castle. "I want to check with my men. I'm assigning Conner to stand guard outside your door until I get back."

Skylar tossed a look at Conner, who was several feet away with his back to them. She grabbed Rio's hand. "Your men have already given you a report. Why are you going anyway?"

"Because I like checking things myself at times, plus I want to look at the log-in sheet again."

"Can't that wait until tomorrow?" she asked, not releasing his hand.

"No, I need to do it tonight." He had to find answers, and fast. "You'll be safe."

"All right, but hurry back."

He hesitated, then opened her bedroom door and stepped inside with her. "When I do, it won't be in your bed."

Her eyes narrowed in that mutinous way of hers. "And why not?"

"Although my men probably know we were together, I'm not going to flaunt it in their faces. They won't talk, but still . . ."

"Then I don't see a problem. I want you here with me." She hugged him. "We're not going to let that creep keep us apart our first night together." Her head lifted, determination staring back at him. "Are we?"

His hand swept her tangled hair back from her face. "You can't always have your way."

"I know that, but I also know that, once you check out the perimeter, you're going to be working on that computer of yours. You can just as easily work in here as you can in the command center." She raised her right hand. "Girl Scout's honor, I'll behave."

"For how long?" he countered.

She kissed him. "Isn't it wonderful that we know each other so well?"

His hand fisted in her hair and he pulled her closer for another taste. What if something had happened to her? "I'll be back. To work."

She held up her hand again.

Smiling, he left the room. He'd known from the first that Skylar would be a handful.

Skylar took another bath and pulled on a long white cotton gown. The oversized neck bared one shoulder. Delicate white lace and ribbon was stitched around the hem and on the long sleeves. She planned to keep her word, but that didn't mean she didn't want Rio to see her as beautiful and desirable.

With a sigh, she straightened the bed they'd wrecked, her hands smoothing out the bottom sheet. When she picked up the pillow on his side of the bed, she pressed it to her nose and inhaled his faint scent—man, soap, and the outdoors. She exchanged it for the one on her side.

Finished, she grabbed her iPad and crawled into bed.

She checked the bids and did a quick sideways bounce. They were all trending up higher. Tomorrow, she thought, she might take some photographs of the auction items and post them on the Web site that could only be viewed by the people attending the auction.

Her smile faded. She leaned her head back against the four-poster's headboard. She couldn't for the life of her think why anyone would want to harm her because of the work she was doing for the auction. Those attending were all upstanding citizens or she wouldn't have considered inviting them and Rio wouldn't have cleared them.

There was no connection that she could figure, but if there was one, Rio would find it.

She sighed and brought up her e-mail. She almost sighed again. There were four e-mails from Matt Hampton, the man whose invitation had been rescinded by Blade because he'd tried to invite Sherman Tennyson, Blade's enemy.

The poor man was pleading to come. Not happening. He'd picked the wrong horse to back, as her Grandfather Dupree would say. She deleted three and answered the fourth.

The decision is final. S. Dupree.

Short and to the point. Hopefully, he would get the message.

But she didn't think so. She answered calls or e-mail daily from others trying to finagle, bribe, or cajole their way into the auction. Or they'd use the old ruse that their invitation must have gotten lost in the mail. The rude ones just asked why they hadn't received an invite.

As she'd expected, the auction was becoming one of

the most talked-about events of the year. The rich and glamorous, the movers and shakers, wanted to be there or it would seem they weren't on the A list. It had been extremely difficult to limit the number of people she invited to two hundred. Of course the Graysons and their friends the Falcons and Taggarts were coming. Mary had already volunteered to babysit. Luckily there were enough bedrooms for everyone.

She smiled as she wrote the next email.

Mother, there's someone joining us for dinner Friday evening. I've mentioned him before. Rio Sanchez. He's a very special man and very special to me. I know you, Father, and the grands will know I'm right when you meet him.

Her mouth tightened for a second. Her father still thought she was ten years old and he needed to intervene on her behalf. He could be tenacious and stiffnecked. If anyone came down hard on Rio, it would be her father.

I'll e-mail Father as well, but I don't want either of you drilling Rio about his past or anything else. Suffice to say that since he's head of security for Blade, and all of his properties, he can be trusted. I can't wait to see all of you again. The auction is going well. Granddad and Grandmother Dupree are in a heated bidding war for Pure Bliss. From their e-mails, I can tell they're having fun on their vacation and trying to top the other bidders. I'm blessed to have each of you, and now there's Rio.

Love, Skylar

Skylar reread her e-mail, did a spell check, and sent it. The e-mail to her father was a variation on the one she'd sent her mother. Only with his, she had bolded the part about not drilling Rio. She doubted it would stop him. But she'd just remind him again. No one, not even her father, was taking him away from her.

Her door opened quietly. Her head snapped up. Joy spread through her. She was reaching for the cover to throw it back when Rio held up one hand. It could have been to stop her headlong flight into his arms or to remind her of her earlier Girl Scout's promise. Either way, it was effective in stopping her. His hair was up again. He was back to being all business.

"Why aren't you asleep?" he asked. "It's almost two."

She held up the iPad. "Working, and I wanted to e-mail my parents and tell them you're joining us for dinner Friday night."

He paused on the way to the small love seat near the bed. "Maybe you should invite them here."

"Reservations already made and you'll be with us. Besides, I want to show you off."

"We'll see." He plugged in his laptop and took a seat on the small sofa. Opening it, he began typing quickly.

They certainly would see, she thought. She turned toward him, her gown sliding down her shoulder a bit more. "What are you doing?"

"Rechecking all of the people who requested invitations and were turned down, and those whose names you submitted and were turned down." He never lifted his head.

She sat up. "That's a lot of people. That will take forever."

"Then the sooner you stop distracting me, the quicker I can get it done."

She felt like flouncing back into bed like a spoiled child—but then she looked at Rio, his head bent over the computer, his shoulders hunched, all for her. He had to be uncomfortable.

"You can go back to the command center and send Conner to guard the door."

His head did come up then. He stared at her.

"All right. I did intend to tempt you back into bed, but you look so uncomfortable all hunched over, working to keep me safe." Her head tucked briefly. "I was being self-ish and I'm sorry."

Putting the computer on the table in front of him, he went to her. His hands bracketed her hips on the bed. "There have been times I didn't have a desk to work on or had to stay in a certain cramped position for hours, but there has never been a time that I felt for a woman the way I feel about you. No discomfort is too great to be here with you."

She blinked back tears. She wanted so badly to tell him she loved him. "I told my parents what an amazing man you are."

He kissed her nose. "They already know what an amazing daughter they have."

"My father thinks I'm headstrong."

Rio merely lifted a dark brow.

"And where would we be if I wasn't?" she asked, removing his hair clamp and threading her fingers through his hair.

"I probably would have eventually gotten around to it." He kissed her bare shoulder.

"I wanted you now." And she wanted him again.

He lifted his head. "I really need to do this."

She started to ask what fifteen minutes would hurt, but

knew from past experience that wouldn't be nearly enough time. They enjoyed savoring each other. She gathered her hair, pulled it over her shoulder, and put the clip on. "You have to sleep sometime. You can do it here, guarding me inside my room."

"Thin."

"Since your men respect you and, I hope, kind of like me, thin is all we need."

He straightened. "Try to get some sleep."

"I just have a few more things to do and then I'll shut it down," she told him.

He went back to the love seat and picked up his computer. He smiled at her, then went back to work.

Skylar blew him a kiss and also went to work, wishing again that she'd been able to give the intruder a whack with the poker.

It was almost dawn. Skylar was asleep on her side facing Rio. With the first shadows of night fading from the room, she looked ethereal and beautiful. Her lips were slightly parted, her black lashes lush against her delicate skin, her slender fingers pillowing her cheek.

The bedding was to her waist. He'd pulled it up over her bare shoulder, but she'd always shoved it away moments later. He didn't like heavy covers on him when he slept, either.

He should still be working to find the bastard behind the hit. He'd checked and rechecked fifty names, while three of his best men divided the others. Ten names popped up as having questionable business dealings or not being on good terms with Blade or Navarone Resorts and Spas. But none had any history of violence—at least none that they knew of. They were digging beneath the first layer, but that would take time.

And while they worked, Skylar's and possibly Mrs. Grayson's lives were in danger. His jaw tightened. Nothing would happen to either of them.

His little warrior hadn't panicked. Even if seeing her naked with a poker in her hands, ready to help, had given him a bad moment or two. Like her, he didn't think the threat came from any dealings her parents had as corporate attorneys. He'd checked the last cases they'd been involved in. They'd won for their clients, but both cases were up for appeal—and there was no telling how long that would take.

In any case, the ruling had been against a multibillion-dollar company and, until they had to pay up, they'd let their lawyers drag the case on. Since it was copyright infringement, there was no possible loss of good public will. But if they lost, it could potentially mean a big financial hit. If the company wanted to put the lead attorneys out of commission, they'd go after them, not their children.

So he was back to the auction. He had to find the connection. He picked up the computer again.

"Rio."

He looked up to find Skylar frowning at him. "Go back to sleep."

She rose up on one elbow. "Have you been to sleep at all?"

"I'm used to all-nighters on the computer."

"Emm." She lifted the cover to show a shapely leg and scooted backward. "You need to sleep. I'll wake you up in an hour."

His heart turned over. She wanted to protect him.

Watch over him. "We both know what will happen if I get into bed with you."

"You'll sleep better afterward, and I'll still wake you in an hour. Come on, my arm is getting tired holding the covers."

He *was* waiting for some data on those ten men to load.

"I should get some reward for leaving you to work, and you deserve one, too," she reasoned.

He laughed, toed off his shoes, jerked off his shirt, and shucked his jeans and underwear. He was rock-hard. Skylar's eyes narrowed in anticipation. She licked her lips.

"You always have a reason to get what you want." He got into bed with her, removed the hair clip, and dropped a kiss on her bare shoulder. "Guess it comes from your days on the debate teams in high school and college."

She kissed him quickly on the lips. "I need all the help I can get where you're concerned."

He stared at her. "All you need is you." He took her mouth.

She quivered at the tenderness of his kiss, his hard, muscled body pressed against hers.

Grabbing a handful of her gown, he drew it over her head and tossed it aside. For a long moment he stared at the perfection of her body; then he lowered his head and took her nipple into his mouth. Slowly his hand skimmed downward over her flat belly and beyond to caress the inner flesh of her thighs before moving upward again to find her hot and damp.

Moaning, she arched against him, raising her hips to meet his touch. He'd intended to love her slowly, but the need to feel himself buried in her satin heat, to feel her arms and legs clasped around him, was too great.

He'd almost lost her. He released her and quickly sheathed himself, then brought them together with one sure thrust. She gasped in ecstasy as he surged in and out of her, stroking, filling, loving.

Their bodies were in perfect harmony as pleasure built and they succumbed and found their release. He continued to hold her as aftershocks rippled though her body.

"Rio."

She murmured his name with such tenderness and pleasure, his hold tightened. He felt an overwhelming need to protect, to possess, to love her. He was familiar with the first, and out of his depth with the last two. However, he wasn't going anywhere.

"Sleep. I'll wake you."

He didn't need sleep; he needed her. "I've a better idea." He rolled on top of her. This time he'd take it slow.

Skylar met the entire Grayson clan and their wives at the front door. Patterson was still in bed, and she had called Mary and the other members of the house staff to give them the day off. Rio had cautioned Patterson to keep the attack to himself. He'd said he would.

"Good morning. Please come in."

"Good morning. Thank you," they greeted.

"Conner, we'll be in Blade's office," Skylar said to the man Rio had assigned to be her shadow if Rio himself wasn't with her.

"I'll be outside the door," he said.

"This way." Skylar led the family into the office where Rio sat behind the desk. He nodded and motioned Mrs. Grayson to take his seat. On the twenty-one-inch computer screen was Blade, with Sierra perched on the arm of his chair.

"Good morning. You two look happy," Mrs. Grayson said.

Sierra yawned. "Good morning, Mama. It's two AM our time."

Blade's arm circled Sierra's waist. "She's turning into a sleepyhead here. Is that Luke behind you?"

"Yes," Mrs. Grayson answered. "I'll get up and let Rio explain."

Rio briefly touched her shoulder. "You can just slide over." When she complied, he looked into the computer screen and told them everything. "Sierra, Mrs. Grayson was never in any danger and Luke is going to be with her."

Luke moved into view of the screen. "He's right. He's good at what he does."

"I'm coming back." Sierra was on her feet.

Blade caught her hand. "We're coming back. If Shane can tear himself away. I'll pick him up on the way. Together, we'll figure out what's going on."

"There's one more thing." Rio stepped in front of the monitor. "I think we should cancel the auction."

"No!" The loud protest came from Skylar. "We are not doing that. What reason would Blade and Mrs. Grayson give?"

"I don't want you paying for my ineptness," Rio said.

She went to him. "What did I tell you about talking nonsense? I'm alive because of you. Even if you cancel, there's no way to tell if some other creep won't come after me."

"Then you'll go back to Tucson."

"Where I'll be even more vulnerable because you won't be there to protect me. Wouldn't it be better if you find the person behind this while I'm here?" She touched his stiff arm. "With you, I'm as safe as I can be."

There was complete silence for several seconds until Blade spoke. "She's right, Rio."

Rio hated that she was stubborn and right, but it knotted his guts to know that someone wanted her dead. If the person was determined enough, devious enough, it could happen.

"I have faith in you. Please have a little in me."

"Skylar." He swallowed.

"I won't move unless I'm with you or Conner." She held up her right hand.

"All right."

"Now, if there is nothing else, I have work to do." Skylar turned to Mrs. Grayson. "I'd like to show you and your lovely and gracious daughters-in-law the collection. It's quite amazing."

"I'd love to see it." Mrs. Grayson spoke to the monitor. "Good-bye, Blade and Sierra. Safe travel."

"Good-bye," they bid.

Skylar led the women from the room. As she did Mrs. Grayson commented on the beautiful clip in her hair. Skylar barely kept from blushing. "Thank you. This way." The clip belonged to Rio, and she had a sneaky suspicion that Mrs. Grayson knew it.

Luke whistled as the door closed behind the women. "That's one brave woman."

"Bravery won't keep her safe," Rio muttered.

"But you will," Sierra said.

"She's right." Blade agreed. "Now, what's the plan?"

An hour later Rio found Skylar in the auction room, working at a large French-inspired desk. Around the room were elegant chairs and a laptop if bidders didn't want to use their cell phones to bid. Stationed at the door would be one of

Mrs. Grayson's senior students with a list of names to re-check anyone entering the room. Jason would be there with the student if problems arose. Rio's men would also be in the room dressed as guests.

Skylar glanced up when Rio was several feet away. She crossed her arms. She wasn't pleased with him.

"It was for your own safety."

"Good thing I don't have a complex since you're always trying to send me away," she muttered.

He knelt by her chair and took her hand. "A day without you in my life would be like a thousand, but knowing you were safe would help me greet the day with joy."

She hugged him. "That's beautiful. You're forgiven."

He kissed her on the lips. "Don't thank me too soon. Your safety will always come first."

"Since I feel the same way about you, you're still forgiven."

Holding her hand, he came to his feet and leaned a hip against the edge of the desk. "We're checking the ten people I told you about this morning. Have you thought of anything else? Anyone who sticks out in your mind?"

"Matt Hampton," she said. "He sent me four e-mails yesterday. I kind of feel sorry for him."

Rio's gaze sharpened. "He say anything about Tennyson?"

"No. Rio, he was almost begging to be allowed to attend. And I understand a little bit. He's trying to follow in his famous father's footsteps in the oil industry and not being very successful." Skylar's other hand covered Rio's. "I know what it's like to try to live up to your parents' image."

"Your heart is too soft. Besides, you'd never take some of the asinine risks Hampton has taken or associate with a devious person like Tennyson," Rio told her.

"Maybe he didn't know," Skylar defended. "You said yourself that some of Blade's associates believed in Tennyson. He might have been duped like the others."

"And one of them might still believe Tennyson over Blade." He got to his feet. "I need to check a few things out and go into town." The bail hearing for the man who'd intended to kill Skylar was that day, and Rio planned to be there.

"Should I wait on you for lunch?" she asked.

"No. I'm not sure what time I'll get back. You need anything?"

"A good-bye kiss."

He needed one as well. His head lowered, his lips moved against hers, exploring the infinite pleasure of her mouth with greedy hunger and endless need. After a long time his head lifted. Her lids fluttered open to reveal dazed eyes.

"My. My. I'm glad I'm sitting down," she said slowly.

"Behave while I'm gone, and don't give Conner any trouble," he told her.

"I'll be on my best behavior."

"Somehow I doubt that." Because he couldn't resist, he kissed her again quickly and then was gone.

Shortly after lunch, Skylar was working in the auction room when her phone rang. She looked at the readout. Unknown. Aware that many people didn't want their phone number made public, she answered. "Skylar Dupree, event manager for Navarone Resorts and Spas."

"Ms. Dupree, this is Matt Hampton. I wonder if I might have a moment of your time. Please, I beg of you."

Her hand flexed on the phone. She should just hang up.

"Please."

She really was a wimp at times. "Mr. Hamp—"

"I've flown down on my jet. I'm near the Navarone Castle. I can be there in five minutes. Please," he begged.

Another thought hit. She might be able to find out if Tennyson was behind the request. She didn't think Blade or Rio would want the man in the house. She also didn't think Conner would drive her to meet Hampton without telling Rio. Rio would insist he come and scare the spit out of the man.

"Ms. Dupree?"

"I'll clear you through security and meet you out front." That was the best compromise she could think of.

"Out front?"

"It's that or nothing." Where others were concerned, she could be firm.

"Thank you. I'll be there shortly."

Skylar disconnected the call, then called the front gate to tell them of Hampton's pending arrival. Finished, she waited a few minutes to tell Conner of her guest. He'd call Rio and spoil everything.

"Rio know about this?" Conner asked, following her out the front door. He was a big man with yard-wide shoulders and roped muscles. He was a good-looking sandy-haired man who topped six feet. He kidded with her a lot, but at the moment he wasn't smiling.

"Rio and I talked about Hampton this morning," Skylar evaded. The car had been checked and cleared through the security checkpoint.

"That doesn't answer my question, Skylar," Conner said.

She gave her best smile. "He'll be here and gone in five minutes."

Conner pulled out his phone just as the car pulled up.

Skylar wrinkled her nose. He was calling Rio. She didn't have much time. She quickly went to the bottom of the steps to greet Mr. Hampton as his driver jumped out and opened the door to the limousine. From the corner of her eyes, she saw Jason come from the direction of the garage. They'd spoil everything.

She extended her hand. "Good afternoon, Mr. Hampton." He was at least six feet tall and weighed about 210. His stomach bulged over his black crocodile Gucci belt. His expensive suit was wrinkled. He looked as if he'd slept in it. And he hadn't slept well if the dark smudges beneath his eyes were any indication.

His questioning gaze went behind her, then to the front of the car where Jason stood. Both he and Conner had guns. Hampton ignored her hand and began to perspire.

"Jason. Conner. Please give us a moment," she asked.

Jason took one step back. She didn't have to look at Conner to know he wasn't moving much farther—if at all.

She smiled at the nervous man, took his arm, and started walking. "Security for the auction, and this is Mr. Navarone's home. How can I help you?"

Hampton mopped his forehead with a white handkerchief. "I—I've come to plead with you to change your mind."

"Mr. Navarone's decision is final."

"He has to change his mind." His eyes flashed with desperation. "You don't understand. He'll—" He put his handkerchief to his mouth.

"Tennyson."

Fear widened his blue eyes. "I—I don't know what you're talking about?"

"You're lying. Tennyson is behind this." She took a

chance. "I wonder what he'll say when Blade contacts him about your visit."

"You can't. You don't know what he's like," Hampton wailed.

"Suppose you tell me."

"No. No. Forget I came here." He turned to leave.

"I can't do that."

He turned back around. "You have to."

"I'm sorry."

"You don't know what you're doing." He lunged for her.

She heard Conner's curse. Jason yell.

Skylar blocked the man's hands, and this time she didn't hesitate to slap both of his ears as hard as she could. When he grabbed them, she kneed him in the groin. He dropped like a stone, moaning and clutching between his legs.

Conner and Jason were there before the man hit the ground. Conner eyed her and then the man. "You ever see Rio really mad?"

She wisely kept her mouth shut. That was one image she didn't want to think about.

Chapter 14

The front door slammed so loudly she jumped. She didn't dare look at Jason or Conner. At least Hampton had stopped moaning and asking for a doctor. He hadn't wanted the ice pack she'd offered. She took heart that they were in Blade's office and not in the room across from the command center. She didn't like to remember the men converging on her and Hampton, swarming the car. She'd thought the driver of the rented limo would faint.

Blade's office door opened and slammed. Rio stood there, vibrating with anger. He went straight to her. "Why?" he snapped out.

She looked past the eelskin boots, sinfully tight blue jeans, chambray blue shirt stretched over a toned and muscled chest, square chin, slightly bent nose, and high cheekbones to piercing black eyes snapping her with rage. She made herself unclamp her hands. "I thought I could get information from him more easily, and I was right. His requests are connected to Tennyson."

Rio's hands fisted. "At what expense?"

"He never touched—"

He struck so fast she didn't see him reach for her. One second she was in her seat. The next her feet were dangling off the floor and she was eye level with Rio. "I'm saying this once. Don't you ever put yourself in harm's way again. Understand?"

She tried to think of some witty comeback, but it was difficult when nerves were jumping in her stomach. "Yes."

For a long moment, he just stared at her as if trying to decide whether he should shake her or turn her over his knee. "I'll let you handle it from now on."

If anything, his gaze intensified. He didn't believe her. His eyes shut. He clasped her tightly in his arms. She felt him trembling. She'd frightened him. Despite his men being there, she hugged him, swept her hand over his head, his back. "I was never in any danger. Conner and Jason were there in seconds. You know he wouldn't have passed through security with a weapon. I—"

"Skylar."

She shut her mouth and just held him until the trembling lessened. She hadn't meant to scare him.

He pushed her away from him and sat her gently on the seat. After taking a few breaths, he pinned Conner and then Jason with a look. She was sure they would talk later. She'd have to do something to make it up to them—if possible.

Rio walked to Hampton, his steps slow and predatory. The picture of a large cat stalking its pray leaped into her mind. He didn't have to hurry; the intended target knew he couldn't get away.

Apparently Hampton had the same impression. He leaned back in the chair, his eyes bugging. The poor man was terrified.

"Rio—"

His gaze pinned Skylar to the chair. She snapped her mouth shut. She'd pushed Rio as far as he was going to let her. She crossed her legs and clasped her hands in her lap. Hampton was on his own.

"Try to harm her again, and I'll come after you. Hard."

Hampton gulped, mopped his perspiring forehead. "I wasn't going to hurt her. I have a daughter her age. I—I just wanted her to listen and understand that she couldn't . . ." His voice trailed off. His head lowered.

"Couldn't what?"

Hampton shook his head. "I'm sorry."

"Not good enough." Rio struck, lifting the man by his shirt collar with one hand. "You talk, or we're going to go someplace and have a private conversation and you'll beg to tell me everything I want to know."

The man clawed at his throat. Rio released him. He fell back in the chair, almost toppling it. He gasped for breath.

"I'm not a patient man, Hampton. You have three seconds to tell me all you know about Tennyson and why it's so important for him to attend the auction or you and I are going to take a little walk," Rio told him.

"I don't know." Hampton looked near tears. "I barely know Tennyson. I was at the club about a month ago and it was mentioned that I'd received an invitation to the Navarone auction benefiting the Music Department of St. John's College. He was there and asked if he might come with me." He looked wildly at Rio. "I told him it wasn't possible. He seemed to take it well and invited me to his home the next night. My wife was out of town, so I went."

He put his head in his hands. "We were drinking. There were women there, but I swear I don't remember being in a bedroom with one. I love my wife. Tennyson has pictures of me and this woman. He's threatened to send them to the newspaper unless I get him an invitation."

Hampton's head lifted. "My daughter is getting married in December to Senator Williams's son. My wife is not in good health. The board of directors aren't pleased with me as it is. The scandal would be financially and emotionally devastating for my family." He looked at Skylar. "I was desperate. If he doesn't get the invitation he'll release the photos."

"Why is it so important to him?" Rio asked.

"I don't know. I swear I don't know." Hampton put his head in his head again. "He'll ruin me."

"If you don't grow a backbone, he will," Rio snapped. "Go to the police. In Chicago, your name carries more weight than his. Tell them what happened and Tennyson's attempt to blackmail you."

"I can't. My family—"

"If they care about you, they'll believe you. If you don't go to the police, Tennyson will always hold those photos over your head," Rio told the frightened man.

"You don't understand. Some women aren't as strong as others," Hampton murmured.

"That's where you're wrong. If Skylar wasn't strong, you'd be in a lot more trouble and pain by now."

The man's head snapped up. He swallowed.

Rio pulled out his cell phone and went to its photos. "Do you recognize this man?"

Hampton leaned forward to look at the picture, then shook his dark head and sat back. "No."

"You're free to leave. One of my men will drive you to the airport," Rio told him. "When you get back, tell Tennyson you talked to me and the answer is still no. Don't mention Ms. Dupree's name in any way."

"I can go?"

Rio leaned down to within inches of the man's face. "I

want you to think—who poses the biggest threat to you, Tennyson or me? Mess this up, involve Ms. Dupree, and there'll be no place, not even hell, where you can hide. You won't see me coming until it's too late."

Hampton's hand went to his throat. Perspiration beaded on his forehead.

Rio straightened and stepped back. "Jason, take Hampton to the airport. Make sure you return his wallet and cell phone before he boards his plane. Got it?"

"Got it," Jason answered.

Hampton slowly rose to his feet as if expecting Rio to change his mind or attack him. He carefully edged around Rio. Almost to the door, he stopped and looked at Skylar. "I'm sorry."

"Me, too. Why don't you take your wife on a surprise holiday until the auction is over? Somewhere you both could relax," Skylar suggested.

"I might just do that," he said.

Jason opened the door and followed Hampton out, closing the door behind them.

"We'll talk later, Conner." Rio stared at Skylar. "And thanks for the phone call."

Conner left quietly.

Skylar sat demurely in her chair. She wasn't sure how much trouble she was in. Rio had his unreadable face on.

"I don't believe I've ever seen you this quiet for this length of time before," Rio commented.

"I'm trying not to dig myself into a deeper hole," she said truthfully.

Rio crossed the room to her. "Take his wife on a holiday after he attacked you."

"He was scared and I did knee him, so we're more than even," she reasoned.

"Only you would think that way." He stopped with his boot touching the toe of her four-inch heels. "When I received Conner's initial call my cell was on vibrate, so he sent me a text about you meeting Hampton. I wanted to shake you. I instructed him to take you back inside and heard him curse." His eyes narrowed to slits. "Those five seconds before he came back on the line were the longest of my life, only for him to tell me you'd been attacked."

Skylar didn't know what to say except, "I'm sorry. I wouldn't have you worried about me for anything."

"I finally figured as much. Once my mind cleared, I realized you'd handled the situation well."

She smiled, pleased beyond words.

"But don't do it again," he warned, his face hard.

"Anything you say." She was forgiven. She'd try her best to stay out of trouble.

"I wish I could believe that. You fight for those you care about. You'll always put their well-being ahead of your own." His hands around her forearms, he tenderly lifted her to her feet. "You have strength and courage. You just need to temper it with caution and thought."

"I was concerned you'd scare him." She played with the button of his shirt. "I wanted to help."

"You did, although you might have given me another gray hair." He finally smiled.

She pretended to inspect his hair. "Nope. Not a one."

"The day isn't over yet," he countered, and they both laughed.

"What was the photo you showed Hampton?" she asked.

"Stu Ryan, the man in your room," Rio answered. "I went to town for his bail hearing. It was denied. There's a warrant out for his arrest in Chicago. His lawyer is trying to fight extradition, but he'll lose."

"Another connection to Tennyson and Chicago," she murmured.

"Exactly. Tennyson is tied to this in some way." Rio frowned. "I just can't figure out how."

"You will." She palmed his cheek. "What time are Sierra and Blade due back?"

"In a couple of hours, but they're going straight to Mrs. Grayson's house."

She tucked her head. His strong fingers beneath her chin lifted it. "What?"

"I don't think you're going to like it." In fact, she was sure of it.

His dark brow arched. "What did you do this time?"

"Your hair clip. I wore it today and Mrs. Grayson mentioned how beautiful it was in my hair." His heart thudded beneath her hand. "I don't think it was an idle comment."

"Neither do I."

"I'm not ready to get married and you're not, either," she quickly said, praying she was convincing. She'd marry Rio in a nanosecond. "Brandon is right about her perfect record being broken. We're just enjoying each other." She brushed her lips across his, ran the tip of her tongue over the seam of his mouth, hoping to convince him.

His mouth opened, deepening the kiss. His hand held her head as he slowly drove her to the edge of reason. The man certainly knew how to kiss.

"What kind of dress are you wearing for the auction?" he asked.

Skylar blinked and tried to clear her fuzzy head. She slid both arms around his neck. "It's a secret, but it's sinfully seductive."

"That's everything you wear," was his comeback.

"Glad you noticed." She ran her finger over the shell of his ear. "A woman has to use all the weapons at her disposal."

He grunted. "During your defense training, did you learn how to use a gun?"

She realized there was a reason behind Rio's questions. "Tracy wanted to learn, so I learned with her. I probably can't break down one as fast, but I still should be pretty good with a handgun and a rifle."

Rio glanced down at the V-neck violet-colored dress and sexy spiked heels. "Please go change into something more appropriate for the shooting range. I want to see how good you are."

"Take your pick." Rio shoved his hands toward an arsenal of pistols and revolvers. She'd never seen so many guns in person at one time except at the gun store. He was testing her again. It didn't help that Conner, Jason, Henderson, and a few of Rio's other men were at the shooting range as well.

Skylar folded her arms. "To do what?"

His expression didn't change. "Defend yourself."

She matched him look for look. "Against what?"

"The person trying to harm you."

"In what situation?" she asked, then continued when his arms uncrossed. "Did he catch me unaware? Is the gun in my pocket? My purse? How many shots might I need to bring him down? The distance? Lighting?"

"Your gun is in an ankle holster. Lighting unknown. Distance close. If you're good, only one shoot is needed," he replied in a flat voice.

She snatched her arms to her sides. "Ankle holster? I can't wear an ankle holster. My red strapless gown, created by one of the top designers in the country, I might add, stops just above my knees then cascades down in the back. An ankle holster is definitely out. It has to be on my thigh."

"Which can be felt. And obvious when you're lifting your dress—which you're not going to do," he said, his voice tight. "It also takes too much time. Whereas the ankle holster is undetectable. You can fake dropping something to reach for your weapon or pretend to faint. Even if your hands are bound you can still go for your gun."

"It took me weeks to decide on a dress," she told him.

Rio crossed his arms again.

He wouldn't budge. The stubborn man. In the movies, it always looked easy, but this was real life. How many times had her uncle pointed out inconsistencies with actors firing weapons and the weapons themselves? "If I can't find another dress I like, you're in trouble."

Rio didn't seem the least bothered. She was caught between kicking him and laughing. Before she could get her foot up, he'd stop her. Her mouth twitched. "Good thing I kind of like you," she whispered and turned to the guns.

"The SIG and Beretta are out. So is the Glock 17, although I kind of like the thirty-three-round expandable magazine—but where would I hide it." She glanced over her shoulder and couldn't tell if she'd impressed Rio or not. "No to the Heckler and Koch 795 semiautomatic that holds nine rounds, although it's small enough at just five point four inches with a four-inch barrel. But I think I'll go for the Guardian with the pearl handle. It's smaller than the H and K, has a nice balance, no problems with misfiring." She checked the chamber and placed the gun in front of her. "Safety goggles and earmuffs."

"Drawer beneath the table," Rio said.

"Thanks." She put them on and picked up her pistol. "Let it rip." The targets, male and female shapes, were moving. She hadn't expected it to be easy. "Where should I put the bullets?"

"Anywhere you can," Rio answered.

"I think the men deserve it right between their stubborn eyes." In quick succession she placed the bullets dead center. "I'll be lenient with the women since we have to put up with so much, er, crap." They received shoulder wounds. Finished, she pulled off the goggles and earmuffs. "Uncle Joshua always required that we clean our weapons after shooting them. If you show me where, I'd be happy to do it. That is, unless you want me to shoot at something else?"

There was complete silence as they stared at each other. Finally, Rio took the weapon from her. "That won't be necessary."

"Is there any other demonstration you'd like?"

There were a few coughs from the men. Rio's eyes narrowed just before he leaned over and whispered, "It's a good thing I kind of like you, too." Out loud he said, "I guess we all know who won this round." He lifted Skylar's hand. "The little warrior."

His men cheered loudly. Skylar beamed.

"You're full of surprises," Rio said when they returned to the castle. "All good."

"I'd thank you if I didn't have to try to find another dress." She sighed. "It really was beautiful."

He stared at her. "Where is this designer?"

"Boston," she answered.

"If you can reach him or her and they can meet us, I

can fly you there in the small jet. You can sleep on the way back."

"Rio." Her lips trembled.

"You've been through a lot since you've been here." His hand swept down her face. "You should least be able to wear a dress you like."

"I have a better idea." She glanced at her watch. "The dress was for you. Since Blade and Sierra aren't returning until later, why don't we have a cozy dinner in my room and I can wear the dress. You, of course, can keep on your jeans."

"What about a dress for the auction?" he asked.

She stuck her tongue in the side of her cheek. "I was teasing you a bit. I brought three just in case one didn't feel or look right. One is an emerald strapless ball gown that should meet with your approval."

"You never cease to amaze me," he said.

"That's the idea." She looped her arms around his neck. "I kind of figured you wouldn't want a wimp for a girlfriend, so whenever I went home or got a chance, I tried to keep up my skills."

He dropped a kiss on her nose. "You have skills all right, and not just in self-defense or with a gun."

"Why, thank you." She pulled her hands free. "Go do whatever it is you do. Dinner in one hour in my room. If you're running late, just call."

"I won't be late." With a short wave, he left the house with Skylar staring after him.

She stunned him with her beauty. He didn't know how long he stood in the doorway just staring at her. Her shoulders were bare, her waist was cinched, and the gown showed off her great legs. "I'm kind of glad I'll be the only one to see you in that dress."

She ran to him, her long legs flashing. "Then all those weeks of searching were worth it."

He lifted the box in his hand. "For you."

Her eyes widened. She pulled the brown ribbon off the distinctively wrapped box and stared inside. "Truffle lollipops. I love truffles."

He shrugged wide shoulders. "I saw them and thought about you always trying to feed me."

"We'll have them for our dessert." She took his hand. "I had to decide between the table in front of the love seat or the chest at the foot of the bed and discovered that the chest top opens out."

The desk chair and side chair were in front of the makeshift table set with crystal glasses, silver dome-covered plates, heavy flatware, the yellow rose, and five-arm candelabra.

"You went to a lot of trouble."

"I enjoyed every second, just knowing we'd be together." She motioned to a seat, then briefly tucked her head. "If I sat in your lap, I don't think we'd finish the meal, and I'd really like this cleaned up before Sierra and Blade return."

"Good thinking." He pulled out her chair.

She took her seat and said grace after he was seated. Beneath the dome tops were sea scallops with mushrooms and spinach.

Rio took a bite and smiled his appreciation for the great-tasting food. "You cook like a chef, multitask with ease, shoot a gun and defend yourself like a pro, and pull off events like the auction with aplomb, all the while remaining caring and beautiful."

"Thank you, but you're the multitasker extraordinaire. You oversee the security of all of Navarone's properties, plus his personal holdings. All the time emanating that dangerous mystique and looking gorgeous."

Rio snorted. "Eat."

"I will." She sipped her sparkling cider. "I thought we'd listen to music and dance later."

His fork poised in midair. "Dance?"

She smiled over the rim of her flute. "You know, where a man takes a woman in his arms and moves to the tempo of music."

"I don't dance."

She leaned to within inches of his stoic face. "It's easy. I'll teach you."

He went back to eating. "I didn't say I didn't know how."

"Then why don't you want to dance?" she persisted.

His gaze lanced up to hers. "It seems a waste of time."

"Not if you do it right." Getting up, she went to her iPad. Almost instantly, Johnny Mathis singing "Chances Are" came on. "It's Grandfather and Grandmother Carrington's favorite song. I grew up watching them dance to it." She went to Rio and lifted her arms. "If you still think that way after the song is over, I won't bother you again."

He looked dubious, but placed his napkin on the table and took her into his arms. He heard her sigh an instant before she placed her head on his shoulder, softly humming to herself. He inhaled the orange blossom and honey rose fragrance she always wore. His cheek brushed against her silky hair; his arm held her slim body close to his. His blood began a slow throb. She felt good in his arms. She fit perfectly.

His hand swept upward to the smooth bare skin of her shoulders and her neck, and made lazy sweeping gestures.

She stopped humming. Her breathing altered. She leaned her head back and stared up at him. He saw the same desire in her eyes that he felt coursing through him.

"I see what you meant."

"I never doubted."

He wanted to kiss her. Among other things. "You didn't eat very much."

The tip of her finger grazed his lower lip. "Food is the farthest thing from my mind at the moment." Her eyes softened. "Just you."

"Skylar." His head lowered. He brushed his lips across hers, once, twice. Then, gently settling against them, his tongue slipped into her mouth to lap against hers. His fingers found the back zipper to her dress and drew it down. When it would go no farther, he moved slightly away and lifted her out of the dress. It pooled at her feet, his mouth still on hers.

She moaned. His breath shuddered as he felt the warm softness of her breasts pressed against his chest. Finally he lifted his head and stared down. His breath stalled.

She wore a gossamer lace bra that cupped her firm breasts, a garter belt over barely there panties, sheer stockings, and evening shoes the same color as her gown.

He tossed back the covers on the bed and placed her with her legs over the sides. With his eyes on her, he undressed. Finished, he leaned over her and kissed her quivering stomach, his teeth nipping at the top of her garter belt, his blunt-tipped fingers brushing over her breasts, her thighs, her woman's softness.

She twisted beneath him, her hands clamped on the sheet. Pleasure swept through her body like a swift tide. All she could do was enjoy.

Undoing the front fasteners of her bra, he took one taut

peak into his mouth and suckled. He rolled the other nipple between his fingers. He switched to the other breast, suckled, blew, gently tugged.

Her fingers fumbled until she removed his hair clamp; then she clasped him to her breast. After one last delicious flick of his agile tongue, his head began to move downward, his sinful lips nipping and kissing all the way. She whimpered when the garter belt and panties slid off her legs. He kissed her at the lowest point of her stomach.

She had a taste, a fragrance that he'd carry with him to his last moment on earth. Both were as unique as she was. Her pleasure became his pleasure as he lavished her with kisses, the slow movements of his hands, and the tantalizing brush of his hard body against hers.

Slipping on a condom, his feet planted firmly on the floor, he slid his hands under her hips and brought them together in one sure thrust. She lifted her hips, then came upward to wrap her arms around his neck and take his mouth in hungry desperation. He thrust again and again into her satin heat. She closed around him like a tight glove, meeting him thrust for thrust.

He loved her the only way he knew how, completely and with a searing passion only this woman could quench. A woman who had given to no other man what she had given him.

A possessiveness rose in him that he'd never experienced before as he took her body and she took his. This woman was his and only his. He felt a surety, as he held her sweat-dampened body and brought them together again and again, that she felt the same way.

He felt her body stiffen and took her cry of release into his mouth. Seconds later, he joined her. His breathing loud and labored, he gathered her to him and lay down with her in his arms, their faces inches apart. She was and would always be all that he desired.

After long moments, her sated, slumberous eyes flickered open. She smiled. "I think we just found our favorite love song."

Chapter 15

When Blade and Sierra arrived at the castle a little after ten that night, Skylar and Rio were there to greet them. Skylar hugged Sierra and hoped she didn't look any different. She and Rio had spent a good part of the evening in her bed. She'd fed them only one truffle before she'd decided nibbling on him was much better.

"I'm so glad you're all right," Sierra said.

"Thanks to Rio," Skylar replied, glancing around at Rio.

Blade slapped Rio on the back. "He does come in handy."

Rio grunted. Blade laughed. "Let's go into my study and we can talk."

Blade and Rio followed the women inside. They met Patterson in the entryway. The older man wrung his hands with obvious unease.

"Welcome home, Mr. and Mrs. Navarone. I'm so sorry about what happened while you were gone," he said.

Blade stopped in front of his house manager. "Not your fault. Sierra and I still trust you to run the house for us."

The servant let out an unsteady breath. "Thank you, sir. I'll see that your luggage is attended to. I don't see Martin and Jenkins."

"We dropped them off in Dallas," Sierra replied. "The two were meeting some friends. They've become as thick as thieves and are flying in early tomorrow. Before breakfast."

The women laughed.

"I'll see to your things and make sure everything is in order." The house manager moved toward the front door.

Blade lifted a brow. "I wonder if you would have married me without Martin to cook for you and Jenkins to keep house for us wherever we go."

Sierra went to Blade and kissed him. "Yes, but one of us would have had to learn to do those things, and I don't think it would have been me."

Blade's grunt was an exact replica of Rio's. He continued into his office. He sat behind his desk, and Sierra perched on the arm of his plush executive chair. Rio seated Skylar in an armchair in front of Blade's desk and stood beside her.

Rio spoke first, telling them about the intruder being from Chicago, Matt Hampton's visit, and Rio's growing suspicion that Tennyson was behind the attacks. He finished by saying, "Tennyson is supposed to be in his office all day tomorrow. He's desperately trying to raise capital and stay afloat. Some of his financial deals have fallen through."

"Imagine that." Blade linked his fingers on the desk as he and Rio shared a look.

Skylar saw it and wondered why any sane person would make an enemy of Blade Navarone. He was fair and honest, but if you went after him or hurt what was his, he went after you fast and hard. With his billions and his connections, and Rio's keen intelligence and dogged determination, there was no place you could hide.

"The jet takes off at eight in the morning for Chicago." Rio folded his arms. "I'm looking forward to meeting Tennyson."

Skylar's head jerked up. Rio's expression was devoid of warmth. She reached for his arm before she thought. "Please don't do something you'll regret."

"I won't be the one regretting it." His voice was deadly quiet.

She stared at him, then pulled her hand back. Rio would follow his own counsel. She could only hope that Shane or Blade would step in if Rio went too far. She faced forward and froze. Sierra gave her a teasing smile and Blade looked surprised. She wasn't sure how Rio felt about anyone besides his men knowing they were involved.

"Ten extra men are coming in from headquarters. I want one of our men on every entry of this house and the other buildings. The gunman had to have been smuggled in and have inside information to know the location of Skylar's bedroom. We're rechecking everyone." Rio briefly placed a hand on Skylar's shoulder. "Creating a diversion at another site would be a good way to take the focus off keeping her safe."

Skylar relaxed. Rio wasn't the touchy-feely type of man unless they were alone. "But if it did happen, I'd have my ankle holster and the gun you provided me with."

Sierra came off the arm of the chair. "Rio is going to let you have a gun?"

"After she demonstrated her knowledge of weapons and placed nine out of nine bullets exactly where she wanted them." Rio crossed his arms again. "You have yet to show me you can use a handgun."

Sierra's chin lifted. "You should take my word."

"I didn't take Skylar's and I'm not taking yours," he came back.

Sierra glared at him. Rio remained expressionless.

"If I did, could I ditch the bodyguards?" she asked.

"No," Rio replied.

"Absolutely not," Blade responded.

Sierra sat back down and crossed her arms. "Then what's the use of showing you I can shoot?"

Skylar realized at that moment that Rio and Sierra liked sparring with each other. She did things to annoy him and he knew it, but he wouldn't give an inch.

Blade cleared his throat. "Since I'll be with you, you won't need a gun, Sierra."

"I wanted a holster a bit higher up, but Rio nixed that idea," Skylar said.

Sierra lifted a brow. "I just bet he did."

"There were logical reasons," Rio told Sierra, then spoke to Blade. "We'll leave here at seven thirty since we don't have to worry about loading luggage."

Sierra's arms uncrossed, her eyes narrowed.

Blade glanced at her and got to his feet. "I'll be ready. It's been a long day. We'll go on up to our room."

Sierra waited until they reached the door. "You know I'll think of a way to pay you back."

"Let's go, Sierra." Blade gently urged his wife out of the room, closing the door after them.

Skylar was up and in Rio's arms in an instant. "You and Sierra like teasing each other."

"I don't tease," he said with a straight face.

"Hmmm," she said with a smile and sobered. "I mean it, Rio. Don't let Tennyson push you into doing anything that will get you in trouble and have me flying up there to show him the error of his ways."

His lips curved as he brushed her hair away from her face. "You would, too."

"In a heartbeat. No one messes with what's mine," she said.

Mine. The single word reverberated in his brain. His hand stilled in her hair just as she did in his arms, her expressive eyes wide.

He didn't know if the admission caught her off guard just as it did him, or if there was another reason. He just knew that it felt right hearing her say the word.

"Mine," he repeated and kissed her until she trembled in his arms, until he banished every thought from her consciousness except him.

She was *his* and anyone who tried to harm her had a ticket to hell.

Shane Elliott was waiting for Rio and Blade at the downtown Chicago office building that housed Tennyson Corporation. Shoulder-to-shoulder, the three well-dressed men, each over six feet, with dark, piercing eyes, swept through the glass door and headed straight for the elevator. Neither looked to the left or the right. However, the interested or curious looks of those in the lobby followed them until they stepped on the empty elevator.

Rio, his eyes hard, jabbed the button for the forty-ninth floor.

Shane glanced at Rio, then Blade, then back to Rio. "What changed?"

"Skylar," Rio answered. The three men kept no secrets from one another. They'd been through hell and back together and would remain lifelong friends.

Shane grinned and slapped Rio on the back. "About time."

Rio didn't comment. Shane might have resigned from his position as head of security to live in Atlanta with Paige, but the three men always managed to get together monthly. They never planned to let their friendship take a backseat to anything, except their wives. Luckily, Paige and Sierra got along well so they didn't mind entertaining themselves while the men did their thing. Rio couldn't help thinking that maybe Skylar could join them.

Two women got on the elevator and spent their time going three floors up eyeing the men. None of the men even glanced at them.

When the elevator was empty again, Shane said, "You'd think Tennyson would have learned by now."

"He will this time," Rio promised.

"Skylar told me to make sure you came home with me," Blade said. "Sierra also extracted the same promise. She said I might hire someone else who was even more difficult to deal with."

"I'll do what has to be done." The elevator doors opened on the forty-ninth floor. Rio stepped off first and went down the plush carpeted hallway. Blade and Shane followed.

Up until he'd tried to smear Blade's name and reputation nine months ago, Tennyson had almost the entire forty-ninth floor, Rio remembered. Since that time his business had steadily declined. He'd had to let employees and office space go. Presently, he had only ten employees. He'd kept his lavish office suite, but the rest of his employees, other than his executive secretary, were in a smaller office suite down the hall.

"For a braggart like Tennyson, this has to hurt his pride," Shane sneered. "Couldn't happen to a more well-deserving man."

"He tried to put the word out that he's looking for office space on the Magnificent Mile or even thinking of building and intentionally downsized," Blade said. "No one believed the lie."

They stopped in front of a polished wood door with TENNYSON CORPORATION—SHERMAN TENNYSON PRESIDENT on a plaque. Rio looked at Blade and Shane. "I handle this my way. No one touches Tennyson except me."

"Rio—" Blade began.

Rio ignored him and opened the office door. His gaze took in the office at a glance. A woman sat behind a U-shaped desk on the phone. To her left, a large man slowly rose from a seat on a plush sofa. The rise hadn't been easy for the bulky man, who had a sixteen-inch neck and bulging muscles that stretched his jacket and revealed the weapon beneath.

"Gotta go," the woman whispered and turned to them, her smile slipping. "May I help you?"

"I got it. Thanks." Rio kept walking.

The muscle-bound man moved to block the door to Tennyson's office. "Mr. Tennyson is not seeing anyone today."

"I say he is." Rio stepped to one side as if going around the man.

The man jabbed an elbow toward Rio's face. Rio went low and punched the man in the gut. He staggered back an inch, then lunged. A hard kick to the chest sent him crashing against the door. He shook his head, his face enraged, and reached for his gun.

"Unless you want a broken wrist, which will put you out of work for a long time, move your hand. Now," Rio ordered.

The man hesitated, his gaze going beyond Rio to Shane and Blade, who hadn't moved.

"Last chance and the clock is ticking," Rio said.

With a sneer, the man plunged his hand deeper into his jacket. Rio moved, grabbing the man's right wrist and twisting it backward. Bones snapped. With a cry of pain, the man crumpled.

"My wrist! You broke my wrist," he moaned. "I'll kill you!"

Bending, Rio removed the gun, put the safety on, and tossed it several feet away on the carpeted floor. He rose to his feet and opened the door of Tennyson's office. He found another man, this one thirty pounds leaner and, from the squinted eyes, meaner, waiting for him.

"Better and better."

The man ran at Rio, then high-kicked. Rio dropped and sent his booted foot straight into the man's knee. He went down, moaning and holding his leg.

Tennyson shot up from his desk, his face enraged. He had added the second bodyguard two days ago. He was running scared.

Rio had given Jason the code to place a bug on Hampton's phone. He hadn't contacted Tennyson and, as Skylar had suggested, Hampton had taken his wife to St. Croix.

Rio straightened and went to Tennyson's desk. The middle-aged man's thin lips tightened beneath his mustache. Behind the guise of a businessman was a poisonous snake. His eyes were filled with hate. He picked up the phone. "I'll have you arrested for breaking and entering, and for assault."

Shane held up his iPhone. "That might be difficult to prove when the authorities see he was attacked first, see the weapon your first guy had, and hear Rio warning him to not reach for said weapon."

Tennyson slammed the phone down. He looked beyond Rio and Shane to Blade, who stood in the doorway near the first bodyguard, sitting on the floor rocking with his hand in his lap.

"Your secretary promised to hold all calls." Blade leaned against the doorjamb.

"You bas—"

Blade slowly straightened. "Say it and give me the pleasure of stuffing your teeth down your throat."

"He's mine," Rio reminded Blade.

"Remember, Rio," Shane said.

Tennyson's gaze snapped back to Rio. "I've heard that name before."

"You'll hear it again, and you won't like it unless you call your dogs off," Rio told him.

Tennyson straightened the jacket of the five-thousand-dollar fine wool suit and took a seat. "I don't know what you're talking about."

"You're lying." Rio leaned across the desk. If he were closer, no power on earth would keep him from beating the living hell out of Tennyson. "If you send someone else, once I finish with them I'm coming for you."

"I'm a respected businessman." Tennyson idly picked up a gold pen on his desk. "You know the way out."

Rio straightened. "You've been warned."

Tennyson's hand tightened on the pen. "I'd heard that you were some kind of Rambo. Guess you aren't so much if you have to threaten an innocent man."

"You're going down, Tennyson," Rio threatened. "I'm going to see to it."

Slowly, Tennyson came to his feet. "You know nothing of what I'm capable of. In every war, there are innocent causalities." He smirked. "Retribution is a son-of-a-bitch, isn't it?"

Rio jerked Tennyson by his silk tie and hauled the man halfway across his desk. Blade and Shane rushed to grab Rio's arms. "Harm her and I'll unleash hell on you and there'll be no place to hide."

"That's enough," Blade said. "Remember the promise."

"His eyes are rolling back, Rio," Shane said.

Rio shoved Tennyson away as if he were distasteful.

"What's going on here?" a male voice asked. "Mr. Tennyson, your secretary called."

Blade turned to see a wide-eyed security guard. Extending his hand, Blade went to greet the gray-haired man. "Blade Navarone. We were engaging in a security practice drill with two of Mr. Tennyson's bodyguards to test their abilities." He bowed his head briefly. "I'm afraid they forgot we were doing a practice drill and . . ." Blade looked down at the two injured men. "Suffered the consequences. Perhaps you should call an ambulance."

The guard pulled out his radio, then paused when he saw Tennyson sitting behind his desk, his breathing labored, his tie loose, and his shaky hand at his throat. "Mr. Tennyson, are you all right?"

He leaned forward in his chair. "You fool! Do I look all right?"

The security guard flinched as if he'd been struck. "I'm sorry, sir. I—"

"Dammit, man, call us an ambulance," the second bodyguard cried. "I think the bastard shattered my knee."

The guard looked overwhelmed.

Blade took out his cell phone and dialed 911. "Perhaps you should go downstairs and wait for them."

"I'll do that." The man left in a hurry.

Blade saw that the secretary was gone and came back

into Tennyson's office. "We probably have ten minutes max before an ambulance arrives. Probably the police as well. I say we make good use of the time so we won't have to come back and have another . . ." He paused meaningfully. ". . . practice drill."

Tennyson glared at Rio, but he kept his mouth shut.

Blade was right about the police arriving with the ambulance. So did the head of building security. It helped that the man knew Shane and obviously didn't like Tennyson. Once the police officer realized Blade's identity, he called his sergeant who called his captain who called the chief of police who called the mayor.

Tennyson and his two bodyguards corroborated the story Blade made up. The mayor and chief of police barely glanced at Tennyson. Their focus was on Blade and the two men with him.

"I've always heard you had top security," the mayor said. "Seems I heard right."

"Thank you," Blade said, trying to keep an eye on Rio.

"Since you're in town, why don't we all go out to lunch? A good friend of mine has a small yacht and an excellent chef," the mayor urged. "Maybe this time I'll be able to convince you to build here."

"Chicago is a great city," the chief of police said.

Blade smiled. "Never hurts to talk." Or to show Tennyson who held the trump card. "We accept the invitation to lunch."

"Mayor." Tennyson got to his feet behind his desk, but after a glance at Rio the man didn't move toward the city official. "I'd like to take you to lunch or dinner anytime your schedule is free."

The mayor never lost his jovial smile. "I'll have my secretary check my schedule." He turned to Blade. "Let's go. Nothing like eating on the water."

Blade wanted to laugh. The mayor had just blown Tennyson off—and from the man's angry expression, he knew it. "Sounds good. Our car is downstairs. After you, Mayor."

Shane, having kept himself between Rio and Tennyson, followed Rio and the other two men out the door.

Blade looked over his shoulder to Tennyson. Pure hatred stared back at Blade. "Come after me or mine again, and you won't know what hit you." He left the door open and joined the chattering group of men.

Except Rio. He stared straight ahead, his eyes cold. Blade, Shane, and Rio knew that Tennyson might be their man, but they had no way of proving it.

As soon as they were seated in the back of the limo, Rio pulled out his phone. Blade and Shane did the same.

Skylar answered before the second ringtone. "Please tell me you're all right."

"I'm all right," he told her, still trying to control the urge to stop the car and go teach Tennyson a lesson he wouldn't forget.

"You don't sound all right. Was there trouble?"

"Nothing to worry about," he told her, unsure if Blade would tell Sierra everything or not. They didn't keep secrets from each other.

"Well, I am, and I won't stop until you're back here holding me."

Warmth replaced some of the anger. "We're having lunch with the mayor and, if I know the mayor, it will be a long one."

"As long as you're with the mayor, I feel better. Thanks for calling. I was worried."

"You shouldn't worry about me. I can take care of myself."

"I know that, and I still worry. Hurry home. I have something to show you. Bye."

Rio's mind went into overdrive as he thought of what Skylar might be talking about. Probably something to tempt— He slowly turned to see Blade and Shane studying him. "What?"

"You had this look on your face I've never seen before," Shane said

"Your voice changed," Blade added.

"So?" Rio looked at them sideways.

"So, we're happy for you," Blade said as he and Shane both caught Rio around the neck and laughed.

If was after nine that night when Rio pulled up in front of the castle. Blade was in the passenger seat. Rio had been right about the long lunch, which included a cruise and late cocktails.

"That bastard Tennyson is going to keep coming," Rio gritted out. "He's probably going after her because he sees her as the reason his plan to sneak in didn't work."

Blade laid a hand on Rio's tense shoulder. "And we'll stop him. He won't get by us. He's not going to get anywhere near Skylar. She's a strong woman."

Rio nodded. "And stubborn."

"And you wouldn't want her to be any other way," Blade said. "Sierra is the same."

"You have more patience than I do," Rio told him.

"You'll find out that when you really care about a

woman, you're capable of doing a lot of things you once thought impossible."

"We're having dinner with her parents tomorrow night," Rio said slowly, trepidation in his voice.

"You never cared what other people thought about you, unless it was important to me. Now it's important to you. I've seen you with Skylar. You're different, happier, and so is she." Blade laughed. "A woman can sure change a man's outlook on life."

"You can say that again," Rio said, his brows bunched.

Blade opened his door. "Let's not keep them waiting any longer."

Rio got out of the Jeep and pocketed the keys. Once he saw Skylar and the surprise, he'd come back and put the Jeep in the garage.

Blade punched in the code and opened the door. Rio entered behind him. He saw Sierra in a large terry-cloth bathrobe and flat sandals. He frowned when he didn't see Skylar.

"Hi and bye, Rio." Sierra caught Blade's hand. "I missed you. We're going to the grotto."

"Good night, Rio." His arm around his wife's waist, Blade kissed her on the cheek.

Sierra stopped at the top of the stairs heading down to the heated underground pool and snapped her fingers. "I almost forgot. Skylar went to get something in her room. She said if she wasn't back down when you arrived, you should go up and knock."

She clearly hadn't forgotten, but Rio was already hurrying for the stairs. He took them two at a time. Conner was standing guard at her door. "I'll take over from here."

Conner nodded. "'Night, Rio. I'm turning in. See you in the morning."

"'Night and thanks." He waited until he could tell by the sound of Conner's boots that he was off the stairs. He knocked on Skylar's door.

"Come in."

He opened the door, saw Skylar standing at the foot of the bed with her left arm propped against the bedpost, and knew his Jeep wasn't going to get moved for a long, long time. Shutting the door without taking his eyes from her, he reached for the button of his shirt.

Chapter 16

Skylar was nervous and, although she tried not to show it, she knew Rio could tell. They were meeting her parents and maternal grandparents for dinner tonight at Casa de Serenidad, where they were staying. Since reservations were difficult to obtain, she'd booked their rooms when the charity event was just an idea.

She'd issued the invitation because she wanted them to see how happy she was so they'd finally stop trying to get her to quit and move back to Boston. At the time she thought she'd be staying at the same hotel. Thanks to Sierra and Blade's graciousness, that had changed—and so had her life.

Thanks also to the handsome man walking beside her. She looked up at Rio, tall, handsome, with a mysterious edge that had women in the lobby of the hotel turning for a second or third look. *He's mine,* she wanted to say. Thank goodness that when she'd blurted it out the other day, it hadn't scared him off. Rio didn't want a permanent relationship. While it saddened her, as she'd told him she was going to enjoy every second with him.

Last night was a prime example. They'd loved each

other most of the night and awakened this morning for more of the same.

"You still think we should have come early?" Rio asked as they passed the registration desk of the hotel.

"Yes. They can't wait to see you," she admitted, some of her nervousness returning. She was her father's little girl, no matter that she was grown and gone. He still thought she needed guidance and protection. She'd warned all of them not to ask—translation, drill—Rio about his past or his family. But her father was a loose cannon and unpredictable at times.

Rio took her hand. "It'll be all right. Your parents love you."

"They're also overprotective, and that goes double for my father." She almost bit her lower lip before she stopped herself. She loved and respected her parents, but there was no way she was going to let them ruin things between her and Rio.

Her hand tightened on his, and when he glanced down, probably thinking she was even more worried as they neared the restaurant, she rose to her tiptoes and kissed him. "With you, I can face anything, do anything."

He smiled. "Of course. You're my little warrior."

"Works for me." She grinned up at him.

"Come on." He placed his hand on the small of her back and approached the maître d'. "Reservations for Skylar Dupree."

"Yes, sir." The man in a black tux bowed to Skylar. "Ms. Dupree?"

"Yes," she answered and scanned the restaurant. "My parents and grandparents are probably already here."

He smiled and picked up two menus. "They were just

seated at one of our best tables. It's in a quiet area, as you requested. I'll show you to their table."

"Thank you." Skylar was infinitely glad she'd requested a quiet area when she made the reservations. She hoped her father would behave, but she wouldn't bet on it.

They hadn't gone five steps before Rio said, "To the far right at the round table in the alcove."

Skylar tried to look around the maître d' and failed. "I'm too short."

"Another time I might lift you up," Rio whispered.

She giggled and glanced up at him. "I kind of like the sound of that."

The maître d' stepped aside. "Here you are."

Skylar turned and saw her parents and grandparents staring at her. For a second, she thought she might have spoken the words too loud—or perhaps she wore a look on her face that clearly said, *I can't wait for us to make love again.*

Rio's fingers tapping against the small of her back brought her back on track. She realized they weren't staring at her, they were staring at Rio. "Hi, it's so good to see all of you." She hugged her maternal grandparents. "Grandfather and Grandmother, you both look wonderful." Next she went to her parents and rested her cheek against each of theirs. "Mother and Father, it's so good having you both here. You're looking pretty incredible yourself."

"So do you, Skylar." Her mother caught her hand, her smile filled with warmth. She'd always been a beautiful woman, with thick black hair she wore in a razor cut. She wore a soft blue Valentino suit.

Her father's hazel eyes narrowed. Any opposing attorney knew to watch out when Beau Dupree did that. "She'd look better in Boston."

Behave, she mouthed. At fifty-eight, handsome, successful in his own right, and distinguished, her father liked doing things his way. He seemed to have forgotten that so did she. She reached for Rio's arm.

"Rio, I'd like you to meet my maternal grandparents, Cecil and Olivia Carrington, and my parents, Beau and Meredith Dupree. Everyone, this is Rio Sanchez."

"Good evening." Rio shook hands with the men and nodded cordially to the women. They smiled, but he could tell they were sizing him up. He pulled Skylar's seat out, then sat next to her at the round table.

The patient maître d' handed them their menus. "Would you like anything to drink, or should I send the sommelier over?"

"We'll have sparkling water," Skylar said.

"You usually have wine with dinner," her father said and picked up his own red wine.

"Not for a long time, Father. How was the trip? Do you like your rooms?" she asked.

"Your father was late getting to the airport as usual." Meredith cast a scathing glance at her ex-husband sitting next to her. Their chairs were at least eighteen inches farther apart than everyone else's.

"I told you, business detained me," Beau said, his voice crisp.

"So you said." Meredith picked up her glass of white wine. "The rooms are lovely, Skylar. Thank you for arranging everything. It's so good seeing you again."

"You look happy and beautiful," her grandmother said, looking lovely in a toffee-colored St. John suit.

"Thank you," Skylar replied.

Rio felt Skylar's leg touch his. He was aware she was telling him he was the reason; he just hoped she didn't keep doing that during dinner. "Have any of you been to New Mexico before?"

There were murmurs of "no." "First time," her father said. "Interesting town and friendly people. Like Boston, it's a bit crowded."

"Have you decided what you want to order?" Skylar looked over the top of the leather-bound menu. "The chef is excellent."

"Don't let Brandon hear you say that," Rio said.

"Why? Who's Brandon, Rio?" Her mother placed her wine on the table.

"It's a bit complicated, Mrs. Dupree, but Brandon Grayson is a chef and owner of the Red Cactus restaurant. His mother is Ruth Grayson. His wife's family owns this hotel. He and the executive chef here have a running feud about who is the best chef." Rio looked at Skylar. "Brandon thinks you're in his corner."

Skylar smiled up at him. "He would be right, but Brandon's restaurant is for casual dining. He'd understand."

"I wouldn't bet on it," Rio said.

Skylar just grinned up at him.

Her father cleared his throat. Skylar held up her menu. Rio slowly turned and caught the disapproving look of Mr. Dupree. Rio's expression clearly said he didn't care. Skylar's father's lips tightened.

"Let's order." Mrs. Dupree signaled the waiter. "Have you ever dined here, Rio?"

Rio's face lost the hard look. Mrs. Dupree was willing to get to know him. "Several times in here and too many to count in the other restaurant on the terrace. Blade's wife, Sierra, is Brandon's sister. She and Faith are close friends. While the Grayson family booth was being enlarged at the Red Cactus, they ate here a lot."

Mr. Dupree's frown deepened. "What have—"

"Not now, Beau," Meredith cut in. "The waiter is here to take our order."

Her ex snapped his mouth shut. Skylar's shoulders slumped. Beneath the table, Rio nudged her knee with his. She glanced up. He smiled. She smiled back and sat upright.

As Rio glanced down at his menu, he noted that Skylar's grandparents sitting next to him had witnessed the exchange. Her grandfather looked thoughtful; his wife, pleased.

The waiter took their food orders, asked about wine and drink orders, then withdrew.

"Can I continue now, Meredith?" Mr. Dupree asked.

"Only if you have to, Beau," his ex came back. "Personally, I'd like to hear more about the auction tomorrow evening. I can't wait."

"I'm a bit anxious myself," Mrs. Carrington admitted. "There are a couple of things I have my eye on."

Her husband shook his gray head. "What if I left my checkbook and credit card at home?"

She smiled at him. "I made sure you didn't."

Everyone laughed, including her husband.

Rio saw Skylar in fifty years in her grandmother, still having the last word and making him like it.

"Well," Beau began, only to be interrupted again.

"Your salads." The server placed the food on the table. "Appetizers will be out shortly."

"What has your employer and his wife eating here have to do with you?" Beau asked in a rush.

"I hardly think that's any of your concern, Beau." Meredith frowned.

Rio agreed, but he answered anyway. "When possible,

Blade and Sierra are together. Sierra has four bothers, including Brandon. All are married. They're a close family and enjoy being around each other," Rio explained. "I'm head of Navarone security worldwide, and Blade's personal bodyguard."

"Father," Skylar said, impatience and annoyance in her voice. "You already know that. I told all of you about Mrs. Grayson and her children when I explained about the auction."

"She certainly did." Her mother picked up her salad fork. "Now drop the subject and let's enjoy our meal."

Beau pushed his salad aside and stared across the table at Rio. "I'd like to know more about the man taking my daughter out."

"Which means the private investigators you hired were too inept to find out anything," Rio said, his voice flat.

Skylar gasped. "Father, you didn't."

Beau's uncompromising gaze swung to his daughter's. "I love you. I'd do anything to protect you." His attention switched to Rio. "You're the first man our daughter ever mentioned more than once. Even before now, your name had come up in conversation. Protecting her and keeping her happy is what's important."

"That's why I'm still sitting here," Rio replied evenly.

Skylar's mother was appalled. "You're just pushing her farther away."

"I'm seeing to her well-being."

"Like you saw to it by sleeping with that woman and destroying our marriage," Meredith snapped.

"I've told you that—" Her ex shoved his hand over his neatly trimmed head of hair. "What's the use? You only believe what you want to believe."

"Because it's the truth. You make me ill," Meredith said tightly. "To think I trusted you. Believed in you, and it was all a lie. I wouldn't be anywhere near you, and certainly not sitting beside you if it wasn't for Skylar. Let her run her own life before you mess it up any further."

Beau braced both hands on the table. "I—"

"Please stop," Skylar said, her voice shaky. She wanted to hide her face and crawl out of the restaurant in embarrassment. How could he act this way? Have Rio investigated and then try to interrogate him after she'd specifically asked him not to.

Rio's hand covered Skylar's, clamped tightly in her lap. His thumb gently stroked the back of hers. She couldn't look at him.

"Father, I'm removing your name from the guest list for the charity auction." She swallowed. "Good night, Mother, Grandmother, and Grandfather."

"You can't mean that, baby," her father said, his handsome face a study in disbelief. "I was just trying to protect you."

"You went about it in the wrong way." She stood on unsteady legs. Rio curved his arm protectively around her shoulders. "Good night."

"Don't worry, Mrs. Dupree. She'll call you and her grandparents a little later," Rio told them.

Her father stood, his face angry. "Now, you're running her life and telling her what to do?"

"You were so focused on me, you forgot that Skylar is her own woman," Rio said quietly. "She loves you and you hurt her. Don't make it worse." His arm tightening around Skylar's trembling shoulders, he led her from the restaurant.

* * *

"It's all right, Skylar. It's going to be all right."

Rio had repeated the words on the way to the valet station, and after seating her in the BMW SUV and fastening her seat belt. She hadn't responded, just closed her eyes and leaned back against the headrest.

Feeling helpless to soothe her misery, he got in and pulled off. She'd been looking forward to him meeting her parents and grandparents, showing him off. He didn't mind for himself. He'd been judged and found lacking in the past, and it would probably happen again.

He didn't care what others thought of him. As the Man With No Name had taught him, know who you are and whose you are, and then no man can make you think or feel less of yourself. If it had been anyone but her father, Skylar would have blown him off or put him in his place. She respected and loved her father too much to say anything more than she had.

Uninviting him to the charity function, however, made it very plain that she was disappointed and upset with him. He'd been shocked. Her mother angry. Her grandparents upset.

Rio kept looking at her to make sure she wasn't crying. When he wasn't shifting gears, he was holding her hand. At least it wasn't trembling any longer. He wasn't sure if he should talk or leave her to her own thoughts. He finally figured she'd talk when she was ready.

He found a station on the radio that sounded like the same kind of melody as the Johnny Mathis song they'd danced to, hoping the music would help. "We'll be at the castle soon. We can take a walk or sit out back or anything you want."

Her eyes closed, and her head remained against the

headrest as it had been since he'd seated her in the car. Silence. He vividly recalled the other time when she had been upset. She'd thought some other woman was after him.

He turned into the driveway, rumbled over the draw-bridge, and stopped in front of the castle. He went around and opened her door. "Your father didn't bother me. Your being upset does."

Silence.

"Come on, Skylar." His hand swept down her arm. "It's all right. Talk to me."

Her head lifted. Slowly her eyes opened. "He had no right to investigate you. None. I can't apologize enough."

"You have nothing to apologize for." He let out a relieved breath that she was talking. "Luke made inquiries about Blade."

"But I bet he wasn't sneaky about it," she said, her eyes narrowed angrily.

"No," Rio admitted. "I think her entire family pretty much let Blade know they were watching him. I think Shane and Paige's mother had a talk as well."

"Their families probably didn't try to stop them from dating Shane or Blade. Or interrogate the men at dinner," Skylar said.

Rio gently cupped her face. "I'm not sure that would have worked with Sierra or Paige; although she's quiet, she not weak. Otherwise she and Shane wouldn't be together. When a family loves you, sometimes they overstep."

"I'm not such an idiot that I can't tell when a man is trying to con me. Father should know that!"

"Then you'll just have to convince him otherwise. You made a good start tonight by canceling his invitation." He almost smiled at the memory.

"I never expected he'd do anything like that. I wanted

them to get to know you, you to know them." She leaned her head against his. "Instead, I was embarrassed and angry."

"There's no reason to be." He lowered his hands and helped her out of the car. "Check your phone, I'm sure you have calls."

"I didn't feel it vibrate," she said, but she opened her small purse and picked up her cell phone. "Five calls. Mother and Father each called twice. My grandparents once."

"Let's go inside and you can call them while I fix you something to eat." Catching her hand, he started up the steps.

"I'm not calling Father until he apologizes to you."

Rio entered the code and opened the front door. "If you don't call him, how will you give him a chance to apologize? He doesn't have my number."

She stopped. "You sound like you want me to forgive him."

He placed his hands on her shoulders and stared down at her. "Skylar, it isn't in you to hold a grudge against those you love. You'll be miserable if you try. So sooner or later, you're going to have to talk to him. It might as well be now."

"I can try," she stubbornly said.

"Come on." He started toward the kitchen. In the great room, he saw Blade and Sierra curled up on the long sofa watching a movie. "Maybe I won't have to cook if Sierra left any of the food Martin prepared."

Sierra's dark head popped up. "Martin cooked a fantastic dinner for us. I don't think—" She stopped when they neared and she saw Skylar's miserable face. Sierra stood, her questioning gaze going to Rio.

"Maybe Sierra should tell you what overprotective Brandon and Pierce thought of Blade while I raid the kitchen." Rio kissed Skylar on the top of her head and kept walking.

"They hated my guts, especially Brandon." Blade got to his feet and chuckled. "Luke and Morgan were a little bit more restrained, but Luke made it pretty clear that if I messed up he'd be standing on my doorstep."

Sierra rounded the sofa, hooked her arm through Skylar's, and followed Rio toward the kitchen. "Brandon and Pierce were pitiful. You should have heard them go on and on about Blade's reputation, as if I was a ninny. They actually thought about trying to keep me in Santa Fe instead of entering into the selection process for the position of executive Realtor at Navarone Place in Dallas."

"What happened?" Skylar asked.

"Mama," Sierra said simply. "She said I could go. We might be grown and gone, but we still listen to her."

"As I understand it, there was a meeting and a caveat to Sierra's going to Dallas," Blade said. "They would be watching me and if I caused her any pain, they'd be there and I'd regret it until the day I died."

"Family can be a blessing, but they can also make you want to send them to another planet to live," Sierra said.

"My father would be on the first flight," Skylar said tightly.

"Good timing." Rio placed a plate with a thick slice of prime rib, red potatoes, and broccoli on the table. Bread and butter were already there. "I'll get you something to drink."

"I'm not hungry," Skylar murmured.

"Sit down, Skylar," Sierra urged. "I'm trying to picture

this new Rio. Perhaps the next time Martin is away or on vacation, Rio can do double duty."

Rio placed the glass of lemonade on the table. "As long as you do the grocery shopping, wash and chop the vegetables, set the table, clear the table, wash the dishes, and do a few other things to help."

Sierra crossed her arms. "You're good at multitasking. Why can't you do it all?"

Rio crossed his. "Because you're going to be doing it."

"We're missing the movie." Taking Sierra's hand, Blade pulled her from the kitchen.

Skylar finally smiled. "You and Sierra don't give an inch, and Blade loves both of you."

"I like that smile." He sat in the chair in front of the plate and held out his arm for her to sit in his lap. "Come and sit down so we can eat."

She placed her purse on the stone counter and sat on Rio's lap. He hugged her, kissed her cheek. "It's going to be all right."

"I believe it when you say it," she said softly.

He kissed her again. "Eat. You were running around so much today you missed lunch."

"I thought I'd eat—" She jumped up and reached for her purse. "I might not be the only one that didn't eat." She punched in her mother's cell phone number. "Mother." Skylar reached for Rio's hand as soon as her mother answered. "I'm fine. Rio and I were about to eat and I thought about you and the grands." She shook her head. "If you don't order room service, I'm going to be annoyed with you. Besides, you want to be at your best tomorrow evening.

"Yes, I arranged a car to pick all of you up so you can arrive a bit early and view the pieces unencumbered." Skylar bit her lower lip. "I'm not sure I can talk to Father tonight, but I'll call the grands. Yes." She smiled up at Rio. "I've already apologized. Being such a great, understanding guy, he understood. I love you, too. Good night."

Releasing Rio's hand, she called her grandparents. "I'm fine. Did you enjoy your meal? You left Father at the table? I'm glad you ordered room service. Yes, we were about to eat. Love you both. Good night." She ended the call, then rubbed her forehead.

Rio massaged her stiff shoulders. "Go on and call him."

"Grandmother said when I walked away, he just stood there staring after me, then sat back down. She said the only time she'd seen him look so lost was the day Mother filed for divorce." She leaned against Rio's chest. "They all left him sitting alone at the table."

"You won't be able to sleep—and like you told your mother, you need to be at your best tomorrow." He lifted her hand. "Put him out of his misery."

"Why do you care?"

"Because you care. I'll reheat the food while you call." Rio picked up the plate and went to the microwave.

Skylar stared at the phone. She was worried about him. Despite what he'd done, she loved him and knew he hadn't acted maliciously. Then there was the very real threat against her life. She didn't want his last memory of her to be of her angry and walking away. She punched in his number.

"Skylar, baby. I'm sorry—I . . ." He blew out a breath.

"You should be. The man you tried to investigate and browbeat is the reason I'm calling. Unlike you, he knows and understands me."

There was a long silence. "Is he with you now?"

"Yes, and he's not going anyplace!"

"Could you put on the speaker, please? I want him to hear this."

She glanced at Rio. "Why?"

"To apologize."

She put the phone on speaker and went to Rio. "You're on speaker."

"Rio, I'm sorry. What I did was uncalled for. I lost her mo . . . Never mind. I just miss her and I don't want to lose her, too."

"She loves you, Mr. Dupree. Neither I nor anyone else will ever be able to change or diminish that love. I think she has something else she wants to say."

"What is it, baby?"

"You can come tomorrow night. And don't you dare make me regret my decision. The auction means a lot to people I care deeply about, and some well-deserving students," she told him.

"Thank you. I'll arrange my own transportation. Meredith . . ." He sighed again. "Thanks for calling."

"Did you eat?"

"No. Just sat there like a fool as the waiters placed everyone's order on the table. Which might be apt."

She'd never heard him sound so down. "Like I told Mother, order room service."

"You think she listened?"

There it was again, the deep concern her father always had for her mother. "You still care about her, don't you?" She'd never had the nerve to ask before.

"Of course, she's your mother," he answered.

He'd evaded, but what else had she expected from one of the best lawyers in the country? "Good night, Father."

"Good night, and thanks again. I love you, Skylar."

"I love you, too, Father. Good night." She ended the

call and heard the ding of the microwave. For a moment she just stood there, then put the phone back in her purse.

"Come here." Rio extended his arm.

She went to him, curving her arms around his waist and placing her head on his chest. "I think Father still loves Mother. He wouldn't admit it." She lifted her head. "You were right. He sounded miserable. Mother has her parents with her. He has no one."

"You can have the world and it still won't help the ache of loneliness," he said quietly.

"I understand that now." She rubbed her finger across his lower lip. "I miss you when you're gone, and nothing else can fill that void except you."

"One day I'll be gone."

Skylar ignored the pain in her heart, and lifted her lips to his. "But you're here now."

Later that night, Rio lay awake with his arms around Skylar's shoulders as she lay with her arms draped loosely around his neck, one of her legs thrown across his. Before Skylar, he'd never slept with a woman, never stayed longer than the act of intimacy. He'd never wanted to. He'd simply engaged in a biological need. And never the same woman twice.

Even before he began working for Blade, women were never difficult to find. He was in his teens when he realized he presented them a challenge—bending him to their will. More often than not, he walked away. The Man With No Name had taught Rio that a man who couldn't control his baser needs would never control his destiny and would always be at the mercy of someone else.

Holding Skylar while she slept, watching over her, taking care of her, he felt a peace and true contentment for the first time in his life. The oddity was that he hadn't realized anything had been missing in his life. Before Skylar, he could have named nothing that he wanted and didn't have or have access to.

Blade had the billions, but he was extremely generous and Rio and Shane had access to anything he owned. No questions asked. Money wasn't an issue, nor was holding his own around the wealthiest people in the world.

The woman sleeping in his arms, sprawled halfway on top of him as if ensuring he didn't slip out of bed and leave her, was. Even before their first kiss, he'd realized as much.

He was stuck on her father's comment that she had mentioned Rio before. Of course, he'd known she watched him, but not that she had mentioned him to her parents. As he'd imagined, she wanted more than an affair. She wanted what he couldn't give her: marriage and happily ever after.

He had no idea how a marriage worked, how to compromise. Yet he'd walk through the fires of hell before he'd hurt her. Once he nailed Tennyson's hide to the wall and the men he'd hired, Rio would take one day at a time with Skylar.

If he felt that either of them was in danger of getting in over their heads, he'd walk away. He'd give his life to save her, but he'd never ruin her life to have her.

Chapter 17

Saturday morning dawned bright and clear. By seven, Skylar had eaten a quick breakfast with Rio and iPad in hand met with Patterson, Rio, and the men he'd assigned to mingle with the guests and guard the entry doors of the castle.

"No food or drink will be allowed past the doors into here. There'll be wait staff on one side of the doors to take those items and wait staff on the other with drinks and finger foods when they leave," Skylar said. "Stationed around the room will be students from St. John's Music Department with computers connected to the Web site to assist with bids. Or the guests can do it themselves."

She pointed to a large screen on the wall. "The items are listed alphabetically as they are in the catalog and will be updated as quickly as possible so bidders can easily see if their bid has been topped. Between eight thirty and nine, we'll clear this room of guests so chairs can be brought in. Everyone will come back at nine when I, with the help of an auctioneer, will go through the bids. If no one tops a bid, we'll move on to the next item. Any questions?"

There were head shakes and murmurs of no. "If you think of anything later, I'll be the one running around like the Energizer Bunny." She laughed, and everyone laughed with her.

"Although the invitation said seven, we know some will come early to beat the rush. For those of you in here, please be on duty by six thirty. The main dining room is where the buffet will be set up with tables and seating. Dancing will be in the ballroom next door." She glanced at the house manager. "I've coordinated with Mr. Patterson for you to eat at six in the small dining room."

The room erupted in applause. Skylar did a little curtsy. "Thank you. Rio."

Rio stepped forward. He wasn't smiling now, and neither were his men. "We've already talked this morning. I expect each of you to be on high alert. With family and friends coming in before the guests, it's going to be an almost constant stream of vehicles and people. No one gets on this property or in this house without clearance. You know what to do. That's all."

The men piled out of the room.

Patterson stepped forward. "The small dining room will have an assortment of food and beverages for the arriving houseguests. All their rooms are ready. Jefferson will help with luggage and Mary will see that the dining room is kept stocked. The extra staff to assist is already here. At six this evening, Mary will assume charge of the children."

"Excellent, Mr. Patterson. You're a lifesaver." Skylar touched his arm. "I would have been lost without you."

The older man flushed. "Thank you, Ms. Dupree. If you'll excuse me, I'll go check on things."

"Certainly." She turned to Rio. His expression was hard. "I'll be fine."

"I plan to make sure of it.," he said, his voice tight.

"My guts tells me that Tennyson will have his guy make a move tonight when so much is going on. I'm not risking it. Jason will be with you until you come down for the auction, then Hendrix and Marshall."

"What! Rio, you can't be serious. I can't do anything with Jason trailing behind me, let alone two men tonight. I—" She snapped her mouth shut and stared at him. He stared right back, not saying anything. He didn't have to. When it came to security, Rio had the last word.

"Why can't it be you?" she asked, trying not to sound sullen.

"Because I'll be doing other things." Taking her arm, he started for the closed door. "Don't worry, I'll be nearby."

"I'm not worried. You won't let anything happen to me." She placed her hand on his chest. "Promise you'll take care of yourself."

"I told you not to worry." Rio reached for the door.

Aware he hadn't given her his promise, she placed her back to the door, keeping it closed. "I need something to fortify me for the day."

"What?" he asked.

"You get one guess." Circling his neck with one arm, she lifted her lips to his. He did the rest, hauling her into the shelter of his strong arms, his mouth ravaging hers as his hands molded her lower body to his. Her body caught fire. She strained against him. They'd made love less than an hour ago, yet every nerve ending screamed for him to take her again.

Thunk.

Skylar resisted Rio moving away from her. Finally she opened her eyes, then palmed her face when she saw him pick up her iPad from the carpeted floor. "Is it broken?"

"Doesn't seem to be." He rose to his feet and handed it to her. "Check it. You have a backup disk, don't you?"

She nodded as she ran through her files. "Daddy gave it to me."

"I can fix it if there's a problem," Rio said. "Everything will be all right."

Satisfied that her files were operational and the iPad undamaged, she lifted her head. "Will it? Then why can't you promise to take care of yourself?"

Tenderly he palmed her face. "A promise infers that I will have full control over every situation. I won't."

She closed her eyes, then opened them. He wouldn't lie to her; neither would he shirk his responsibilities. He was strong, courageous. She had to be the same way. "Do you think you'll have any trouble coming to my room tonight with so many people in the house?"

"Nothing is going to keep me away from you," he said, his voice deep, his hot gaze steady.

She smiled despite her fear for him. "Well, then. Let's get this show on the road."

Daniel Falcon arrived shortly before after ten with his wife, Madelyn Taggart Falcon, and their son, a hefty and rambunctious two-and-a-half-year-old Daniel Junior. With them were his sister, Dominique Falcon-Masters, and her husband, Trent Masters. The car following them carried Shane and Paige and her mother, Joann Albright, along with her son, Zachary "Rolling Deep" Albright Wilder, the renowned music producer, and his world-famous concert violinist wife, Laurel Raineau Albright Wilder.

They were barely out of the car before Luke drove up with Catherine, his mother, her brother, John Henry Falcon, and his wife, Felicia. Sierra, Blade, Rio, and Skylar were there to meet them. Jefferson couldn't carry all the luggage. The men eagerly helped while the women talked and passed a grinning Daniel Junior around before he settled with his Granny Felicia.

"I have refreshments in the small dining room," Skylar said. "There are two guest bathrooms on the lower floor where you can wash up, or I can show you to your rooms."

All the women staying overnight opted to go to their rooms. While Skylar took them upstairs, Ruth showed Felicia, who, with her husband, was staying with her sister-in-law, to a guest bath.

It was a noisy, happy bunch that finally settled in the dining room. The doorbell rang and more guests arrived. This time it was Madelyn's older brother Kane Taggart and his wife, Victoria, with their seven-year old twins, Kane Junior and Chandler. Behind them were Matt Taggart, his wife, Shannon, and their two-year-old daughter, Tempest. The little girl immediately wanted to get down and go to Daniel Junior.

Daniel and Matt looked at each other and shook their heads as the two cousin toddlers held hands and jabbered. Kane Junior and Chandler were asking Mary in Spanish if there were any soft drinks.

"I heard that," Victoria answered. "No sugary drinks."

The twins looked at their brawny, six-foot-plus father for help. "Sorry, guys. She's the boss, but Sierra and Blade have horses. Why don't you ask nicely if we can all go for a ride?"

The twins' eyes widened. They rushed to Sierra and Blade. They received a yes just as Patterson let in more relatives. Morgan and Phoenix; Pierce Grayson and his wife, Sabra Raineau Grayson, Broadway and movie star;

Brandon and his wife, Faith McBride Grayson, with her older brother Duncan McBride and his wife, Raven.

"Hi, Skylar." Faith greeted her with a hug. "Cameron and his family couldn't make it due to a NASCAR race this weekend, but he wishes the auction the best."

"I understand. Your brother's NASCAR package of a weekend with him at a race of their choice is doing fantastic. I'm pulling for him to win the Sprint Cup this year."

"Thanks, I'll tell him," Faith told her.

Skylar glanced around the room to ensure everyone was all right and didn't need anything. Rio, Shane, Blade, and Luke were talking quietly among themselves. It wasn't difficult to imagine what the subject was. She hated that she had brought trouble to Sierra and her family, and had told her as much that morning. Typically, Sierra had responded just as her mother had the night the intruder broke into Skylar's room: "I can handle trouble." Then she'd added, "Good friends are hard to find."

"Hello, Skylar."

Skylar jerked around to see Felicia Falcon, the woman who might be working with Mrs. Grayson to try to take Rio away from her. Or try to push them together. Skylar wished she had enough courage to ask.

Felicia, as beautiful and as youthful looking as ever in one of her knockout dove-gray Chanel suits, frowned. "Is something wrong?"

Skylar mentally shook herself. "Mrs. Falcon, I'm sorry. I was thinking. It's good to see you again. Thank you again for steering me toward Navarone."

"You're welcome, although for a while Meredith wasn't thrilled with me," Felicia admitted, sipping her mimosa. "It's not good when you're at odds with a good friend and sorority sister."

Skylar hadn't known. "I'm sorry, but Mother seems happy for me."

"Now. She mentioned you were meeting them for dinner and bringing someone special," Felicia said. "Anyone I know?"

"Rio," Skylar said proudly, her gaze intent, hoping Mrs. Falcon would pass the message on to Mrs. Grayson to back off. Expecting at the very least mild annoyance, Skylar was surprised to see a flash of excitement in the other woman's eyes.

"Rio is an interesting man. I don't recall seeing him with a particular woman," Felicia went on to say.

"I guess it took the right woman," Skylar told her, aware there was more than a little pride and a hint of naughtiness in her voice.

Mrs. Falcon laughed softly and touched Skylar affectionally on the shoulder. "Well said. It takes a strong woman to grab the attention of a strong man. What time is your mother arriving?"

"Around six." Skylar wasn't sure why, but she felt as if something had gone over her head. Perhaps the two women were on her side after all.

"I won't keep you. John Henry gets lonely if I'm gone too long." Lifting her glass in a salute, she walked straight to her husband. He curved his arm around her slim waist and kissed her on the cheek. Their marriage might have been rocky once, but it certainly wasn't that way now.

"Can I have everyone's attention please?" Sierra tapped a knife against her juice glass. "That means you, Brandon."

Brandon grinned. Faith blushed.

"Navarone, over here." Sierra beckoned to her husband.

"I'm coming as fast as I can pull this ball and chain."

Blade dragged his leg for a couple of steps, then hurried to his wife's side.

"Ha. Ha," she said.

Unrepentant, he grinned, kissed her, and threw his arm around her shoulders. "It's wonderful having family and friends together under one roof. Sierra had an idea that she wanted to tell you about."

"Catherine had the first Christmas with family and friends before Brandon, Pierce, and I were married. It was wonderful. We're so happy you're here to help Mama and the Music Department at St. John's, but also to get together as a family. Time will be limited this weekend, but Blade and I would like to invite everyone in this room, and a few not here, to spend next Christmas week at Navarone Castle."

Husbands and wives looked at each other, and couples began accepting the invitation. Less than a minute later, everyone had accepted except Rio and Skylar.

"Skylar, I know you'll want to spend Christmas with your family in Boston, but I hope you can spend some of the week here," Sierra said. "We'll get you there on time, even if the small jet has to take you."

Rio and Christmas, playing in the snow, skiing, sitting in front of a fire talking. "I'd love to. Thank you."

Sierra pinned Rio with a narrowed gaze as he stood with Luke and Catherine. "Rio, I have something very special planned for you for Christmas."

Crossing his arms, he grunted.

Sierra just grinned.

Skylar had a nonstop day. Surprisingly, Jason, her bodyguard, didn't slow her down in the least. Most of the time she forgot he was with her. She was too busy making

sure the band, the caterers, the delivery service, the flo-
rist, the wait staff, and the gift boxes shaped like Navarone Castle with chocolate musical instruments inside all
arrived on time.

One thing she didn't have to worry about was Mrs.
Grayson's students. They arrived eager and excited in the
luxury van Blade had arranged for them. She and Felicia
greeted them. Skylar felt they were watching her, but she
never caught them. Too busy to worry, she went to check
the dining tables.

They were draped in white linen with fresh-cut rose cen-
terpieces. If desired and present, the highest bidder of the
night could take his or her centerpiece choice, and continue
until all were gone. Napkins and flatware were already on
the table, and would be removed and replaced with a fresh
place setting when the draped seat was vacated.

In the kitchen, she again checked over the menu with the
catering company Brandon had recommended. There
would be smoked salmon, roast tenderloin, avocado spheres,
mushroom risotto fries, assorted vegetables, breads, raspberry macaroon lollipops, raspberry cake with fresh rasp-
berries and raspberry sauce.

She saw Rio at a distance in the early afternoon with
Shane. She waved and he waved back before getting into
one of the speedy golf carts. Continuing, she met with the
man in charge of valet service. Thankfully, an area behind the garage was paved as the original owner had
planned to entertain lavishly.

Then it was back to the house to speak with Patterson
on checking the guests' coats and wraps. On and on the
day went. She saw little of the houseguests as they were
scattered over the estate riding, boating, on the archery
range, or just relaxing out back.

"It's five thirty, Skylar."

Skylar looked around at Jason, then at her watch. She couldn't believe the day had rushed by so quickly. She'd asked him to remind her of the time. She wanted to be dressed so she could recheck everything before her parents and grandparents arrived. She was already cutting it close. She hurried to the stairs. "Thank you, Jason."

At her door, Jason said, "The boss said to tell you that he'd see you before you went downstairs."

"To give me my accessory, I suppose."

Jason's lips twitched. "That would be my first guess."

Wondering what his second guess would be, Skylar entered her room. She headed straight to the bathroom. By the time a knock sounded on her door twenty-two minutes later, she was zipping up her gown.

"Yes?"

"Rio."

"Alone?"

"Yes."

Unzipping her dress she answered the door. "Come in."

His gaze swept over her in one hot sweep. The emerald-green, high-waisted gown was hand-embroidered with a bateau neckline. Green chiffon peeked from beneath the elbow-length sleeves. The silk skirt flared from thighs to end in a short ruffle train.

She did her own looking. With his muscular build and broad shoulders, Rio was magnificent in a black tux. And for the time being, all hers.

She presented her back and thought, hoped, she'd heard a sharp intake of air. The V draped to the middle of her bare back. She'd piled her hair on the top of her head so nothing could impede his view of all that naked skin. "Can you help with the zipper, please?"

She didn't know he'd moved until she felt the warmth of the back of his fingers on her skin. She shivered, fought the urge to lean back against him, then turned around and let them feast on each other.

"I'm going to enjoy taking this off you."

"That's the idea, and I'll enjoy it as well."

He kissed the middle of her back, letting the tip of his tongue lightly graze her skin. "I'll make sure of it. Zipped."

Her breath trembled over her parted lips. "Now, if my legs weren't shaking."

"You can sit while I put this on."

She frowned on seeing the ankle holster. "I still think I'd like the one on my thigh better."

"Do you want to sit or stand?"

"One of these days you're going to meet someone who can stare you down." She lifted the hem of her skirt and extended her right foot.

Rio knelt, slipped off her shoe, placed her foot on his leg and strapped on the ankle holster. He stared up at her. "I hope you don't have to even think about using the gun, but if the time comes, don't second-guess yourself, don't try to reason, just place the bullet where he won't get up. Understand?"

He was worried again. "We have a date back here tonight. If necessary, I won't hesitate."

He slipped on her shoe, came to his feet. "You look beautiful."

Her smile trembled. "Because I'm with you."

He reached into his pockets. "Wear these. They have a transmitter. You won't be able to hear me, but I'll be able to hear you in case you get separated from the men."

Skylar gasped when she saw the emerald earrings.

Oval in shape, they were at least three inches long in a gold setting. "They're exquisite." And very expensive.

"I picked them up while I was in Chicago."

Skylar blinked rapidly and put on the earrings. "If I ruin my mascara, I'm going to be very annoyed with you." She sniffed. "How do they look?"

"No one will be able to tell."

She started to swat him before realizing she was looking for compliments and he was concerned about her safety.

He reached for her door. "Ready?"

"Ready." She preceded Rio into the hall, her skirt rustling. She had no idea what the night might bring; she just prayed that when it was over, she and Rio would be safe in each other's arms.

She looped her arms through his as they went down the stairs. She had another surprise waiting. A few steps from the bottom, one of the photographers she'd hired stepped forward.

"One moment, please."

Rio stopped and stared at her. He wasn't pleased.

"Please turn this way, sir."

"He's taking everyone's picture as they come downstairs, and of the children playing upstairs," Skylar said. "I'm giving the album to Mrs. Grayson, but I'm keeping ours for myself. Now, please, look at the camera."

"I don't like my picture being taken."

"I'll make it up to you later, and that's a promise."

His expression stoic, Rio looked at the camera. The photographer took several rapid shots. By the time they reached the bottom, her mother and grandparents were coming though the front door. Skylar hurried to greet them.

"You look beautiful," her mother said. "Those ear-rings are stunning. Where did you find them?"

"I'll tell you later," Skylar evaded. "Why don't I show you the auction room?"

"Let's go," her grandmother said, patting her small evening bag. "I'm ready to shop."

Her husband laughed. "She checked twice to make sure the credit card was in her purse before we left the hotel room, and once in the car coming here."

"As if you're not interested in that signed baseball," his wife teased back.

Her grandfather turned to Rio. "I hope you're coming with us. At least I won't be so outnumbered."

Rio glanced at Skylar. "For all the good it will do. I'm learning that some women don't always play fair."

"Took me two years of marriage to figure that out." Her grandfather studied Rio. "Smart man, Skylar."

"I think so. This way."

They weren't in the auction room three minutes before the houseguests, led by Mrs. Grayson, joined them. Intro-ductions were made and then people wandered around the room marveling at the various objects up for bid. Soon they were joined by newlyweds Richard and Naomi Youngblood with their daughter, Kayla, as well as Rich-ard's cousin Lance Saxton and his wife, Fallon. Patterson took Kayla, Naomi's daughter, up to play with the other children.

When the first guests arrived at six twenty-nine, every-one on duty was in their place and Sierra, Blade, Mrs. Gray-son, and Skylar were there to greet them. So was someone to take their wraps, offer drinks, and show them to the auc-tion room. People probably thought the two men behind them were there for Blade and Sierra instead of for Skylar.

There was a steady stream of people afterward, all thankful to be invited, excited about the auction, and marveling at the beauty of the castle. By seven, the hosts decided to mingle. Skylar received compliments on the wonderful collection up for bid, her gown, and her stunning earrings.

Every once in a while she'd catch a glimpse of Rio, but he seemed always to be moving or watching. He didn't even have time for a short dance with her on the ballroom floor. She knew neither of them would eat and had already asked the caterer to leave food for them in the refrigerator for later tonight. Afterward they'd feast on each other.

"Things are going very well," Mrs. Grayson said.

Skylar started. Lost in her naughty thoughts about Rio, she hadn't heard anyone approach. "Yes, they are."

"I knew you were the one to pull this off," Mrs. Grayson went on to say.

"You and your students are a great help. They seem to be having fun."

Mrs. Grayson warmly smiled. "They are. They're my honors students. I'm so proud of them. I'm hopeful that those who haven't pushed themselves will want to strive to do better once they hear about tonight. If this turns out the way I believe, this could be a yearly event."

Skylar agreed. "The last time I checked the minimum bid on anything was twenty-five hundred and seventy-five dollars."

Mrs. Grayson took her hands. "You're a strong, resilient woman, Skylar. Your courage served you well. I knew you were the one when I first saw you. You never know when an act of kindness will change your life. By the way, lovely earrings. We'll talk later."

Her heart thumping, Skylar watched Mrs. Grayson disappear into the crowd mingling in the hall and touched her earrings. *I knew you were the one.*

Skylar was no longer unsure. Mrs. Grayson had definitely been talking about Rio. She'd been almost afraid to hope even with Mrs. Grayson's comment about them being well matched and the hair clip. She wanted to hug herself. Rio was all hers, just as soon as she could change his mind about marriage.

"Ms. Dupree, this letter is for you." Patterson handed her a small sealed envelope on a silver tray and left.

Still thinking about what Mrs. Grayson meant, Skylar opened the letter. Her world crashed. Her mouth dried. Her body trembled.

If you want to see Rio alive, ditch the bodyguards and come out the back door of the solarium. Tell anyone and they'll find a corpse.

Chapter 18

The note and envelope clutched in her trembling hand, Skylar whirled to Hendrix and Marshall, working to keep her voice calm. "Please radio Rio. I need to speak with him."

Both men jerked their earpieces out at the same time. "Something's interfering with the signal."

"It's being jammed," Hendrix said, his mouth tight, his gaze going to the letter. "What did it say?"

"Personal." She left the auction room and went into Blade's office. "Rio, if you can hear me, please call Blade's private line."

She stared at the phone on the desk. It remained silent. "Can you call the control room and see if Rio is there?"

Marshall pulled out his cell phone, mumbled under his breath. "No go."

"Blade's phone is a landline," Skylar told him, praying Rio was all right.

In seconds Marshall was talking to the control room. "Rio isn't there. He's isn't tagged, so we can't locate him."

"Find him now!"

Both men looked at the note in her hand. "Our orders were to stay with you."

Opening the door, she quickly walked to the entrance

of the auction room. "I'll stay here with the other men until you find him."

"I don't—"

"Find Rio and stop arguing with me," she said tightly. "Now!"

"If anything happens to you, he'll have our necks," Hendrix told her.

"And if anything happens to him, you'll have me to deal with," she came back. "One of you go notify Blade and Shane. The other, look for Rio."

"Don't worry, Skylar, we'll find him. Let's go, Marshall." Hendrix went in search of Shane and Blade, while Marshall left through the front door to search for Blade.

Skylar headed to the solarium at a slow walk when she wanted to run. The solarium's door was the only one in the castle that didn't have one of Rio's men, because it only opened from the inside.

Cautiously, she opened the door and peered outside. The lights along the path were out. Only the lights high above were on. Once she let go of the door, she'd be locked out. "Rio, I don't know if you can hear me, but I received a note that someone had you. I'm to meet them outside the solarium."

She waited a few moments, hoping for Rio to come through the door behind her. Nothing. She considered getting out the gun, but reasoned that if someone did have Rio, they'd have a gun as well and in the light she'd be a clear target. Or they'd threaten to shoot him if she didn't drop the gun. No, keeping it hidden was her best option.

"Keep coming or he dies," ordered a cold, menacing voice.

Her heart slammed against her chest. She stepped outside, letting the door swing shut behind her. Her skin prickled. She bit her lip. If she'd been had, Rio was safe and she was the one in danger. Hoping the signals were no longer jammed, she said, "I'm here as you wanted at the back entrance by the solarium. You can come out and bring Rio with you."

A man dressed in black, holding a Glock 17 with a silencer attached, stepped out of the shadows. "Let's go."

Recognition dawned. "You're the man from the restaurant, but you had a mustache."

"If you would have cooperated then it would have saved a lot of people a lot of trouble."

He didn't have any bruises on his face; nor were his clothes disheveled. She couldn't imagine Rio being taken unaware. "I didn't see you on the tape."

"Reversible coat. Dark glasses." He jerked his head. "Let's go. A man wants to see you."

"I'm not going anywhere until I see Rio and know that he's all right."

"This gun says differently."

"I know exactly what a gun can do to human flesh, but I'm still not moving. You said a man wanted to see me. If he'd wanted me dead, we wouldn't be talking."

"I don't like smart women."

"And I wouldn't like being dead. You wouldn't like it, either."

He frowned. "What's that supposed to mean?"

"My fiancé, Rio, would come after you and you'd die screaming." She thought that a gruesome touch. She must have heard or read it someplace.

The man's dark eyes narrowed a bit. "That's the dude with the ponytail. He broke Keith's wrist like a matchstick and shattered Joe's knee."

"And he referred to it as nothing much." Skylar casually crossed her arms. "Just think what he'd do to the man who dared harm the woman he loves."

"You talk too much." The man's voice hardened.

She snatched her arms to her sides. She had to stall. "You would, too, if someone was about to kill you. I came out to the back door by the solarium just as you said, so I'm willing to talk. You didn't keep your end of the bargain by showing me Rio. However, I'm willing to negotiate. The man who hired you has money problems. I can double, triple what he's paying you."

"He said you might try that."

"Tennyson is sinking in debt. You should have checked."

"I didn't say Tennyson hired me."

"If he hadn't, you wouldn't have repeated his name."

He took a step closer and leveled the gun at the middle of her chest. "No more talk. Move your butt over here, or we're gonna test your theory about your boyfriend."

"Fiancé."

"Now."

"This place is well guarded. How do you plan to take me?"

"That's my secret. You can do it walking or unconscious," he threatened.

If she went with him, she'd be going to her death. Skylar took a few wobbling steps. "I'm so scared I can't walk in these high heels."

"Well, take them off. I've wasted enough time!" he snapped.

She started to bend and the door behind her burst open. She whirled, seeing Rio with a gun, his face enraged. She accepted that part of the anger was aimed at her for disobeying.

"Stop right there and toss the gun unless you want her to get a bullet."

Rio tossed the gun. "Let her go."

"Is that him?" the gunman asked Skylar.

"No, it's Brazos, his brother. He looks mean, but he's kind of slow," Skylar lied. Tennyson probably hated Rio for showing him up and Blade for destroying his business.

"I can tell." He sneered. "He said if I popped that Rio dude and you saw it, I'd get double."

"I told you I'd pay triple."

"Look, sister, shut the hell up and bring your butt over here before I put a bullet in this dude's stupid mug." He frowned. "I wonder if I could do him instead. He's got a ponytail."

"And I'd tell him the truth," Skylar threatened.

"Not if you were dead."

Rio took a menacing step closer.

"Do it. I'm just pissed and tired enough of her talking my head off, I'd do you for free."

"Don't. They're very close," Skylar quickly told him. "I'm just going to take my shoes off, like you suggested."

"No." Rio stepped in front of her. "She's not going anywhere with you."

"Move to one side," the man ordered.

Skylar moved since she knew Rio wasn't going to. "One shoe off." She tossed the shoe toward the gunman, but he never took his eyes from Rio. "Reaching for the next shoe."

"No, don't," Rio told her.

"Begging for your life. What a wimp." Rio started for the man. "So be a dead—"

Skylar fired. The man yelped as the bullet tore into his arm, shattering the bone. His gun tumbled to the stone walk.

Rio quickly retrieved the Glock and checked for other weapons. Ignoring the man's groan, Rio bound his wrists, then snapped out his position on the radio, adding that he had the man. He straightened and advanced on Skylar. "What the hell did you think you were doing coming out here alone?"

"I thought he had you. I'm sorry. I was wrong."

"Wrong! Wrong is when you make a wrong turn or pick up the wrong tape. Wrong is correctable," he said, his voice inching higher with each word. "You could have gotten yourself killed."

"So could you. You didn't have your gun," she said.

"Do you think that was my only weapon?" He pushed his jacket back to reveal another gun. Lifted his pant legs to show a knife strapped to each. He tapped his chest. "Kevlar. I'm an expert in self-defense. I told you to let me handle it. Going for your gun was an idiotic thing to do."

"You're the one who's idiotic if you think I was going to stand by and let some creep shoot you," she yelled right back at him.

"Then why didn't you put a bullet between his eyes instead of risking him getting a shot off and hitting you?"

"Because he can tell us where Tennyson is. He was taking me there."

The back door bust open. Men piled out. Blade, Shane, and Luke led the charge.

"You two all right?" Blade asked, glancing between the two silent people. He didn't receive an answer.

"We should have known Rio would get him." Conner pulled the whimpering man to his feet, ignoring his cries of pain.

"I don't think so," Shane said.

Blade slipped the still-warm gun from Skylar's hand. "I guess she can shoot."

"Like I said, she's some kind of woman," Luke said.

"Conner, take him to my office and hold him for Dakota. He was in the auction room earlier," Blade ordered. "I'll go reassure the guests. I'm sure Skylar and Rio will be in shortly."

"I have your gun, Rio," Shane told him as he passed. "I'll leave someone at the door to let you back inside."

When they were alone, Skylar placed her hand on Rio's galloping heart. She took his hand and placed it on hers, which was beating just as fast. "I didn't want you hurt. You'd protect me no matter what. I couldn't let that happen. Just like you, I protect those I care about."

He jerked her into his arms, then kissed her until she was trembling for an entirely different reason. "I couldn't find you. I wanted to beat Hendrix and Marshall for leaving you. We managed to jam the frequency jamming our systems and I heard you on the radio. All the time it took to get here, I was praying."

She brushed her lips across his. "God and the Master of Breath heard you."

He stared down at her. "You're determined to give me those gray hairs."

"You have a long way to go yet. Come on, I suppose Dakota will want a statement. We better grab Patterson on the way. He gave me the note."

"Hendrix mentioned a note," Rio said. "Where is it?"

"By the door. I left it there in case I was wrong and you had to come get me."

"I put two tracking devices in your dress after I left you this morning," he told her.

"Smart." She started for her shoe.

He reached it first. "I'll do it."

With one hand on his shoulder to balance herself, she lifted her stocking foot. He brushed off the bottom, tenderly kissed her leg, then slipped the thin gold-buckled strap over her heel. "You're not moving out of my sight the rest of the night."

"My thoughts exactly."

"Who gave you the letter?" Rio asked the moment they had Patterson in the small dining room with the double doors closed.

Patterson blinked and caught his throat as if he was having trouble breathing. Skylar, standing behind Rio, felt sorry for the older man. He had enough problems. However, she wasn't going to interfere. They needed the information.

Rio held up the crumpled letter and note card. "Who gave you this letter to give to Skylar?" he asked again, his voice as hard as his face.

"Why—why no one, Mr. Sanchez. I was walking though here, checking to see that things were in order as usual, and I saw the letter on the table. It had Ms. Dupree's name on it so I immediately took it to her." He swallowed, his frightened gaze jumping from one to the other. "Is there a problem?"

"Because of this letter, a man almost kidnapped Skylar," Rio snapped out.

Patterson's eyes widened even more. His hand reached for the chair beside him and missed. Rio caught him with one hand, then pulled out a chair with the other and eased him into the seat.

"I'll get some water." Skylar rushed into the kitchen, trying to stay out of the way of the caterers, saw a tray of sparkling water, and grabbed a glass. When she returned, Patterson was still pale.

"Mr. Patterson, drink this." Skylar held the glass up to the man's thin lips. He managed a couple of swallows.

"T-thank you." His breath shuddered out as he opened his eyes. "Ms. Dupree, I'm truly sorry. I—I don't know what to say." He looked around the room as if dazed. "Nothing like this has ever happened before." He sat up abruptly. "Does Mr. Navarone know about this?"

"Yes," Rio answered.

"I—I must go and apologize." Patterson attempted to stand.

Rio and Skylar gently urged him to remain seated. "There's nothing to apologize for, Mr. Patterson," Skylar told the trembling man. "It wasn't your fault."

"But I feel responsible. If I hadn't given you the note . . ." His voice trailed off.

"Then someone else would have," Skylar finished and glanced at Rio. "We have to go speak with the police. I'm sure Blade and Sierra will understand if you wish to lie down for a bit."

"No." The house manager struggled to his feet, then steadied himself. "I couldn't do that with guests in the house. I'll be fine. Thank you for your concern."

"Let's go, Skylar." Rio reached for her arm.

Outside the door, Rio saw the crowd gathered in the hallway. He could still hear the band playing, but from the difficult time he had maneuvering through the crowd he figured no one was dancing or at the buffet. It was even tougher once he neared Blade's office.

"Police. Let us through. Police."

People stepped back, but just enough for the four uniformed officers to pass. Two stopped in front of Blade's office door; the other two continued inside. Rio nodded to the officers outside and entered Blade's office.

Luckily, it was big enough to hold the twenty or so people inside. Dakota, in a black tux, stood in front of the man Skylar shot. Just behind the police chief were Blade, Shane and Luke, Morgan, Daniel, and John Henry. It would be Rio's guess that the Grayson and Falcon men wanted to ensure Mrs. Grayson—mother, aunt, and sister—wasn't in any danger. Rio's gut told him she wasn't.

Skylar was the target. Rio could understand Tennyson's hatred of him and Blade, but hiring men to harm her because he couldn't get into an auction seemed excessive even for a bastard like Tennyson. Still, people had been murdered for a lot less.

"Skylar." Mrs. Grayson said Skylar's name, and every person except those standing in front of the gunman looked around. She rushed to Skylar, followed by Sierra, Felicia, Catherine, Sabra, Laurel, Mrs. Albright, Paige, Faith, Phoenix, Fallon, Dominique, and Raven.

All Rio could see was the top of Skylar's head. He wondered where the other women were just as the door opened and Victoria, Madelyn, Shannon, and Naomi arrived. It hit him that they all were mothers. Even knowing there had been no danger to their children, they'd needed to see and hold them.

Skylar would make an incredible mother, he thought. She'd be gentle and loving, but like a mother lion if anyone tried to harm their child. Rio tensed, fought against the image of Skylar holding their baby in her arms. Marriage and children weren't for him. He was only thinking that way because he'd come so close to losing her, because of seeing her that morning in the small dining room playing patty-cake with Tempest and Daniel Junior.

Rio skirted the men behind Dakota and held the letter in front of the handcuffed man. "Do you know anything about this letter?"

"I want a doctor and a lawyer." He clenched his teeth in pain. "I'm entitled."

Rio leaned down to within inches of the man's sweaty face. "You're entitled to roast in hell and I'd like to send you on your way."

"Now, Rio," Dakota said jovially. "Let me talk to him first."

The man leaned back in his chair and winced. "Rio? She—she said your name was Brazos."

"Because I knew you'd shoot him," Skylar said tightly. "You said Tennyson offered double if you killed Rio."

"I—I don't remember." He licked his lips.

Dakota glanced around at his officers. "Maybe me and my men should step outside so Rio could help you remember."

"You—you can't do that! That's against the law," the man yelled.

"So are attempted murder and kidnapping. Federal offenses." Dakota peered down at the man. "I'm betting you have a rap sheet a mile long. You're looking at life with no chance of parole. You tangled with people whose power reaches all the way to the White House. Once the judge bangs that gavel and those prison doors clang shut, you'll never breathe fresh air again."

"You—you don't scare me." He licked his dry lips. "I got connections, too."

"Rio, why don't you take out that fancy phone of yours and show Mr. Big Mouth how much trouble he's in?" Dakota asked. "I'd go outside and ask the governor to come in, but just in case you walk out of here a little worse for wear than you came in . . ." He spread his callused hands wide. "I wouldn't like to put him on the spot. I voted for him."

Rio started with Blade and Daniel. "If you even thought of going after Mrs. Grayson, you're a dead man walking."

Sweat beaded on the man's face. "I . . . I don't know nothing about no Grayson woman. He hired me to—" He snapped his mouth shut and looked away. "I never heard of her."

"Skylar Dupree was the only target?" Rio asked, his voice cold with rage.

The gunman looked at Dakota. "I need medical care. My arm is killing me."

"Strange words from a man who wanted to kill me or at least take me to Tennyson, who would." Skylar's eyes narrowed furiously. "Rio was right. I should have placed the bullet between your eyes."

"If Dakota and his men leave, we can make that a reality." Rio opened his jacket to reveal a gun.

"Won't do," Skylar said, matter-of-factly. "Needs to be the same gun. Ballistics and all that." She sniffed, dabbed beneath her eyes. Her voice hitched as she said, "I tried to just wound him, but he just kept coming. I—I was so afraid. I warned him." She looked around wildly. "I had no choice. No choice but to shoot again and make sure he stayed down and wouldn't kill me."

"You're crazy," he yelled frantically. "You can't kill me in cold blood. Cop, do something."

Dakota stared up at the beamed ceiling. "I wonder how they got them so straight."

"Blade, do you have the Guardian you took from me?" Skylar held out her hand.

"Here you go." Blade placed the gun in her palm.

Her fingers closed over the pearl handle. "Thanks. So

small and beautiful, yet so deadly. I was taught always to check my gun before using it." She opened the chamber, closed it, and sighted down the barrel. "We're good to go."

The man tried to scoot back in his chair. "You can't kill me."

"I was always taught turnabout was fair play," she said sweetly.

"He said you'd be an easy target. That I wouldn't have any trouble," the man blurted out, his words tripping over one another.

"And I told you, Tennyson is a liar with little money and no friends." She glanced around her. "Whereas I have plenty of friends, buckets of money, and Rio. If you want to see tomorrow, I'd advise you to talk. Last chance."

"You won't get another one." Rio's voice was deadly quiet.

"Wait! Wait a minute!" The gunman swallowed, perspiration beading his face. "Tennyson hired me and a pal to take you out. When I couldn't pick you up at the restaurant, we followed you in the rental until the police came. Lonnie and me came out here Tuesday night. I drove him. He never came back. I took off when I saw beams of light in the woods. I found out later that you'd caught Lonnie." He paused for a breath. "After this dude busted into his office and took his bodyguards out, Tennyson wanted you alive. I was to bring you to him."

"Where?" Rio asked.

"You got all you're gonna get from me. You'll have to find the rest on your own," he said. "I'm saving the rest as a bargaining chip for my lawyer."

"Not good enough," Rio snarled. "How did you get in here? How did you know the solarium door was the only one not guarded? Who delivered the letter? Who is your contact here?"

"I guess you don't hear good," the man taunted.

Rio reached for the man. Dakota caught one arm, Skylar the other.

"Get him away from me!" the gunman yelled, gritting his teeth in pain as he shrank against the chair. "I'm telling my lawyer about you threatening me and that the police didn't do squat."

"You tell your story, and I'll tell mine." Dakota pulled the man from the chair by his uninjured arm. "We'll just see who they believe."

"Where—where're we going?" The gunman tried to pull back.

Dakota lifted a brow. "Didn't you ask for medical care?"

"Yeah, yeah. It's about time," he grimaced. "I'm gonna tell my lawyer that, too."

"I'm trembling in my boots." Dakota kept walking. "I'm sure everyone else in here is doing the same."

The man looked around at the many faces in the room. The men's were filled with hatred, the women's distaste. No one would speak on his behalf. He gulped.

"Take him to the ambulance. Tell them to do the eval on the road. There's been enough talk and speculation already." Dakota handed the man to one of the uniformed officers. "Put out an APB on Tennyson. Rio, can one of your men give my office the particulars?"

"I will." Shane stepped forward and followed the police out of the room.

"According to my contact guarding his house in Chicago, Tennyson is supposed to have been there since late last night." Rio's mouth tightened. "I bet anything he's not there."

Blade stepped forward. "He has a private plane. He could be anywhere."

"With the FBI involved, we'll have a better chance of running him to ground." Dakota turned to Skylar. "You're something. You got him to talk."

"Unlike the man who broke into my room." Skylar handed the gun to Rio.

"This one was sweating a lot more," Dakota said. "I took a chance that he'd break, and he did."

Skylar smiled. "I've always wanted to play good cop/ bad cop."

Dakota chuckled and glanced at Rio's hard face. "I think it was bad cop/baddest cop." He went to Ruth. "Glad to hear you weren't involved. Thanks for the invite. Best party I've been to in a long time."

"I'm glad you could come, Dakota," Mrs. Grayson said. "Please join us here for brunch around nine in the morning."

"I'll be here." He tipped his hat to Sierra and Blade. "'Night."

"Conner, I want everyone to stay on high alert. He and his pal got information from someone working here. Until we find out who it is, we don't take chances," Rio told him.

"Got it." Conner and the three other men left the room.

Skylar sighed. "I guess I should go talk to the family about what happened."

"You can use my office," Blade offered.

"Thanks." Skylar sighed again. "If you hear shouting, just ignore it. It will be my father."

Chapter 19

"What!" Beau Dupree shouted. "I can't believe you were in danger and no one told us!"

"Baby." Meredith enfolded her daughter in a hug. Her grandparents wrapped their arms around both of them.

"I'm fine," Skylar told them for the umpteenth time. "The men responsible are in jail, and the authorities are searching for the man who hired them."

"Which might take days or weeks," Beau said. "In the meantime, this nut could hire someone else."

"His assets have been frozen," Rio said.

Her father rounded on Rio. "How do you know that? It takes time and a court order for that to happen."

"Rio has contacts," Skylar offered. Rio was in one of his moods. He wanted Tennyson in the worst way. Skylar could only hope the authorities found him before Rio's people did.

"I think your father might be right about you coming home," Meredith said.

"Not happening." Skylar pushed out of all their arms. "I'm safer here with Rio than in Boston."

"Safer!" Beau yelled. "A man held a gun on you!"

"And there's not a scratch on me because Rio made

sure that I wouldn't be helpless. He even went so far as to put a mini microphone in these earrings and tracking devices on my gown." Skylar stared at her family. "I'm staying here."

"He also had two bodyguards who left you," her father reminded her.

"Because I insisted they look for Rio," Skylar explained.

"They'll be dealt with," Rio said, his voice flat.

Skylar turned on him. ""If you do more than talk to them, *we're* going to have a talk. I was worried sick about you and—" She took a deep breath to try to stem the tears. "They saw how upset I was."

Rio's glacial eyes warmed, comforted.

"Baby." Her mother pulled a tissue from her small purse and dabbed her daughter's eyes. "It's all right."

"How can you say that, Meredith?" Beau asked.

"Because she is fine, thanks to Rio," Meredith told him.

"She wasn't a victim like I was," her grandmother said. "I'm proud of you, Sky."

"Me, too," her grandfather added. "Rio, I'm liking you more and more."

Beau threw up his hands. "Are you all crazy? Did you hear what I heard? Skylar was almost killed."

"We could ask you the same thing, Father." Skylar clenched her hands. "Why do you continue to act like I have no sense in my head? That I can be easily led? So I come back to Boston, then what? You drop by once a week, if your schedule isn't too busy. What about the other days when I don't see you because you and Mother are divorced?"

He flinched as if he'd been sucker-punched.

Her voice softened. "I'm sorry if what I said hurt. I love you both, but perhaps it's time I told you the reason I left Boston. It was because you, especially you—and you, too, Mother, but you're not nearly as bad as Father—put me in the middle. You made me feel as if I was being disloyal because I still loved and wanted to be with both of you."

Her mother briefly closed her eyes. "I'm sorry. I didn't know. I was just so angry at him for cheating."

"I didn't cheat! That woman lied!" he yelled.

"Pictures don't lie," she shot back.

A muscle leaped in Beau's jaw, but he remained silent.

Skylar held up her hands. "Please. No more. I thought you should know what happened tonight so you wouldn't be blindsided by reporters or friends. As for me, unless Navarone Resorts and Spas moves its headquarters, I'm staying in Tucson." She took her mother's and grandmother's arms. "I have an auction to run. My mother and grandmother have things to buy."

Rio opened the door. "Don't forget Mr. Carrington's signed baseball."

Her grandfather smiled. "Yep, more and more. Let's go."

Rio fell in behind them as they left. Skylar urged her family to go on in. Seats were waiting for them in the front row beside Mrs. Grayson. Speaking briefly with the headwaiter, she took Rio's hand and squeezed. "I have plans later for you."

"Behave," he said.

She grinned and walked to the front where item number twenty-six, the NASCAR package, had just sold for fifty-one hundred dollars. Skylar applauded the sale and reached for the microphone from the auctioneer.

"Good evening once again, and thank you for coming. I guess you got a little more excitement than you expected."

She winked to laughter from the audience. "Thanks to the excellent security of Mr. Navarone, the intruder is in custody and we can get on with tonight's events." She lifted her hand. Waiters came in bearing trays of champagne, sparkling water, and hors d'oeuvres.

"I'm going to relax one of my rules and let you eat in here. The buffet line is still open and the band will play softly if you have what you came for and want to romance that certain someone. Delivery can be arranged. In the back of the room, St. John's honors music students can answer any question or assist you in any way. Now, let's go to our next item, number twenty-seven, a painting by the very talented Kara Simmons-Landers. I see the current bid is thirty-five hundred. Remember, some invitees were unable to attend, so there could be bidding online as well as in this room. So, let the bids begin."

Skylar was sensational. She had the audience in the palm of her competent hand. Rio couldn't have been prouder of her. It was difficult to believe that earlier she had faced down a gunman and threatened to put a bullet between his eyes. The announcement of the final total—$2,789,000— brought screams from the students and applause.

Blade and Sierra came to the microphone. "Sierra and I would just like to add our thanks to all of you here tonight; to Skylar, for doing such an incredible job organizing this wonderful event; and of course to my fantastic mother-in-law, Mrs. Ruth Grayson, department chair, for her dedication and pride in sharing her love of music with the outstanding Music Department of St. John's College."

There was more applause that grew as Ruth stood and waved. She started to sit down, but Blade beckoned her. He stepped aside so she could stand between him and Sierra. "I'll make this quick. Sierra and I believe in you, the students, and St. John's. All of your children earned their degrees there. So Sierra and I would like to donate two million, two hundred and eleven thousand dollars to make tonight's total an even five million."

Ruth's eyes widened. She turned to hug her daughter and Blade, then Skylar. Everyone was on their feet cheering. The students chanted, "Go, Professor Grayson," over and over.

Skylar spoke into the microphone. "What do you say we have one last dance, one last trip to the buffet, and one last drink if you're not driving—to cap off this extraordinary night. Ladies, grab your dance partner because I'm grabbing mine."

Rio met Skylar halfway. "I suppose you want to dance?"

"It will do for a start." She grabbed his hand.

She had a reckless look in her eyes. Rio felt his body harden and couldn't wait until he had her alone. In the hall, he saw her father, his face tight with disapproval. He wasn't finished with them.

They'd bid the last guest good night shortly after midnight. All the hired help was gone and just the family and close friends were relaxing in the great room. Women had kicked their shoes off, the men had loosened their ties and pulled off coats. Upstairs, the children slept peacefully.

"I'd like to speak with you, Skylar."

If her father hadn't looked so miserable, so alone, Skylar might have refused. Her father was a strong man. Tonight, he looked as if had lost everything and wasn't sure how to get it back. She felt even more certain that he loved her mother.

"Beau, please," her mother said quietly from beside Skylar on the sofa. "Just let it go."

"I can't. I'm sorry," he said.

Her mother seemed as shocked as Skylar. Her father wasn't the apologizing type. He was a bulldozer in a Tom Ford suit. Skylar got to her feet. "Say what you have to say, but I won't change my mind."

He glanced around the room. "I'd like to speak to you in private."

"This will have to do, Father. They all know about what happened tonight," she told him.

"All right." He placed his untouched cup of coffee on a side table. "I'm asking you to come back to the hotel with me. You can have my bed. With Tennyson still free, it would make me feel better."

"He's not free for long," Rio promised

"But the fact remains that he is now," her father said. "I'm concerned about your safety."

Meredith stood. "Beau, can't you see that she's safe with Rio and that's where she wants to be, here with him?"

"Mother is right." Skylar rounded the sofa to stand by Rio. "I'm staying here with Rio. If it hadn't been for him, I'd be dead. I should have trusted him to take care of himself and stayed inside. My fault. Not his. I love my family, but my life is with Rio."

Skylar kept her head held high in the ensuing silence. She had to believe and trust in Rio, but just in case, she looked up at him. His face told her nothing. "If you make me regret what I just said, I'll make your life miserable."

"Skylar, I . . ." His voice faltered.

She took his hand. "I trusted you, now you have to trust in me."

He gazed down at her. Strong, fearless, the woman who had slowly stolen his heart. "Can we talk for a minute?"

Her mutinous gaze narrowed, but she allowed him to lead her away from the others. Once he stopped, she pulled her hand back. Rio was in trouble and knew it. She was slipping away from him.

"Skylar, you're asking for something that I can't give you."

"Bull," she snapped, fighting the pain in her heart. "You can give me everything. If you love me."

Love didn't begin to encompass all that he felt about her. She was his everything. That's why he had to let her go. Eventually he'd fail her. He didn't know anything about keeping a woman happy.

"Skylar—" He faltered when he saw tears in her eyes. Anguish seared him. "Don't."

"You're going to miss me." Her chin lifted. Angrily, she swiped away the tears. "But you better not wait too long to come to your senses. Good-bye."

The pain worsened. "No!" He didn't know if he shouted the word or desperately needed to. He just knew he couldn't let her walk away from him. He reached for her.

She whirled, even in the wide skirt, her right hand going up to knock his hand away, and then she aimed at his face with the heel of her palm. Surprised, Rio's instinct took over. He blocked her hand as gently as he could. She aimed for his chest.

"Skylar, stop. You're going to hurt yourself. I still have on the Kevlar vest."

She didn't stop. For every chop he countered, she came back with another that pushed him backward. "Skylar." She was royally pissed at him. "Stop before you hurt yourself." It wasn't happening.

"If I didn't have this dress on, I'd put you on your stubborn butt!"

"Blade. Shane. If she hits me, she'll hurt her hands."

"I never interfere between a man and a woman," Blade said.

"Same here," was Shane's response.

Rio glanced up to see if her father would help, but her family held him. She caught him square in the nose.

"Got you."

She said the words with such pride, he dropped his hands. Perhaps she deserved to give him a few licks.

She dropped hers. "You fight, or I'm going to play dirty."

She already had. She'd swooped in and stolen his heart.

Her eyes softening, she moved closer. "Didn't the Man With No Name teach you to reach out and fight for what you want?"

His hand lifted to touch her face, then curled into a fist instead. "Strong, courageous, beautiful. You deserve so much."

Her smile trembled. "And that's what I'll have with you."

"I—"

"There's probably not a couple in this room who hasn't hit a bump or two, but look at them now. Happy. Deeply in love. Think about the children sleeping upstairs, Rio." Her arms slid around his neck. "That's what I want for us. I want to be the mother of your children."

His eyes shut tightly. He'd already pictured it. She was killing him. He couldn't have it all.

"But you have to reach for it. Reach for me." On tiptoes, she brushed her lips across his. "I'll always be there. I'll never let you down. I'll love you forever."

Reach for me. Her words reverberated in his mind and opened his heart to the possibility of a lifetime with this one special woman. *I'll never let you down.*

"Fear has never ruled you, Rio. Don't let it keep us apart. Dare to love me."

He'd dare anything, risk anything for this woman. He stared into her steady gaze and saw his future. If he was brave enough to reach for it.

Doubts slipped away. His heart gladly surrendered. Without a moment's hesitation, he reached for her. "I love you, Skylar."

"What's the rest?"

"Rest? You said—"

"I lied."

Rio threw back his head and laughed until his sides ached, then lifted Skylar until their faces were inches apart. "I'll be gray before I'm forty."

Her hands tenderly cupped his face. "I'll do my best to behave."

He cocked a brow. "I seriously doubt that."

"We'll have love and happiness and each other."

All that he desired and never thought to have. "Skylar, will you marry me?"

She beamed. "Yes! Yes! Now put me down so I can put my arms around your neck and really kiss you."

He kissed her lightly on the lips, then placed her on the floor. "That will have to do."

"Giving orders already?" She grinned up at him. "Here's one for you. Find out where we can get married the quickest."

"I better go ask you father for your hand first." He figured she wanted the traditional approach. At least he knew that much.

"If he says no?"

"It will be his choice if he wants to come to the wedding or not," Rio answered, his voice flat.

She threw her arms him and kissed him until he felt himself teetering on the brink of losing control. He'd been afraid of that happening. Skylar put her entire body into a kiss, wrapping a man in pleasure. He removed her arms and didn't waste his time scowling at her. Skylar had a mind of her own, and thank God and the Master of Breath for it. He curved his arm around her slim waist and went to her father.

"Mr. Dupree, I want to marry Skylar. I'd like to ask for your consent."

"And if I say no?" Mr. Dupree asked.

"Beau," Meredith said softly. "Mess this up, and you'll lose everything."

There were shadows and regret in his eyes when he briefly turned to her. "I lost that long ago. I know what it feels like not to be with the one you love. I wouldn't do that to Skylar." He extended his hand to Rio. "You both have my blessings."

"Father, thank you." Skylar hugged him, then her grandparents.

People gathered around to congratulate the couple and take pictures with their cell phones. With his arm around Skylar, this time Rio smiled.

"Rio is going to find out where we can get married the quickest," Skylar said, giddy with happiness.

"No!" Her mother shook her head emphatically. "You're going to have a proper wedding."

"Mother."

"You're my only daughter." Mrs. Dupree sought help

elsewhere. "Rio, please. I've thought about this since she was in high school. She'll listen to you."

"Up to a point," he replied.

"Please," she repeated.

Rio thought of how long it took Blade and Shane to get married. "Define *proper* time-wise?"

"A year at the very least," she responded.

"Four to six months seems better," Rio told her.

"Even with a wedding planner we can't possibly plan a wedding in that length of time," her mother almost shrieked. "There's too much to do."

"What if you had help?" he asked.

"Who?"

Rio looked straight at Mrs. Grayson and Felicia Falcon, who were smiling. "Well, you started this."

"Thank you," Skylar said, grinning at the women. "Although you had me worried you'd picked out someone else for Rio."

Amid groans from Brandon and Pierce, Mrs. Grayson said, "We'd be delighted to help. Felicia and I both have had experience planning weddings."

"It will be the most fabulous event of the season," Felicia said excitedly.

Other women in the room volunteered to help as well.

"Count me in." Sierra shook her head. "Although I hope you know what you're getting into, Skylar."

"Same question I asked Blade," Rio shot back

Skylar laughed. "I do, and I couldn't be happier."

Blade's laughter joined Skylar's. "That's the same thing I told Rio." He stood, bringing Sierra with him. "Now let's toast the happy couple. I know Martin will make the brunch even more spectacular to celebrate the engagement of Rio and Skylar, and Mrs. Grayson's perfect record continuing."

Groans, cheers, and laughter filled the room.

Chapter 20

Arms wrapped around each other, Rio and Skylar walked her family out to the waiting limousine. She motioned to the driver standing by the open back door that he could get back inside.

She and Rio had just gotten off the phone with her paternal grandparents in Spain. Skylar e-mailed pictures of her and Rio to them. They couldn't be happier for her and were cutting their vacation short so they could return to meet Rio in person and help plan the wedding. Skylar was shipping *Pure Bliss* to their home.

"I don't see my car," Mr. Dupree said.

"I tipped the driver and dismissed him." Skylar went to her father. "You can ride with Mother."

His gaze cut sharply to his ex-wife. "I don't think she wants me near her."

"Perhaps if you told her you loved her, she'd change her mind," Rio told him.

A soft gasp came from Meredith. "You're wrong, Rio."

"Father, this might be your last chance," Skylar warned. "Tell her. Do whatever it takes to get her back." She swallowed. "I can't imagine being away from Rio for three years. I would have gone insane."

"If it hadn't been for you and work, I would have," her father admitted softly. "It's the parents who are supposed to teach the children, but tonight you taught me to fight." He went to his ex-wife. "I'm telling you again, I didn't have a one-night stand with the woman I met in the bar. Yes, I was foolish to go up to her hotel room because she said she wasn't feeling well." His mouth tightened.

"I didn't expect her to come out of the bedroom in her lingerie or for her to grab me. I certainly didn't expect someone to be taking pictures. I got out of there as fast as I could. My mistake was in not calling and telling you what had happened," Beau finished.

"The pictures didn't look like you were resisting," Meredith said, agony in her voice.

"Pictures can be altered, Mrs. Dupree," Rio told her.

Meredith swallowed. "She tried to blackmail me when Beau refused to pay up."

His handsome face twisted in anger. "I put the fear of God in her when she came to see me. I had security escort her out of the building, and I made a police report. I have faults, Meredith. You know that better than anyone," he said. "If it suits my purpose in court I will bend the truth, but I didn't cheat on you then or since the divorce."

"What do you mean?" she asked.

"I figured if I ever got the chance to ask for forgiveness, I better be able to tell you there hadn't been another woman in my life." He blew out a breath. "I know you've dated and I under—"

"Dates. Just dates," she murmured. "You broke my heart. You broke my heart."

"Honey, please forgive me." He pulled her into his arms, kissing the tears away before finding her mouth. She clung to him as much as he clung to her. "I never stopped loving you, Meredith. Just let me prove it to you. Please, don't push me away again. I'm not sure I could survive this time."

"Give him a chance, Meredith," Skylar's grandmother said. "You know you want to."

"Beau made a mistake, Meredith. Don't you make one by holding on to anger or pride," Meredith's father told her. "I believe him."

"Trust your heart, Mother," Skylar advised. "That's what I did."

"One chance, Beau." Meredith's voice trembled, then firmed. "That's all you'll get."

He held her hand tenderly. "Thank you. That's all I'll need."

"Let's get going. We'll see you at celebration brunch in the morning." Skylar's grandfather helped his wife into the limo, then carefully handed her his signed baseball, and the box with her diamond-and-ruby brooch. Beau assisted Meredith after she gave a quick hug to Skylar and Rio. They waved as the car pulled off, then went back inside.

Arms in the air, Skylar twirled in a circle. "I'm so happy."

Rio picked her up in her arms and headed for the stairs, taking them two at a time. "I'm about to make both of us a lot happier."

Skylar bit on his earlobe, suckled. "I'm going to hold you to that."

"I know." He stopped in front of her door. "The code."

Skylar pushed her skirt of her dress out of the way and punched in the code. Rio was inside in seconds, closing the door after him, turning her away from him. His warm lips brushed over the velvet smoothness of her skin as his arms circled her waist to cup her breasts. Even through the material he felt the nipples harden, reaching for him.

He quickly undressed. Once he touched her again, he wasn't going to let her go for a long, long time. Finished, he pulled the zipper of her gown down, enjoying the material slowly opening to reveal more of her bare skin to him. As it did, his mouth, tongue, hands followed every dip and curve. By the time he reached the bend of her knees, she was trembling so badly she could hardly stand.

Kneeling, he glanced up at the flawlessness of her body. His hardened even more. All she wore were the earrings he had given her, lacy panties, thigh-high stockings, and her heels. He stood and walked in front of her. She took his breath away. His hands were unsteady when he unclamped her hair, ran his fingers though the thickness.

His fingers still in her hair, he took her mouth with passion and greed. She moaned deep in her throat. He lifted her out of the dress. She clamped her legs around his waist. He heard her shoes hit the floor. Gauging his steps, he walked backward until he reached the bed. The covers were turned down.

With her securely in his arms, he lay down and scooted until they were crosswise on the bed. He took her nipple into his mouth, sucking and teasing. His hands slid downward. The lace gave under his strong hand. She was bare and open to him, her woman's softness rubbing against his erection. He sucked in a breath.

She leaned over to lick the hard point of his nipple. "I'm going to make it better." Her fingers trailed over his length, brushing, rubbing, skimming. He lifted his hips to increase the incredible pleasure of her touching him.

She reached beneath the pillow, pulled out a condom,

and rolled it onto his stiff erection. She'd barely finished when he lifted, guided her onto him. The fit was tight, the sensation exquisite.

Her hands splayed in the middle of his chest, her eyes closed as pleasure rippled through her. She rocked against him. Each tantalizing movement took him deeper. She rode him with wild abandon, savoring the feelings rippling though her until she could hold back no longer. She stiffened, calling out his name as she went over, taking him with her.

"I have a surprise for you." Her chin propped on her folded hands, Skylar lay stretched out on top of Rio.

"I'm not sure I can handle it." His hand lazily swept up and down her bare silken back to her hips.

"I bet you can." She rocked against him, felt him respond. They'd made love twice. It was after one in the morning. "See, but I'm talking about another kind of surprise."

She kissed his chest, rolled out of bed, and picked up her discarded dress. "I will always have fond memories of this gown." Going to the closet, she hung it up. On the way back she stopped to pick up fresh lingerie and continued to the bathroom.

In less than five minutes, she was back. She'd combed her hair and put on a pair of black low-cut panties and a demi-bra. She went straight to his white shirt and put it on. "Let's go. Food is waiting downstairs."

Rio rolled out of bed to pull on his briefs and pants. "You can't wear my shirt. There're other couples in this house who might have the same idea."

She wrinkled her nose and pulled off his shirt. "When

we're at my place or yours—" She stopped on the way to her closet. "I can't wait to see your place. Anyway, we can walk around naked if we want."

With her bent over to slip on black slacks, Rio thought he might be up to a third time after all. She slipped on a black cashmere sweater and flats, and reached for his hand. "We can always bring the food back up here. I'll take the tray back early."

"You naughty man."

He started for the door. "Behave and be quiet."

She put her finger over her lips.

Shaking his head, he led her quietly down the stairs, past the great room and the dining room into the kitchen. He switched on the light.

The house manager Patterson whirled around from the refrigerator, dropping a carton of half-and-half. He held a small brown vial in the other hand. Fear widened his eyes. His mouthed worked like a fish out of water. He turned to flee.

Rio had him by the collar of his robe and pajamas before he'd gone two steps, snatching the bottle out of his hand. "Start talking before I pour whatever this is down your lying throat."

"This isn't my fault. Tennyson threatened my sister and her family. He had pictures of them at their home, where she and her husband work. Even where their three children go to school. He threatened to harm them and break both my legs if I didn't help him discredit you and Mr. Navarone." He began to cry.

"I called Blade. He's on his way." Skylar stared at the sniveling man with hurt confusion. "I trusted you."

"We all did," Rio said. "I checked you and your sister

and her family out again after the first break-in. Her family is doing well in Amarillo."

Patterson's frail hands tried ineffectually to remove Rio's. "But they wouldn't be if I hadn't agreed to help Tennyson. It's not my fault. He made me do it. I wouldn't do anything to harm Mrs. Navarone if he hadn't made me."

"What did you say about Sierra?" Blade's voice was dangerously chilling.

"If you kill him, we'll never have the whole story," Rio said.

The man whimpered louder.

"Before he died, he'd tell me everything I needed to know." Blade started for the man.

Sierra stepped in front of her husband. "I'm fine. I won't be if you beat the crap out of Patterson. We need to find Tennyson and put an end to this." Sierra grabbed Blade's arm. Shane moved to the other side.

"Keep talking," Rio ordered as the kitchen filled with more houseguests. Two of Rio's men positioned themselves behind Patterson.

"Two of the paintings sold tonight were fakes. I switched them out and gave the real ones to Tennyson. He'd planned to raise questions about their authenticity a couple of weeks after the auction, but things changed when Ms. Dupree saw me talking with Tennyson's right-hand man. If she could identify him, it would lead back to Tennyson." Patterson, growing paler, reached for a chair. Rio lowered him into one. "He hired new people to be at his office just in case and kept the other man out of sight."

"So that's why you were so nervous when I asked you if things were all right and you asked me not to tell anyone,"

Skylar said. "His back was to me. I only caught a glimpse of him."

"I didn't know that. When I told Tennyson, he was infuriated. At first they hadn't wanted you to be able to connect us, then Tennyson became enraged because Mr. Navarone didn't want him at the charity event." Patterson swallowed. A jerk of his collar got him talking again.

"I didn't want to do it, but he made me. Martin dotes on Mrs. Navarone and planned on making her crepes for brunch this morning. Tennyson sent the drugs to make her ill along with a gunman. I smuggled him in the trunk of my car tonight. The same way I smuggled in in the first man. Tennyson said he was just to tie up Ms. Dupree, scare her so she wouldn't talk if his plan was ever discovered. She wasn't to be hurt. He wanted you and Mr. Navarone to suffer for causing his downfall. He said it was fitting."

"Tennyson lied," Rio snapped. "The gunman planned to kill her."

Patterson shook his head in disbelief and horror. "No. No. You're wrong. He gave me his word."

"The word of a liar isn't worth warm spit," Blade tossed out.

"You should have told someone, Patterson," Shane said tightly. "Now you're going to prison."

"I don't want to go to prison. I was just scared for my sister and her family, and for myself. Surely, you see I had no choice." The house manager looked from one person to the other. "You have to help me."

"You could have come to me," Blade said, fury in every syllable. "Instead you were willing to cause harm to two innocent women."

"Skylar felt sorry for you, and you were willing to let

that bastard have her." Rio's hand fisted in the man's collar and cut off the circulation.

Skylar grabbed his hand. "Don't let him ruin our lives. Turn him loose. Rio!"

His hand unclamped. The house manager crumpled to the floor crying. "He said he was just going to frighten her."

Shane dragged the man to his feet. "Where's Tennyson?"

"He's nearby. The—the man tonight was to sedate Ms. Dupree and put her in the trunk of my car. He was to wait in the backseat. Once she was missing, Tennyson knew Mr. Sanchez would turn this place upside down looking for her. He gambled on you not searching my car." Patterson rubbed a shaky hand across his face.

"When things settled down, I was to—to put the drugs in the half-and-half, then fake chest pains and leave to deliver the gunman and Ms. Dupree, and then return. He wanted to know how both of you reacted once Ms. Dupree was missing, and Mrs. Navarone became ill." He dropped his head. "I'm supposed to call back after I finish in here."

"Where's your phone?" Rio snapped.

"My pocket."

"Call Tennyson and put it on the speaker," Rio ordered.

Pulling his cell phone out of his pocket, Patterson punched in the number. "Mr. Tennyson. I—I did as you instructed."

"Good. Your sister and her family might survive, and you might not end up in the hospital after all. I wish I could see that bastard's face when his wife is convulsing and dying."

Patterson jerked, almost dropping the phone. Rio caught

his hand and steadied it. "D-dead? You said it was to make her sick."

Tennyson laughed nastily. "I was afraid you'd be too big a coward to go through with it otherwise." His voice hardened. "And if you even think of going back and disposing of the milk, I'll do more than break your legs, I'll have my man carve you into little pieces. Understand?"

"Y-yes, sir."

"Good. Is the Dupree woman secure? I haven't heard anything on the news."

Rio nodded.

"Y-yes. They're keeping it quiet."

"I bet that bastard Rio is going out of his mind searching for her when she's right under his stupid nose. He won't be so bad now." Tennyson laughed again. "Bring her to me. I have some things planned for her before she dies. We're on the tarmac at the Santa Cruz private airstrip three miles out of Santa Fe. Do you know how to get here?"

Once again, Rio nodded.

"Yes, sir," Patterson answered again.

"I just wish the man I sent tonight had taken out Rio, but you can't have everything."

"No, sir."

"What did you say?"

"I—I meant, yes, sir. Mr. Tennyson, you deserve only the best." Patterson's voice quaked.

"That's what I had until that bastard Navarone and his guard dog Rio interfered. Well, I'll have the last laugh," Tennyson said with contempt.

"Yes, sir."

"Bring that woman to me as soon as you can, then I want you to go back and call me the second you can after Blade's wife is dead. Don't keep me waiting this time.

The poison works fast. There's no way he can save her."
Tennyson laughed. "I wish I could see his face." The line
went dead.

Patterson hunched his shoulders as if trying to disappear. "I didn't know. I swear I didn't know."

"This is what the man Skylar shot was holding as a
bargaining chip. The bastard knew about the poison and
was willing to let Sierra die to plea-bargain a deal," Rio
snarled. "He overplayed his hand. He wasn't wearing
gloves. With his fingerprints on this bottle, he'll be looking at two counts of attempted murder."

"He better pray he never gets out of prison." Blade's
nostrils flared with rage.

Rio pulled Patterson to his feet. "You have one more
phone call to make. Where are the keys to your car?"

"On top of my dresser."

"I'll get them and bring his car around front and meet
you there." Shane hurried out of the room.

Rio started out of the kitchen. His two men followed.
Blade was already gone.

Skylar stepped in front of Rio. "Let Dakota take care
of Tennyson."

"Sure. We're just going to smoke him out," Rio said.
"Don't worry."

"Rio." Skylar glanced at the frightened, crying man.
"He was scared. He was more terrified of Tennyson than
he believed in you or Blade."

"And that's the only reason I didn't come down harder
on him," he told her. "Let's go."

Skylar followed Rio and the whimpering Patterson to
the door. Conner and Henderson got into the back seat of
the waiting SUV. In seconds a black BMW 745 pulled
up. Opening the back door, Rio helped Patterson inside.

Blade got in on the driver's side. Shane moved to the passenger seat. The BMW sped off, with the SUV following closely.

"Rio said they'd call Dakota."

"Do you believe him?" Sierra asked.

"To a point. He'll call, but I'm worried about when," Skylar answered.

"Same here," Sierra said. "Blade has never lied to me, so that means he plans to call *after* they've dealt with Tennyson."

"There's only one thing we can do."

"You read my mind." Together, the women walked back into the house.

"Mr. Tennyson, we're here," Patterson said, his voice trembling.

"That didn't take long. I'll have Hawkins lower the steps."

Rio took the phone from Patterson. "My men are here to guard you. You're in enough trouble so don't move or make a sound."

The car dome lights off, Blade and Rio got out of the car and headed toward the steps of the small Learjet. Shane got out as well. Henderson slipped into the backseat to guard Patterson. Conner, his hand on the butt of his Glock, stood by Shane and waited.

"I want Tennyson," Rio said.

"You can have him—once I'm finished," Blade said, hitting the steps. Rio was right beside him.

Guns drawn, they entered the luxury cabin. The smirk on Tennyson's face died. He bolted behind a man almost twice his size. Without hesitation, the man reached for the gun in his shoulder holster.

Rio and Blade fired at the same time, hitting the man in each thigh. Howling in pain, he went down. Rio and Blade were already moving toward the door Tennyson had fled through. Rio disarmed the man and put a zip-tie on his wrists, then cursed as Blade kept going. Hearing Shane coming up the steps, Rio was up just as Blade shot the door lock, then kicked. The door slammed against the wall.

Blade went through first with Rio close behind. Tennyson glanced up, terror in his eyes as he backed against the wall. Blade's fist landed solidly under Tennyson's chin. Rio caught him before he fell and plowed his fist into his soft belly. Blade pulled the man toward him and drew back his fist.

"That's enough, fellows," Dakota called from behind them. "He's not worth the aggravation. Besides, he looks unconscious."

Blade let the man drop. "Which one called you?"

Dakota squatted to examine his prisoner. "Don't know what you mean."

"Did Sierra or Skylar call you?" Rio asked.

"Confidential." He patted Tennyson on the cheek. "A deputy is outside with Patterson. Which one of you has the vial?"

Rio pulled the small brown bottle out of his pocket in a cloth napkin. "My fingerprints are on there as well."

"Thanks. I expect all of you and Ms. Dupree to be at my office after brunch to give a statement."

"You change your mind about coming?" Blade asked.

Dakota spun. "Wasn't sure the invitation was still open."

"It is," Blade said. "By the way, Rio got engaged to-night."

"Congratulations." Dakota rubbed his nose. "Kind of

figured it wouldn't be long the way you acted toward Ms. Dupree. You got yourself some woman."

"Don't I know it," Rio said. "I'm sure you know about the painting switch. The real paintings are probably on the plane."

"I'll check. 'Night."

"'Night, Dakota," Rio and Blade said.

Rio glanced at Blade, who nodded. "Tennyson threatened Patterson's sister's family, and him. We all heard it."

"So I was told. It will be noted on my report," Dakota assured them, then turned back to Tennyson, his eyelashes fluttering. "Tennyson, you have to be the dumbest man on this planet to go after their women." He pulled the groggy man to his feet. "You'll have the rest of your life in jail to think about it. Starting tonight."

Epilogue

Rio was nervous. It's wasn't the tailored tux he was wearing or the five hundred guests waiting in the flower-filled church; it was the woman who would forever hold his heart.

He paced—something he never did—waiting for Luke to come get him. "I don't have the foggiest notion of how to be a good husband. I'm used to keeping my own counsel." He tossed a look at Blade sitting on the couch and Shane by the window. "Couples, the ones who make it work like you two, talk and share their feelings." He shook his head and continued to walk the length of the groom's room. "I'm afraid I'll fail and disappoint Skylar."

He stopped and lifted his hands. His voice trembled. "She'd stay out of loyalty and love, and that would slowly kill me. I love her more than I thought it possible to love anyone."

Blade got up and went to Rio. Shane joined them, standing on the other side of Rio.

"We didn't know, either," Blade told him. "Love will guide you. In any case, any woman strong enough and patient enough to wait two years on a man who showed no interest in her, and courageous enough to take out an armed gunman, is strong enough to whip you into shape."

"My money's on Skylar," Shane said. "I used to feel sorry for her."

Rio whirled and took a step back to stare at his best friends. "What? You both knew she was watching me?"

"And we watched you trying not to look back," Shane said, smiling.

"You know I made sure my and Sierra's paths crossed again so I could make her mine." Blade laid his hand on Rio's shoulder.

"I took a job to protect Paige from an unscrupulous man because she already had my heart." Shane place his hand on Rio's other shoulder. "Blade is right. Love will guide you."

He stared at the two men he'd gladly lay down his life for. There had always been honesty and trust among them. His fear disappeared. Laughing, he hugged them, knowing he had enough love to last a lifetime and beyond, and every day would be a happy one for him and his little warrior.

Skylar stood in the bridal room of the church she had grown up in. She'd wanted a few minutes alone before she went down the aisle. She'd thought about this day so many times and now it was here.

Tears tried to form in her eyes, but she willed them away. She wanted to look absolutely perfect for Rio. She could hardly believe that they were going to be married.

As promised, Ruth Grayson and Felicia Falcon had been invaluable in helping Skylar's mother and grandmothers plan the wedding. Sierra had been there as well.

She'd reasoned that if Skylar was determined to marry Rio, Sierra, as matron-of-honor, considered it her sacred duty to make the wedding spectacular.

The shower Sierra had given Skylar in Tucson certainly qualified as such. Blade, Shane, and Rio had showed up at the "in" restaurant Sierra had completely booked to make sure the women were behaving themselves. Sierra, Paige, and Skylar had assured them they were—until the men left and they went back to having fun and being naughty.

A smile curved Skylar's lower lip as she thought back over the past months. Rio and her father were actually becoming friends. He'd proudly introduced him to family, friends, and business associates. Her grandparents called Rio son. And if the looks her parents kept giving each other were any indication, their dating would soon lead to another wedding. This time they'd make it work. Skylar was sure of it.

There was a soft knock on the door. "Skylar, it's time," her mother said.

Skylar turned from gazing out the window and heard the soft flutter of her couture ivory gown. It had a barely there illusion neckline and sleeves, a fitted waist, and a wide-sweeping skirt with a flurry of delicate beading and crystal embroidery inspired by her Moor ancestors.

Her maternal grandmother's tiara was attached to a lace-and-embroidery fifteen-foot cathedral veil. On her right wrist she wore her paternal grandmother's diamond bracelet. The diamond earrings belonged to her mother. In her surprisingly steady hands she held her bridal bouquet of lush cascading pink roses and white spray roses. Attached securely was a lace sachet containing the petals of the first pink rose Rio had given her.

Her new life with Rio was ahead of her. She started to the door. Out of the corner of her eye she thought she saw a white-haired man with a long staff. He was smiling. More surprised than afraid, she paused, then continued to the door.

He won't be alone anymore.

She wasn't sure if she'd thought or actually heard the words. It didn't matter. "No, he won't. Thank you," she quietly whispered and left the room.

Skylar joined her beaming parents in the foyer, then watched her mother and the procession of her attendants enter the sanctuary filled with family and friends. She smelled the lovely scent of hundreds of flowers—fragrant garden pink roses, green hydrangeas, pink ranunculus, graduated calla lilies, blush tulips—that filled the church.

As she'd often done, she stared down at her engagement ring, a flawless emerald-cut ten-carat diamond surrounded by pink diamonds, and remembered the pure pleasure and unbelievable happiness when Rio slid it on her finger two days after they were engaged. They'd always be thankful to Blade and Sierra for rearranging their schedule so she and Rio had never slept apart. And they didn't plan to.

Her father swallowed, blinked, and lifted his arm. "You'll always be my baby, but I trust Rio to keep you safe and to love you."

Skylar looped her arm through her father's and kissed him on the cheek. "Thank you. I'll always love you."

"Let's not keep Rio waiting."

Too full of emotion to speak, Skylar stepped into the aisle with her father. Her gaze went immediately to Rio. He waited for her with a wide smile on his incredibly handsome face. Her heart leaped with boundless happiness. He was as anxious and as ready as she was for their new life together.

As she started down the aisle on her father's arm, she knew neither would ever be alone or lonely again.

They had love and each other. They had all that they desired.

Spend more time with the Grayson family and their friends in these wonderful series by Francis Ray